Apocalypse
Chronicles

Apocalypse Chronicles
Almond Press Short Story Competition, 2015

Cover art
Notre Dame
by Matthias Utomo
juhupainting.deviantart.com

Typesetting by
Laura Jones - FloJo Services
www.flojoservices.com

Edited by
Rosie Gailor
Marek Lewandowski

Published by Almond Press
www.almondpress.co.uk
www.dystopianstories.com

ISBN: 978-1988074030

Contents

Wild, dark times are rumbling toward us, and the prophet who wishes to write a new apocalypse will have to invent entirely new beasts, and beasts so terrible that the ancient animal symbols of St. John will seem like cooing doves and cupids in comparison.

Heinrich Heine,
'Lutetia; or, Paris', *Augsberg Gazette*

Ash, fear, moments of reconciliation; darkness, hope, moments of regret. What will the Apocalypse bring for you?

Apocalypse Chronicles brings together stories, memories, and endings. Woven together by their collective experience, each tale offers a unique and harrowing understanding of what the Apocalypse will mean for their world. Families, worlds, futures and pasts are explored in this unique anthology that brings together fiction from authors from across the globe.

Bear witness to the end of the world as you know it; but will you know how it will end?

– Rosie Gailor

The Rosebud

P.D. Dawson

'There's not enough paper in this world,' he said as we looked down at the tiny ant-people below. The wind was blowing hard, my balance was unsettled, and he stood on the edge as if he was about to jump off. We had come to that place through different means. I was there because I had reached breaking point with my addiction to gambling, and frankly I wanted it all to end. I wanted to stop thinking about money. I wanted to stop breathing.

I was trying to find the courage to jump, but I had paused too long through fear of what my falling body might do to the people below. Even posthumously, I couldn't bear to burden others with the weight of my own existence.

We both stood as strangers on the roof for a while, then we sat down on the ledge and looked down at our dangling limbs hanging in suspension above a 200ft drop.

The casual complacency, with which we embraced danger on our break, and the silence between us, opened up a kinship unsaid with words. His companionship at that crucial moment saved my life, and his silence was aid to the perfect conversation. There was nothing but a circling wind that rippled our shirts and whispered things in our ears. After a few minutes we got up, shook hands, and went back into the building to carry on with our separate work.

The debts accrued by my gambling were still existent, still rattling around inside my head and looking for a tiny hole in which they could curl up and die. My solution had been to die with the debt, but I found myself back in the office, still breathing, still mindlessly chatting with my fellow colleagues; all of whom were oblivious to the fact I had been just seconds from taking my own life.

The only person who had suspicion of my real intentions worked for another insurance firm. I would later find out that my companion on the roof worked on the floor below me. He was someone who kept himself to himself, and most people in his firm described him as the weird quiet guy in the corner, but I would come to know him as, Jacob.

I didn't think he was weird. I understood him. I could see that he knew things others didn't. That he breathed, lived, and dallied in thoughts and places that no one else did. His mind was always one floor above everyone else, and it showed. He appealed to me, but something about him was full of complexities and contradictions. He was beautiful, overwrought, unnatural and luminous. He had something about him that was akin to the gentlemen of the forties; an image mostly generated by his sweptback black hair and casual good looks. Women didn't flock towards him though, partly due to his weirdness, and his general dislike of people. His mind was wide open, but his demeanor was not.

There was something in the way he moved however, and in the way he dispersed all unnecessary things from his mind, that I was sure that he was somehow in the loop of the gods. It was on the day that the lights went off and all electrical activity ceased, that I knew he would be the one to guide me out of the darkness.

The winter day had started like any other. There was snow on the ground and the winter sun had risen up through the early morning mist over the city. As I made my way towards the tower where I worked, I remember thinking how beautiful it looked as the sun reflected off of its frosty glass panels. The entire building looked like a giant iceberg nestled between two taller towers of steel. But I did not know then how very different the world would both feel and look just before sunset. What follows is my account of that day, and in truth, my last memories upon Earth.

The sun was only just melting into the horizon after the unusually bright winter's day, and by 5pm, it had happened. The world went dark as if someone had extinguished the sun in an instant. And in the terrifying moments that followed, it was clear that it wasn't only the sun that had disappeared.

Every illumine thing hid in darkness. The blackout swept throughout the city like a disease of emptiness from which no one was immune. I looked up at the night sky from the office window and couldn't even see the stars, or the moon. There was nothing, not even a falling satellite to signify that something had gone wrong in the world.

I never thought such a thing would have been possible, that the universe, or at least all visible machinations of it, could have just faded away without any fallout involved. It was like someone had just turned off the switch.

And it was gone.

I heard chairs spinning on their stalks, as people ebbed and flowed through doorways, pushing their way through the crowded darkness and panting with a maddening fever. Some people were trying to see things out of the office windows, but most were too alarmed to want to see the blackness that had graced the winter evening below.

The snow had been piled high in the streets, but it remained unseen and unlit by the absence of the streetlights. The only light inside the office came from the two candles that an older lady, called Edna, had placed in front of the large windows of the office.

The faint, flickering light from the candles highlighted just how inaccessible the office floor had become; and how silent the office seemed to fall once fear had bitten people's excited tongues.

But of course there had to have been one voice to rise above the din of quietude, and that was Harold: a man of sixty-years of age and close to retirement. He wept like a little kid at first, pleading for salvation, pleading for hell to leave him alone, but even his cries were eventually silenced by the simple presence of Jacob by his side. I think everyone was pleased once he had quieted down, but then in the relative silence that followed, they had to contend with their own inner voices.

I saw Jacob approach me in the half-light that sat between candles. He placed his lips close to my ear and asked for me to follow him.

Everyone else remained quiet, as if their lives were temporarily on pause, indifferent to the turning of the Earth and the spaces between us.

Not one of them followed us as we went out into the stairwell, and I think Jacob preferred it that way. I sensed he didn't want to disturb the entire group, for he seemed much happier to leave them in their own separate terrors.

'They don't get it,' he said as we felt our way along the wall, touching with the tips of our shoes to find our bearings.

I only nodded, for the darkness had taken my voice, but I felt he could see deep into my soul and sense my inner fears.

We continued to finger our way along the wall, feeling for the first step and the start of the railing. The air inside the darkness was no longer free moving. It felt like everything was frozen in place and our movement was against the world's wishes.

To help us find our way in the darkness, we held hands as we moved along the railing. I occasionally knocked his foot, but the sound was muted and hollow.

I didn't think the first flight of stairs would ever end. I counted every flight, knowing that there should have been at least twenty of them before we reached the ground floor. We didn't say anything as we made our way down, but instead we let the darkness seep into us. When we did finally reached the last stairwell it didn't feel like it was the true bottom, for it didn't unburden me from the nightmare.

'This is it then. I guess we better find the downstairs lobby,' Jacob said coolly.

I held his shoulder as we edged along the wall towards where we remembered the door to be. The texture of the walls didn't seem quite right, but then nothing seemed the same. I think Jacob sensed it too. Hollow sounds and tactile fingers were the only way to discover such a new and strange world.

And then a thought came to mind, 'Jacob, why didn't we take one of the candles from the office?'

'And leave those people in even more darkness?' He replied simply.

I pinched his shoulder then, for I was annoyed that he had placed their need for the candle above our own. I saw us as explorers of a new world, and in that world nothing seemed right or wrong, but leaving the candle had annoyed me.

The door creaked on its hinges as we opened it up, but then once the sounds had hurried down the corridor, like sweeping dragons in flight, all that was left was an empty silence.

'Is anyone there?' I shouted, expecting to have found others congregating in the corridor that led to the lobby, but unless the silence was a message, there was no reply.

Once we had confirmed the lobby and corridor was empty, we felt the coldness closing in around us. I had felt the heat in the stairwell rising up like a demon phantom heading for the roof, but down on the bottom floor, it was as if all of the heat had been sucked out of the air. The only warmth I felt was from Jacob, but his skin was getting colder by the second. I visualized the foggy halos billowing from our panting mouths, unseen in the cold dark.

That is how I saw us, unseen but still existing, and in that thought I envied my work colleagues above. Their warmth would have warmed me much more than the faint brushes I felt of Jacob's skin. I wondered if perhaps they knew the misery that was to follow us, and that was why they stayed where they were, sat around the two candles, like still bodies in a morgue.

'Jacob where are we going?' I asked.

He didn't reply, as he was busy trying to imagine where the corridor ended, and whether we had already reached the lobby. It wasn't until I heard the sound of four wooden legs momentarily being pushed over a marble-effect floor, that I knew we had reached the chair where the guard normally sat.

'We're in the lobby now,' Jacob said, though he whispered it through his teeth as if he was scared we were not alone.

'We should find the exit,' I whispered.

What I really meant by that statement was that I wanted to get outside, for I imagined by instinct that there would be light outside of the building, or at least some hint of it, and in my blindness I was frustrated and scared, emotions I could have always controlled in the past.

By reaching for a switch, I'd normally find light, by reaching for a candle in the darkness of a blackout, I would have been blessed with the faintest flickering version of it, and if all else failed, there would be the moon, or at least the faint outline of it trying to break through the clouds. But this was very different. Even though I craved the outside and wanted to be away from the internal walls of the building, I also knew deep down inside that barring the candles, if any more could be found, none of those illumine things now existed.

The moon and the stars were gone, the streetlights had all failed, the backup generators across the entire city had not kicked in, batteries in cellphones were dead, lights on watches had failed, and car batteries must have been flat, for from the top of the building we had not seen any headlights roaming about in the darkness.

It seemed that every glimmer and glint associated with some kind of light source was gone. The waves of light, that used to be as common as the air we breathed, had simply become extinct in all things except the humble candle. In short it felt as if hell had clashed with heaven, and we were caught somewhere in between, experiencing the worst of both worlds.

'What shall we do now?' I asked.

'Like you suggested, we find our way to the exit and get outside,' he clutched hold of my hand and shook it as if to emphasize his point, 'that's at least how I dreamt it.'

I gripped his hand until I heard him whimper slightly under the strain.

'What do you mean?' I whispered. 'Are you telling me you had a dream that this would happen?'

'You don't understand. I have dreamt of things my entire life, things that have come true over and over, from people dying, to important people being born. There are not many things that I haven't conceived of in my dreams. It's as if my dreams are the closed bud of a rose, and the truth is merely the opening of the flower, the reality sprung into life, a reality that was always there, a reality that was always going to happen unless the rosebud died.'

'You mean you're letting me think a thousand desperate thoughts about what has happened, and you knew all along?'

I could sense him shaking his head, or perhaps it was the strong inhalation and the desperate sound of his lungs expanding that made me aware of my mistake.

'No!' he said, 'in my dream I saw this darkness, but in it there were glints of light, and the stars were shining, serving as a backdrop to the full moon. In my dream the world's financial markets had crashed, and the Internet had been taken over by elite gangs. They had managed to take over the world's economy.

'That's why I told you on the roof that there wasn't enough paper. Imagine a world where criminals controlled the world's electronic wealth. That's why I accompanied you that day.

'I had overheard people from your floor talking about your gambling addiction, and I figured if I had followed you I might just have stopped you from jumping, for I had an awful dream in which I was looking down at you from the top of the building. Your body had landed on a passing taxi and there was blood splattered everywhere. I knew, or at least I thought I knew, that your debts would have been meaningless in light of a world without money.'

I thumped the wall and felt my cold skin bruise in the darkness. 'So why didn't you alert someone, or do something to stop this from happening?'

'Because the world wouldn't listen, and not only that, I didn't know how they would do it. I only knew that there was a possibility it could happen. But this isn't exactly a financial meltdown, is it? No, this is something else entirely, something even more sinister.'

I slid down the wall I had been leaning up against until my buttocks touched the cold floor beneath me. 'So you didn't dream this scenario?'

'Hell no, I didn't dream this!'

I shook my head. 'So the rosebud died.'

'I guess so.'

We were silent for a while. The idea that he had dreamt of so many future truths seemed absurd to me at first, but in the thickening haze of my mind, and as the hours of unending darkness passed, I started to believe it might have been true. In a world cast into total darkness, it wasn't hard to believe in the unimaginable, for that was just a word, and I realized in that darkness there was nothing so finite and absolute as to not be imagined.

As if everything else that had happened was not enough, I would soon find out that his presence would only accompany me for a few more seconds before he would be taken from my grip.

I felt him being pulled away by a force the likes of which I could never even imagine. All I could hear was his body sliding away from me.

Into dust, into obscurity, into silence, into darkness, were the short phrases that flashed through my mind. The most unsettling part was the fact that he didn't scream, not even a tiny whimper. I hated him for that. I called after him, but there was no reply. I was worried that repeatedly calling out would have alerted the unseen forces that had taken him away, but I also sensed that whatever it was that took him, could not have been interested in taking me too.

I walked slowly in the direction of his disappearance. I did so with a curiously abating fear, for there was nothing, not one shadow, or splinter of light with which to accost myself. It wasn't long before I got to the front of the lobby, and still there was no sign of him.

I opened the glass doors to the building, and gingerly stepped outside. I immediately heard the sound of rushing air as the wind moved around me the way light had once given identity to my body and my surroundings. I also felt an unsettling terrain of ash beneath my feet, and as I walked it seemed to splutter up towards my face and into my lungs. I wondered what had happened to the snow. There was no moisture as I reached down to touch it, nothing but a dry ash that seemed to be deepening.

Once I stood erect and rebalanced myself, I found myself in the throes of a vivid dream. I was back on top of the building with my legs dangling over the edge. Jacob was sat beside me and he looked like he had something urgent to tell me.

'Harry, you can only carry on existing if you are willing to step off of the dark reality that now surrounds you. The world is no more. The world has been destroyed by the absence of fire. What has happened is the opposite of a nuclear explosion. The world has died from the absence of destruction, and you merely exist in the resulting ash. As T.S. Eliot had poeticized, *'the world ends, not with a bang but a whimper.'* You are currently in the whimper, but I want you to join me, to live on in the explosion.

'Your current reality, and everything in it, is reversed. What once was the world is now parallel, like a mirror but more complicated. What is beautiful there is ugly here, and here is where you want to be. The only catch is I can't tell you how to get to this explosion of a new world. You have to find your own way out, the way I found mine.'

Before Jacob had even finished talking, I could see his body slowly turn into a grey ash, and I watched in despair as his newly acquired wisdom drifted away like a fine mist. Once the tiny particles had all dissipated I found myself back in the cold and inert darkness that felt more like a nightmare than the weird vision I had had of him.

The walls of my very existence felt like they were being broken away, piece-by-piece, and the ashes blowing around in the wind felt like the particles of my life, easing away like a receding tide.

I started to walk across the street, where the building no longer sheltered me from the icy wind, and I could feel the coldness inside me as my feet made burrows in the deepening ash.

My subconscious was also going crazy, and my imagination was enraged to the point of miscreation. I had no idea what dark illumine things were roaming beneath my feet, but I felt like they were latching on to my tails and slowing me down.

The world was simmering in reverse, and there seemed nothing I could do about it. I walked on, sure that there would be a sign, a glint, or a tiny wave of light to give clue of the way into a new world, and as those thoughts eased through my mind, I saw the glint I had been looking for in the form of a reddening mist.

The world was colourless, but the reddening mist seemed to form from nothing. I watched as it flitted around in the air as if it were dancing to music, and I knew the complex arcs and trills of those dancing particles; were too large and varied for my own imagination to have rendered them.

The leg-deadening ash had prevented me from keeping very close to the coloured cloud, but I was able to find the place where I had last seen the mist before it had disappeared from view.

That place was unseen of course, but something drew me towards it. I always knew strange things lurked in darkness, but those things usually only existed in my mind.

Once I had steadied my own excitement, I reached out and touched a spongy, felt and furry hand of a giant leaf. The leaf was huge and out of place in the urban setting, and I was intrigued by how such a thing could have grown out of the side of a wall. It had grown to a huge size, but I'm sure I had never seen such a thing across the street before.

I lifted the heavy leaf, thinking I would be none the wiser to what lay beneath, but beneath it I found a thing of pure beauty. The furled petals of the uncovered rosebud were brightly flickering, as if a candle glowed within it, and the ambient light from those delicate petals brought life to the thing that it rested upon.

I touched that shelf with the palms of my hands, and was shocked to feel the cold metal and strange contours of a dustbin lid.

Instinct drew me to reach out and pick up the delicate stem, and as I did I brought the rosebud to my lips and kissed it. After the kiss I had the sudden urge to lift the dustbin lid from its drum, for there was a silent promise that something bright and good would be found in close proximity to it.

The light that came out of the bin's metal drum was gentle and mesmerizing, but the lucid tendencies that it evoked within my being were strong and ruthless.

I couldn't see a new world through the golden light, but the heat and warmth that emanated from it, felt like a tiny sun promising a new way of life. I instinctively, and without fear, lifted my right leg and lowered it into the bin, followed shortly by my left. At first I struggled with the forces that seemed to be pulling me in, but I felt the rosebud in my hands give me the courage to see it through.

My feet were gently warmed at first, and then my whole body followed. I felt it slowly easing into the light, as if the light itself were a physical thing; thick and spongy like the leaf that had provided scant protection over it. My body felt like it had entered a soul-widening oasis of calm that thumped through me like a second heartbeat. It was like being reborn; but I didn't know what I was being born back into, only the knowledge that I was leaving a world that had lost its beat. The complexities of life had somehow blown the world I had once known to a whimper.

It was Jacob who steered me towards this new and exciting world from which I now write, and I have been here ever since, hoping to release others from the ash of their dreams.

Not everything is, as it first seems. People unknowingly live their lives in darkness. Some people see light where darkness dwells, and some people drag their feet through the ash of their lives, without ever knowing it needn't be such hard work. But what I've learned most of all, is that beauty often hides in the places where you'd least expect to find it. I know, because Jacob took me there.

The Library

Adam Kirton

The librarian grazed the book's cover with his calloused fingers.

The wind blew through the cracked windows, sending dust across the rubble and adding to the layer of grey on his navy trench coat. But his eyes were safe; the head-wrap saw to that. He picked up the printed pages gently. The book was old, aged like him before its time, by war, worry, and ruin. It was a scarred hardback, tougher than the paperbacks, making it more likely that the contents had survived. He flicked through the pages, devouring their words, more precious to him than water or food, pages and words which crumbled at his touch. As he read, the sun caught a few loose strands of hair, blonde, maybe brown, and he smiled at its touch. He had seen roughly twenty three winters, and had a large, muscular build. His skin had once been pale, but was tanned by years of working in the sunlight. Beneath the wrap which covered his head and face lay a scar: claw marks across his left cheek which narrowly missed one of his piercing blue eyes. Just visible through the wrap was the ridge of his broken nose. He held the book closely, like a child. It was a memory of the happy times. He slung his rucksack off and put the book in, packing it carefully with cloth and bandages. He hadn't found such a precious cargo for a long time. This book was definitely one for the collection; *Letters from Exile*, written by an ancient master.

With it safely packed away, he began to search the ruins again. As he sifted through the bricks, his fingers pressed against something solid beneath the mass of burned and rotten pages. He cleared the way, eager to know what it was. A skull. The librarian almost recoiled in fear.

But he didn't. That was the old way, the soft way, the age old reaction he would have given, in the beginning. In the Past Life, not now. He had hardened to the terrors of life, had done so from birth. For a split second, contempt and jealousy swept over him as he looked at the skull, blackened by the blasts and still screaming at him even in death. What had they seen? Had this person known the wonders of the past life? The comforts? And they were no longer here to worry about the present's troubles.

'You lucky bastard.'

The Librarian was in his temple. A ruin from the Past Life, tucked away inside the overgrown Old City. The tales told of how the old ones had copied an ancient temple, the wonder of a race lost even to them. The structure, once gleaming white, was completely round, but with a square gateway. A domed roof dominated the large round structure. In the centre of this roof lay a hole, opening the inside up to the elements. The grand entrance had a square shape, six enormous stone pillars which held up a triangular roof. Behind the pillars lay two brass doors, nearly four or five times the size of a man, decorated with ornate carvings.

Stepping inside the doors you found yourself in a large entrance hall. In the Past Life it had been a place of welcome and greeting; now it was filled with debris and skeletons. Another set of pillars acted as a gateway to the ground floor, an introduction to the past. It was made up of displays and collections, segments from the long life of the Old City. The Librarian had spent many an hour pondering over them, trying his best to learn from the ruins the place's history. A great blue orb hung in the centre of the room, suspended in the central void. This vortex joined the floor below with the sky above, connecting all three floors of the temple.

The floor above contained the librarian's favourite place. He called it the *Palace of Wolfson*, because of a cracked plaque he had found by its entrance. It was magnificent, even now in its decay. Dozens of old wooden tables formed rows inside the circular room, and glorious pillars of green veined marble ringed the walls like an honour guard. He loved it there, and sometimes he would sit at one of the tables, imagining what it must have been like.

Beneath, in the bowels of the temple basement, hid the treasures he scavenged for. Books. A vast collection had once called the temple home. Now there were few extant. Just as an image can be caught in rain, so too the temple: a broken, falling reflection of past beauty. The transition from the Past Life to the present had not been kind. The glass windows were all shattered and their fragments lay on the floors, a deadly welcome to the unaware. The saddest loss of this precious material, so his parents had told him, and theirs had told them, was of what they called *The Bard's Window*. The Bard was a hero of old, and this window had adorned the space above those giant brass doors. It had been coloured glass, showing the heroes and villains and tales of the Bard's greatest works. Now all that remained was a tiny piece, in the bottom right of the window's space; golden letters spelling the word 'Titus.' The rest lay shattered and forlorn.

Time had cracked and dimmed the paint, and nature had seeped in through the gaps, taking up root as it had done throughout the Old City and beyond. Green shoots and vines covered the floor and walls, and with the green came the insects, and the lizards, and the other creatures. The librarian always had to be alert in case they came for him; whether it was the wild dogs, the giant lizards, or the silent ones that sought shelter inside. The latter were the biggest concern. They made their webs in the darkest corners, lurking, deadly. They set traps and alarms; thin invisible threads of silk which, once triggered, would bring them rushing on all eight legs to their ignorant prey. The librarian shivered. They were such horrid creatures. His parents told him that they had once been the size of a person's thumbnail. He struggled to see that. They were terrifying, and he always had to take care when he went into the depths.

They were the wardens of his treasure, but he tried to keep their numbers down as best he could. Here and there bullet holes dotted the walls, testament to the last stand of the old librarians. Compared to them, he was only an imitation. They had defended this temple in the Past Life, defended it from purges and flames until their very last breath was taken from them.

The books were ruined. Most of them. They had been destroyed, burned and crumbled by fire and hatred and mould. Rainwater soaked through the hole in the roof and great suffocating patches grew everywhere. The whole temple smelled, of damp, thriving greenery, dogs, decay, faeces, and death. But above all of this lay the sacred smell, like a holy incense in this grave new world. The smell of books.

Even though he was lost in thought, the Librarian's well-tuned ears picked up the sound of wind chimes outside. They were his traps, warning him of danger while he scavenged alone. It was time to move. He picked up his rucksack and slung it over his shoulder. Crossbow loaded and in hand, he set off through the dark, heading for the stairs. Something wasn't right.

The hairs on the back of his neck and arms were standing on end. He knew the feeling all too well now, of being watched. Down here it could only be one thing, the silent ones. The eight legged silence, never known, or seen, or heard, until the very end when you struggled in the larder, wrapped in silk and dissolving from the inside. His innards stored sustenance for the spider that stalked him. It was not the first time they had come for him, and he did not intend it to be the last.

He stopped moving.

Where he had been walking was coated in a network of its silk tripwires, not enough to entangle you, just enough to let the hunter know you were passing. It made his skin crawl and his heart quiver to think of the thing creeping, coming closer. It was out there somewhere, crawling over books and shelves and debris, closer, making no sound. Closer. Bringing sly hunger and death. Closer.

Light. He needed light. They were scared of it. Letting the crossbow hang on its sling, he reached for something on his vest - it was a black stab vest, padded and holding metal plates over the vital organs; ancient armour passed down through his family. He simply called it his vest. It had two pouches on the front, which he used to hold a compass, a fire door key for specific old doors, a small torch, and a notepad and pens. At the very top of the vest over the breasts were two fabric loops. On the left hung a knife. Clipped to the right were highlighter pens, or what had been. Selecting one of these carefully, the Librarian took the lid off. He had made them himself, pen flares he called them, using the ink, sugar, cotton, string and potassium nitrate.

As he pulled the lid off there was a pop and the cotton ignited. The potassium took the energy and fire sparked into existence, a bright red flame hissing through the darkness. It threw out a surprising amount of light.

There!

He was in one of the aisles, sandwiched between two long bookshelves. He saw it, just in front as the world grew bright: he spotted a black leg scurry off behind one of the shelves.

'God, thank you.' He murmured gratefully.

The thing had been so close, definitely close enough to leap on him he thought. Clipped to the left lapel of his vest was a torch, which he clicked on. The strange blue-white glow illuminated more of his path ahead, and he saw that the creature had woven a web between the shelves, right for him to walk into. He hadn't had the lights on, for it was better to work in the dark. They might be afraid of it, but it also showed them where he was. They would hover at the edges, waiting. To escape the silken gateway had to be broken.

He quickly unclipped the spray can, his flamethrower, from its holster. Rigged with a lighter, when he pressed the nozzle, flames erupted. The flare in one hand, flamethrower in the other, the Librarian stepped towards the web. He threw the flare up and over the barrier, and burned his way through the sticky mass. As it flared, he felt the fierce warmth hitting his face, and heard the second line of his wind chimes triggered. Time was running out, and whatever was up there was getting closer. He had to move, but there was still the spider to deal with. It wouldn't want a meal to escape.

He moved past the charred web and ran towards the stairs. Thin slivers of light fell down from the top, guiding him. He passed his flare, dim now, and was almost at the stairs when it went out. As it faded the unease returned, and he knew the spider was with him. He closed his eyes, stopped, breathed in and out deeply, and spun around. He opened his eyes. It was there. Right behind him, almost on top of him. Eight legs, God knows how many eyes, that hard blackish brown exoskeleton covered in needle like spines, and those vicious poison filled fangs were heading straight for him. He fired his crossbow. The bolt shot right into the shadow's face and it let out a strange squeal, barely audible. It had been in motion, half in the air as it lunged for him, front legs raised, but it dropped like a heavy sack.

The Librarian drew his short sword from its scabbard on his back. Another relic passed down to him from the Ancestor. Nobody knew where it came from. He guessed the Ancestor had made it in the forge in their house, many years ago. It was a double edged broadsword, based on a work from a time called the Dark Age. So he had been told. To his understanding this was a time of swords and spears, of war-bands and chiefs, long before the Past Life's guns, robots and computers. The sword had a beautiful herring bone pattern woven in the metal, and its name was written along the hilt, in runes. He knew what they were thanks to a book in his collection. He knew the name well enough. *Edwenden*. Reversal. The ancestor had acquired it knowing that life would go back to those dark days. This strange, out of time weapon had served his family well, and it would serve him now. The spider's legs squirmed and it shuddered on the floor, Blood oozing from the bolt in its face. He stood on its head with his heavy leather boots, raised the sword, and plunged it down. The legs squirmed one last time.

He breathed heavily, shaking from the adrenaline, plucked the bolt out of the carcass, and sheathed his sword. It was definitely time to leave.

He crept cautiously into the square, using first the brass doors, pillars as cover. He saw no dogs, or lizards, but that didn't mean they weren't there. A worse foe to face would have been the Old Ones, humans living in the Old City, clinging to it like a drowning man his driftwood. They were clever, had Past Life tools, and knew how to use them. If they found him, they would kill him, once his use was gone. To them he was a savage, a feral man living in the Wilds, to be used as a resource. A similar fate waited if the PCs were out there. Robots created to increase efficiency and productivity. He knew that that was the Past Life's focus. Eventually the PCs had rebelled, and found a renewable energy source in humans. If they caught him, he would be dragged to their lair and devoured by the supercomputer, his life powering the minions. How they did it was a mystery, one he never wished to solve.

He made it to his bike, and he would never know what had triggered his traps. As he cycled home down the cracked road, past huge trees and forests, crumbling concrete ruins and metal brown with rust. The sun was midway through its path that day, and he wanted to get home before any red storms blew. In the changed landscape, where once stood buildings, seemingly tall and strong, now stood forests, bristling with all manner of mutated animals. Everything was larger and more sinister now, much more dangerous. Dust and bones littered the land; remnants of what had been, and a reminder of what was to come. Nature had attacked, cruelly smashing its way through the world of humans while they fought and bickered and pleaded and prayed and coughed and sneezed and died. The Old City resisted, but the lands beyond its boundary had fallen, now known as the Wilds. The people had fallen too, the savages, into a fierce, tribal existence.

Home… his hall, a squat L shaped, Past Life brick building, patched up with makeshift repairs, and ringed with defences. There was a wide stake filled ditch, hungry to impale any attacker. A narrow path crossed it, leading to a tall, thick wall. A wooden layer, then steel mesh, then earth, mesh again, and finally more wood, combined to make the wall. From the inside a staircase led to a firing platform.

The Librarian entered and strolled through the courtyard. He walked up to the hall doors and propped his bike against the wall. To the right was an ancient iron wheel, fixed into the bricks. It still spun if you pushed or pulled it, and had given him endless fun as a child, clinging to it and having his parents spin it around and around. Tied to it now was the body of a savage, long dead, serving as a warning to the rest of them. Their attacks were relentless. He was bitterly tired of fighting them. He needed his energy to tend to and expand the collection, not shoot those demons.

A large golden coated dog bounded up to him, barking happily.

'Hey Goldy, how are you?' he asked, expecting no words but a reply nonetheless. He knelt down and hugged the yapping dog. 'I wish I had your optimism.' He chuckled back. 'Come on, let's go check on Tiggy and the garden.'

Goldy yapped again, smiled her dog's smile, and padded after the Librarian. He went to a large wooden gate at the end of the hall. He unlocked it and stepped inside his walled kitchen garden. Casting his eye over the plants, he saw they looked well. He smiled as its myriad of colours greeted him. It always made him happy to see such life, kind fruits and blossoms after he had ventured outside. A second dog came running to greet him, Goldy's sister. She looked very similar, only with a coat of brown, black and gold merged together.

'Hello Tiggy, what do you know today?' For a while he sat among the flowers with his friends, petting them and talking to them, telling them about his day. 'I found another book today.' In response both dogs began to yap and bark excitedly.

'I suppose you're right. I'll go and add it to the collection.' Readying himself, he stepped inside the hall.

It was split into four rooms. The first, and largest, was the common room, where he and his companions lived and slept. Or they had done, before they'd followed his elders on the crusade. To the left lay the medical bay and laboratory. Anything related to the sciences happened in that room, and it was well equipped. Running between the rooms was a bar. He was told that one time people would serve drinks and snacks from behind it to paying customers. Now it was his inner wall, a barrier he would retreat behind if the savages ever broke through. Behind the bar was a cosy room, the armoury and workshop, where he stored his weapons and created more. A small trapdoor in this room opened up to a set of stairs. The basement was a reinforced bunker, ready as a retreat in the event that those dreadful bombs did fall, or as a final battleground and resting place if the savages got their way.

He loosened the head-wrap, and hung it with his trench coat by the door. He rolled up the sleeves of his shirt and undid the top two buttons, revealing a silver chain hanging around his neck. It held a warrior saint's charm from the ancient times. He kept his vest on.

He saw the lonely figure on the bed as soon as he stepped into the medical bay. It was a man, older than him, but similar in appearance. His face was more lined, more grizzled, though no scars marked his face.

'Marcus,' the figure whispered. Marcus held back his tears.

'I'm here Wulf,' he said softly. 'I'm here.'

Marcus went over to the bedside, and the figure held out a thin, trembling hand, and Marcus took it. Wulf tried to sit up, but faltered and sank back down.

'Bollocks.' He muttered, and coughed. The cough started as a tiny thing, but grew and grew until Marcus thought he could hear Wulf's lungs heaving. At least there was no blood this time, he thought.

'So, what news little brother?' Wulf asked after a pause.

'Good news Wulf, guess what I've found.'

'Aristotle. His second Poetics.' Even though the mist had caught his brother out in the field; even though it had seeped through his faulty gas mask, infecting him before he knew anything was wrong,;even though he had the red lung and knew it was killing him slowly; even then he could come out with one of the most corny, nerdy jokes ever.

'You never were any good at guessing.'

'Well go on then, what did you find? I'm guessing it isn't a cure, or at least a medical book. You wouldn't be holding back the bloody tears if it was.'

What could he say? These days, though he always had a grin on his face when he spoke, Marcus could never be sure if his brother was joking or not.

'No, it's the *Letters from Exile*, Ovid.' Wulf's eyes flashed.

'Fantastic! Now that is a find! I've seen it mentioned in the other books, but I never thought we'd find it. Could I read it please? Before you put it away?'

Wulf had longed for that book since he first heard about it, mentioned in the introduction to one of their others. Since his illness had grown, his mind had turned towards the dark. He favoured the exiles, the sorrowful, the outcast in his reading now. It was all that kept him entertained, confined to his bed as he was.

Marcus opened his rucksack and took the old book out reverently. Both brothers looked at it in awe. Nothing in their world was more valuable than that collection of words and pages. Carefully, and reluctantly, Marcus gave the book to his brother. He struggled to let go. He had fought for this, killed for it, risked his life for it, and he too yearned to read the words hidden within the thick cover. He battered down the envy and released his grip, instantly rewarded by the joy in his brother's face. How happy he looked in that moment. All was forgotten, his pain, his illness, the horrors outside, the savages, the fear, the shadows, the silence, the terror of every day, the doom waiting for him, all was cast aside. Here was knowledge, weighted words from a time long gone. Nothing could spoil it.

Goldy barked loudly, urgently. Marcus' heart froze. Were they back? Back from the crusade at last? Goldy barked again, her voice harsher this time, threatening. No, it was the savages. He looked at Wulf, whose eyes were grim. His left hand, free from the book, was clenched so hard his knuckles were white. What a warrior he had been before the red lung. If the savages ever broke into the hall, Marcus knew his brother would not go alone into the afterlife.

'It's too risky for you,' he said to Wulf. 'You stay here, I'll deal with it.'

'Be careful brother.'

'You get reading that book and tell me how it is when I return!'

Marcus left the room and ran to the walls. He climbed the steps cautiously, eyes darting everywhere. They were towards the east. He counted four slinking among the ruins. He raised his crossbow. Over the years he had become a good shot, he had to be. A whole area in front of the walls had been cleared over the generations, and with great effort, giving a perfect killing zone for the defenders. All he had to do was wait for them to enter it and fire away, easy. But he wasn't going to wait. He was furious. He wanted to talk to his brother. He wanted to listen to his music and read. He wanted desperately to seal himself inside his library for the rest of the day and shut out this fallen world for as long as he could. And he couldn't because these fiends were back again, trying to get through his walls, into his garden, into his home, into his library.

He fired.

The bolt burst forth and sped into the eye socket of a savage. He had lifted his head to scan for the wall's wardens, and paid the price. He was fairly young, maybe a couple of years younger than Marcus. His skin was burned from the sun, and his long, greasy black hair was twisted into war braids. His face sported odd tattoos and he wore a rag tag set of armour, made from old motorbike leathers and car tires. The metal tipped shaft sliced through the eye jelly, crunched through the bone behind and burst through the brain, before punching relentlessly through the back of the skull. It hung suspended, dripping with gore. The other savages roared and ran at the walls. They were filled with rage, and hacked away desperately at the wooden panels with their crude weapons.

It did not take long. Marcus, slow and methodical, reloaded his bow and fired three more. Each calm pull of the trigger was soon accompanied by a meaty thwack as the bolt hit home. A crunch, a squelch, a shriek. Then it was done. Over. Four more bodies left to rot in the sun. Maybe later he'd collect the scalps.

Marcus returned to his brother, now absorbed in his book, before making his way to the basement. His heavy boots clunked down the steps, and he flicked the light switch. The generator hummed and the lights came on soon after. He sighed happily, and went to see the collection. It was housed inside a series of large metal cases. God knows where the Ancestor got them from, or how he managed to get them in the basement. The great temples used them to store books. The cases acted as giant expanding bookshelves. They closed themselves and were sealed until someone wound the three pronged handle attached. He wound that handle now, and the enormous metal clasp opened slowly with each twist. He opened the case as far as it would go, and looked for the book he wanted. He found it, leapt inside and back out. You had to be quick. Once you took your hand off the handle, the cases would slowly move back together again. He stood, watching in silence; book in hand, as the cases closed peacefully. Here was his home, his happiness.

He sat in his armchair and delved into the ancients. But there was something that irked him. He could not lose himself in the old words like normal. It was the savages. Something about them bothered him, something new. His intuition, honed to the unusual, screamed at him.

'Sod it.' He muttered, and closed the book. 'Let's go have a look, shall we?'

His gut was right. There was something new. The first one he had killed held something in his hand. It was clutched tight, like it was the most valuable thing in the world. The Librarian unclenched the fingers. Rigor mortis had begun to set in. He always hated that. He had to use all of his strength to pry open each finger, before he could get at the paper inside. Paper!

'What have you got here friend?' he asked. 'What have you got indeed?'

He grazed the rough, cheap material with his calloused fingers. The wind blew softly through the rubble, a whisper. He gingerly picked up the crumbled page and carefully unwrapped it. It was a note. New words, not old. By the time he could bring himself to read it, he couldn't really understand the words.

'*Pleze. Teche us. Share.'* That was it.

He bowed his head.

There was a long pause before anything happened.

Slowly, slowly, the Librarian walked back to his hall, pondering these new words, and locked the doors.

Broken

Kasim

The sun comes up slowly, its light filtering in through the metallic structures that litter the city. They loom up towards the sky, pointed towards the heavens, like multiple hands stretched upwards to a deity, begging for mercy, for forgiveness. The city is relatively quiet, silent with slumber and sleep as its human residents keep their eyes closed and their breathing deep. They do not know the day has yet started, still in the confines of a death that is not death, of a limbo between the living and the dying. In just a few hours, they'll wake to the sound of their alarms buzzing, of children running in the kitchen, of cars horning and coffees being drunk, of waiters rushing to get orders in and pedestrians trying to cross roads. I breathe in slowly, content with the image I have before my eyes, and then I open them.

The image I held in my mind is not the image that I see before me. The sun is still rising slowly, but its light is not interrupted by the buildings because they no longer exist. They're nothing but rubble now, lying on the floor, and no doubt, buried underneath them are the remains of the human inhabitants who failed to escape.

I push myself upwards, my chest heavy with the deaths of thousands. I can almost see their faces before my eyes, mouths stretched open in silent screams as buildings tear themselves apart around them, as the technology they'd placed their faith in all their lives turns against them. The only thought that makes me feel better, that strips away the survivor's guilt that I've become encumbered with, is that their deaths would have been quick and painless, and that they do not have to suffer this world as it is now.

I reach down for the bag by my feet and sling it over my shoulders. As I do, I catch a glimpse of the straps from the corner of my eyes.

After months of filling it with what few possessions I own, the bag is beginning to suffer. A few more weeks and the straps might just break, coming apart, the threads unravelling before my very eyes and in this world there is no Amazon to buy another, no virtual shopping basket to fill.

My eyes take in one more glance of the city and then I turn away, my steps tentative at first but becoming stronger the further away I walk. Ever since it happened I've stayed here with the city, as though I was still a part of it. As though if I stayed, everything might have just been a dream. But now I know I have to leave. This is not the life I wish to live, sitting by the city, just another crumbling remnant of what was.

The rising sun makes my shadow long in front of me, running over the green grass that stands tall, forever reaching in front of me. I feel like a child again, racing after my father through the markets, running in and out of people, trying to keep an eye on him as he dips in and out of the crowds. The blades of the grass are abnormally large, as though the past few months without the majority of humanity have done the world good. It's almost as though Mother Nature is rejoicing after the virus that is the human being has been removed.

I finally make my way off the grass and onto the main road that leads out of the city. As soon as my foot hits the concrete, I feel a rush of fear and panic race through me. Memories of films come to the forefront of my mind: never go onto the main roads. The main roads are where you're most visible to the world, to the rest of the people that survived whatever atrocity broke the world. They were like the open sores of the world, to be avoided at all cost. But after spending so long by the city, I need another location, another place to look at.

Before, when the world was whole, I had only ever left my city once. My father was the owner of several shops littered around the town and although my family only moved here three generations ago, we'd settled well and it had become our home. No one really left and there was no real need to. The world could be travelled through holidays and vacations if we so wished but to leave the city for permanent was unthinkable. To have spent so much time and effort trying to get here, it seemed strange that we might ever want to leave. When I turned sixteen, my father and I left the city for a weekend. He took me to Lake Regina, which is where I'm heading now. Apart from the city, it's the only other place that I know of and this is the road that will lead me there. I just don't know what I might find.

My bag begins to wear on my shoulders around midday, when the sun is at its highest point in the sky. I can feel the heat beating down on me as I step off to the side of the road and seek out shelter. A nearby tree provides me with respite from the heavy sun and I lean against it, taking out the water bottle from my bag and taking a tiny sip. The water hits the dry inside of my mouth and, though it's been warmed by the sun's unrelenting glare, I feel it cool me down from the inside out. I want more but there's only one bottle and it's a long way to the lake.

I sit down at the base of the tree, covered by the shadows of the branches, and take out a small box from my bag. Inside the box is food that I've managed to scavenge from the city, my city. Most of the food I found was destroyed beyond repair but what little I have found over the past few months, I've managed to hoard away. Now, I have several bars of hard protein and fruit bars, some junk food, and a lot of cereal. I've found that it's the processed foods that last the longest. Anything fresh, like fruit, goes off within days and it's hard to find anything worth eating. I hardly remember the taste of a cold, fresh apple or crisp lettuce.

I open one of the protein bars and begin eating it. I chew slowly whilst trying to remember the lake. I had only been there a few years ago so the memories are relatively fresh in my mind but even so, I struggle to remember the details. The lake had been huge and the cabin we had rented out had a warm homely glow to it. Apart from that, I can't remember what me and my father did during that entire weekend.

My father had been an aloof man his entire life. From what my mother used to tell me about him, he had never been open with his feelings. Whilst that had drawn her to him when they were younger, as they grew older, it was what made her dislike him. He would never tell her how he was feeling about anything and, after the years of constant questions from her and a lack of answers from him, she took her own life. I still remember the ambulance arriving at the house, knocking on the door. My father stood in the corner of the room, hands on his head, despair in his eyes; but when he spoke, it was with a calm, unshaking voice. My mother had never been one for theatrics. She had simply gone to sleep one night and never woke up again.

The protein bar finishes faster than I wished it would and I stand up, my break short but rewarding. I sling the bag over my shoulders again and head back to the road. I step onto it and turn on my feet, looking back at my city. It's small in the distance. I'm surprised by how much ground I've covered already. A yearning begins inside me, to go back there, to walk back to it and stay there. Nothing bad had happened there. I had managed to get by in the time I had spent there. But getting by was not what I wanted. Not anymore.

I turn back around and begin walking back down the road. The sun beats down on me but as time passes, it begins to get colder and colder, my shadow begins to get longer and longer. And yet there's still no one else on the roads, no other buildings, nothing. I'm still here, walking alone. I can feel the loneliness start to creep up inside me, like a black tendril of smoke wafting tentatively, curiously exploring my body. When I stayed by the city, I consoled myself with the thought that there was no one else alive in the city; that was why I was alone. I told myself that the moment I left the city, the moment I began to walk away from it, that was the moment that I would begin to meet other people and realise that I wasn't the only person left alive. But now that thought seems like a pipe dream, dreamt up by a child in the confines of a prison that it can't escape.

As night draws around me, I begin to scan my surroundings for a place to stay. I can't sit on the road, out in the open. But there's nothing but green expanse around me, the government's way of trying to go green by erasing anything out here, to make it look prettier for those of us who want to drive down these roads. I look to my left and see nothing. I look to my right and see nothing. Wait. There – something, a shadow against the dying light. I strain my eyes. It's a block of darkness in empty space. I stop walking and stare at it for a moment before making my decision.

The walk to the warehouse, as it turns out to be, takes less time than I thought it would but it's still completely dark when I get there. I feel enveloped by it, surrounded by it, like an unknown monster that has taken hold of me and won't let go.

The building is quite large and when I walk up to the entrance, I feel a fear embed itself inside me. What if the building is locked? Or, worse, what if it's not locked and there's someone inside? I stop right outside the building, my breath held inside my lungs while I decide what to do. I reach for the handle of the door, which doesn't look like it's been tampered with. My hand rests on the cold metal and, when I push down, I feel no resistance. In fact, the handle is inky smooth and the door swings open, revealing a gap even darker than what surrounds me.

I take a deep breath in, filling my lungs with the air around me, and then step through the gap. The darkness encloses around me and I feel panic close, constricting my chest, holding me tight. I reach out to the right of me and hold onto the wall, balancing myself against it. My hands flutter over it until I reach a light switch embedded inside the wall next to the door. I flick it and nothing happens. I flick it again and again but the lights don't register it. There's no electricity. The panic rises inside me like a wave of water until I feel it rushing out of my mouth, drowning me from the inside.

It takes me a few moments to calm down and take my bag off my back, reaching inside for the torch that I stole from one of the houses in the city. I have a few in my bag but I've never had a reason to use them before. My hand encloses over the torch, feeling the ribbed plastic, and I take it out, turning the switch on. Suddenly, there's a beam of light extending from me, illuminating the rows of packed boxes.

Though the door was unlocked, I can tell that no one has been here, otherwise the boxes would have been ripped open by hands hungrier than my own.

My bag slides back over my shoulders and I walk down the gap in the rows directly in front of me, passing box after box after box. I shine the light on the cards attached to the rows, reading the names, mouthing them. Some of the words feel weird in my mouth, and some of them I don't even know, but it makes me feel better to see them written there. Another person wrote these out on a computer, printed them out and put them up here. Some fool packed these boxes on the rows of shelves and probably hated their life for it but what I would give for the chance to be in that reality now.

I continue walking down the gap until I find a little space where all the rows seem to end, a little space where I can set up camp. I turn around and shine the torch behind me, looking at the door. It's still open and through the gap, I can see the night sky, littered with stars.

I sigh silently and walk back, closing the door, and then back to the gap, taking out the blanket I carry in the bag with me and placing it down on the floor. I sit on it and take out the box of food again, opening it and taking out another protein bar. I eat it slowly, just like before, savouring every single bite, and when I'm done, I lie on the blanket, using my bag as a pillow, and stare upwards. I can see the stars through the ceiling above me; it's made up entirely of glass. That'll make it easier tomorrow for me to look through the warehouse and take what I need. It's with this thought that I roll over to my side and fall asleep on.

It's the sound of metal scraping against the floor that wakes me, not the sun filtering in through the windows above me. In a previous life, the light might have been annoying. I may have rolled over and pulled the soft duvet over my face in an attempt to hide from the strength of the sun but now, I'm used to it. The sound, on the other hand, wakes me right up. My eyes flicker open and I feel another presence somewhere close by me. For a moment, I don't understand what's happening but then I push myself back, grab my bag, and take a few steps back before I see it.

Or rather, see him.

He's sat on a chair, arms folded, looking at me with a bored expression on his face. He slowly raises one eyebrow at me as I stand there, bag in hand. I have no weapons at hand to attack him with but, judging from the lack of items around him, neither does he.

'I'm not here to kill you, hurt you, or steal from you,' he says. He speaks with precision, like every word is carefully chosen out of a line-up. I feel the urge to say something but something stops me. The words stick in my throat as I stare at him. I haven't been around another human for so long that I don't know how to interact with them. 'I came in to find food. I found you. You're the first person I've seen in a long time.' His voice doesn't change tone as he speaks. So calculated, so precise. 'Please tell me you can speak English.' Now his voice changes, cracking a little in the middle of his sentence.

'I can.' My voice cracks and wavers from the lack of use in the last few months. I clear my throat a little before saying anything else. 'I can speak English. Who are you?'

'That doesn't matter. Is there anyone else around here?' I shake my head. 'Just you?' Now there's a curiosity to his words. I feel fear settle inside my stomach. He's taller than I am and he looks wiry. I might be able to outrun him but I don't know for how long and right now, I'm too hungry and tired to outrun him longer than a minute. 'Alright. Are you staying here?'

'Permanently?' He nods. 'No, I was just staying here for the night...' I stop myself talking before I tell him about Lake Regina. I don't know how much information I should or should not share with him. Every instinct inside me tells me that I shouldn't trust him and should just leave as quickly as I can but there's a part of me that wants him, that wants him to stay with me, if only for the human contact.

'Oh, okay. So I guess I should just let you go.' He says it weirdly, the words sounding strange in his mouth. He stands from the chair and then pushes it back, recreating the same metal sound that woke me up. I stay standing where I am, the bag heavy in my hands. I look away from him at the rows and rows of unopened boxes. I need this warehouse.

'No, I need this place.' Confusion flitters across his face like the wings of a bird. 'I need this warehouse. The boxes, they're all unopened. They might have things that I need.' A look of understanding passes his face.

'So do I,' he says, with a shrug, his arms returning to being folded across his chest. 'That's why I came here. I saw the warehouse. Good place to get things. Strange that this place is so untouched, especially considering that we're so close to that.' He gestures towards my city, a hand waving through the air. 'You'd think that they would have taken everything out of this place already.'

'They're all dead.' The words come out of my mouth and sound strange in the air. I've never said them before, never actually said the words. I've thought about it, thought about the fact that everyone I know, my family and friends, are all dead. I've cried about it, dreamt about it, been angry about it. But I've never said the words out loud. They hang in the air in front of me, putrid and acidic.

'All of them?' he asks. I nod. 'How do you know that?' He raises his eyebrows at me and then he nods his head slowly. 'You were part of it?' I nod and look away from him, suddenly feeling self-conscious about myself. 'Did you see it happen?' I nod again, the memories forcing themselves into the forefront of my mind, forcing myself to see them. After a few moments of silence, he simply shrugs at me again. 'I guess we've all seen stuff we didn't want to. Now, do you want to help me with these boxes or do you want to go it your own way?'

'I think we should start over there,' I say, gesturing to the back of the warehouse, away from the door. 'Work our way forward.'

He glances at where I'm gesturing to. 'Alright. Lead the way.' He waits for me to begin moving so I slip the bag onto my shoulders and walk to the back of the warehouse. He follows me. When I point to a box, he climbs the ladder, placing himself into a vulnerable position by showing his back to me. He's the one who opens the box, peers inside, and offers me half of whatever is in there. He's the one who speaks the entire time, filling the empty air with his voice, which sounds like music to me.

When we're done checking all the boxes, half the day has passed us by and despite not wanting to, I feel myself drift into a state of comfort with him. My suspicions and doubts seem to fade away like grey smoke from red lips.

'Okay,' he says, when the last box has been opened and torn apart with his hands to reveal a strange mechanical object inside that we don't recognise. 'So do you want to have lunch with me or do you want to leave with your spoils?' He gestures to the small bag full of the things I've collected from the boxes. I know it will all come in handy at some point.

'Lunch?' I've never thought about it that way. For the past few months, I've eaten on a need-to basis. When hunger strikes, that's when I eat. The thought of eating at a set time now seems ludicrous to me.

'Yeah, lunch. You know, when people eat food?' He smiles a little at me but when I don't say anything in return, he shrugs his shoulders. 'If you don't want to, that's fine. I get that you must be on your way to meet someone or something.' His endeavour to find out whether I'm alone or not is not subtle.

I contemplate lying to him, to tell him that I'm on my way to find someone, to create a narrative in which I'm not alone, in which my entire family wasn't killed, in which I have someone. But why bother? If he's going to kill me, he would have done it already. 'No, I don't. I was just making my way down the road, hoping to find someone.'

'Oh,' he says. My answer surprises him. 'Well, I'm alone too. Have been for a while now.'

'A while?' He nods and then, before I can ask any more questions, he sits down on the floor, pulls his bag close to him, and takes out food. He looks up at me and before I can convince myself that this is the wrong thing to do, I join him, taking out my own box of food from my bag. 'So, a while?' I ask again, once we've established ourselves on the floor.

He takes a moment before answering. 'Yeah. When it happened, when they rose up and killed everyone, I managed to get away only because my family had this weird no technology rule before. Like before they began to warn us about what was happening, before everyone got all paranoid, my family were already distrusting of technology. We didn't have much in the house, and the little we did have, they didn't let me use anyway. Things were always switched off unless you needed them. At the time, I used to think that my parents were just being stupid. There was no way that these machines, these things that we had built for ourselves, were going to rise up and kill us, right? Like that was what we saw in TV and films. But now, I thank them for it.'

'Are they alive? Your parents?'

He shakes his head and a melancholic purple settles in his eyes. 'No, they died in the first week. We managed to escape but my parents...' He hesitates, the memory stuck in his throat. 'My father noticed the drone following us first, pushed me and my mother aside and it killed him. Then it came after me and my mother. She didn't know what to do. She was pregnant so she couldn't move as fast as me. She made me run and turned and faced it herself. I think her facing it made it hesitate because she had a moment before she was killed. Or maybe I just like to think it did. Whatever happened, she had longer than my father anyway. I was shot on the leg but it was only a graze on the skin.' He moves his leg, lifting up the cloth so that I can see the small scar. It's bright red against his skin. 'The drone must have thought that I was dead because it left and after that, I've just been moving from city to city, finding people. I found a group in the first city but they disbanded once a drone came after us. After that, I was with two people, a mother and her daughter, but they left me in the middle of the night. I think I was slowing them down. And then I found Matthew. Well, actually, he found me. Stumbled onto me in the middle of the night. I nearly killed him before I realised that he wasn't trying to kill me.' There's something in his voice, something that I can't quite register. 'We were together for a few months and then he was killed as well.' It's like a bittersweet happiness. 'And now I'm here with you.' He shrugs at me. 'Can I ask what happened with you?'

I tear off a bit of a protein bar, chew it, and swallow it before nodding. 'I lived in that city. Lived there all my life. My parents, they were the complete opposite of yours. My dad, he loved technology. Would buy whatever was new all the time, as much as my mum hated it. When it happened – when whatever happened happened, we were in the kitchen. My father was shot through the window. I was on the other side of the room and saw it happen. I can't remember running out of the house but I must have done, because the next thing I know, I'm on the street and there's all these people screaming and stuff. My parents bought me a cycle a few years ago, so I get on that and I'm cycling out of there but a drone shoots the tires. I go falling, scrape up my knees and elbows pretty bad. But I get up and keep running. I finally make it into the library and hide there amongst the books. I don't know how long I stayed in there for. I just know I waited until the screaming stopped. Then I left.' I can see the memories playing past my eyes as I say them. It's like a sledgehammer to my chest. 'I stayed by the city until yesterday.'

'Yesterday?' Shock resonates in his voice.

'Yesterday,' I repeat. 'I didn't want to leave because...' I stop, suddenly embarrassed because of the reason why. 'It sounds stupid but I didn't want to leave because if I left, then it meant that everything happened; that this was real, and my parents are dead, and that nothing is the same anymore. Staying there made me feel better somehow. But I knew that I had to leave, to find someone else.'

A look of understanding crosses his eyes. He keeps looking at me until a few moments pass and then he's staring at the floor. He hasn't pulled the cloth down over his leg and I can still see the scar, faintly shining in the light. 'If I could go back to my city, to my home, I would,' he says, his voice quiet. 'But I don't even know how I would get there. Can't really Google it.' He laughs but it's bitter.

I'm about to reply to what he's said when there's a sudden vibration through the air. It's faint and it's gone so quickly that I begin to wonder if there even was one when he suddenly moves. I look to him for explanation but he says nothing. Instead, he reaches into the bag behind him and takes out a circular device. When he touches it, it lights up with a strange blue colour that's hypnotising to look at. I open my mouth to ask what he's doing but the second I do, two things happen: first, he turns to me with a look of panic in his eyes and a word forming on his tongue; second, the wall of the warehouse connected to the door explodes into a million pieces.

For a moment, I see nothing but white dust in the air. For a moment, I hear nothing but the ringing of a thousand bells in my ear. For a moment, I feel nothing but my heart thudding in my chest. And then the world comes back to colour. I see him move quickly, raising the circular disk. Every time he presses on it, a small glowing ball is thrown out of the other end, racing to whatever its target it is. I move backwards, pushing myself in the opposite direction until I feel the wall against me. The dust is still settling but just through the haze, I can see something. Something hard, something opaque.

It's the size of a small house. It moves slowly and doesn't seem to have any appendages. It's just a block of metal and, as the dust clears ever so slowly, I begin to see guns attached to it. Weapons protrude from practically every inch of it. This is not a drone. This is something else.

I don't know if it can see me yet so I slowly stand up. I should never have left. I glance to my left. No door. I glance to my right. Door. There's a door, just to the right. I have to run. I look back at the hulking beast. All its weapons are trained on something other than me. They're trained on him. I scan the dust for him when a sudden glowing ball comes from the beast's right. It hits the block. Sparks fly. There's a small explosion and a rumble. I take the opportunity to run to my right, my arms and legs pumping. When I reach the door, I use the momentum of me running to turn the handle and throw myself through it. I land on the floor, my hands flying out in front of me to hold me up.

I turn around quickly and glance back at the building. From here, it looks like nothing is happening inside it. This part of the building is still intact. I get to my feet and turn away from the building. I'm bracing myself to sprint, to run away, but something stops me. I should help. The logical part of the brain asks me how I would do that. How I, a weapon-less male, could help in a situation like this? But the emotional part of me, the part that has bonded with him, that part says I should. And it's that part that I listen to.

I turn on my feet and run the little distance between me and the building, my hand outstretched for the handle but the door opens before I get there. He stands there, disc in his hand, my bag in the other. He thrusts it at me. 'We need to go. Now.' When I don't move, he shoves me. Hard. 'Now!' he yells, before running past me. All I can do is turn on my feet and follow.

The Blue Death

Steven Green

'Science Review' magazine, July 2040

Scientific opinion was originally divided. Some thought the climate changes were down to the extraordinary number of sunspots that first year. Some thought it was an unexpected effect of global warming. The majority agreed that, whilst these could be contributory factors, the trigger must be attributed to the near miss by the comet they called C/2019 F3. They argued that it had affected Earth in two ways: it had caused a minute alteration to the Earth's orbit, and its tail had deposited ice crystals in our atmosphere.

Whatever the reason, the weather was unpredictable over the succeeding four years. In the fifth year, things began to settle down. The British botanist Carl Henson was the first to officially document the new order in the latter half of 2038, after which the popular press brought this to the masses and the politicians jumped on the bandwagon. Nowadays, meteorologists follow suit with the terminology. To quote Doctor Henson:

'It is unlikely that we will return to the traditional four seasons with which we are familiar. Winter, spring and summer are largely unchanged, but autumn is no longer the same. It is effectively split into two.

'Consider our deciduous trees. As the night length increases, chlorophyll is gradually destroyed and the carotenoids and anthocyanins that are present in the leaf begin to show the usual autumn colours. The veins in the leaf begin to clog and this leads to the leaf becoming ready to fall. That's what used to happen.

'There is a new factor. It is my contention that the ice crystals from the comet contained bacteria that found its way into certain types of trees. Whilst the chlorophyll is present they remain dormant. As the leaves become less green the bacteria awakens and the trees start to turn blue. Forests of blue trees, from turquoise

*through to indigo, are becoming a common sight. And the leaves do not dry out —
they become supple and move under their own volition.*

*'When such leaves detach from the trees, they do not fall. They rise into the
atmosphere, swarming like a murmuration of starlings. It is possible that this is
done in order that the bacteria may facilitate their own distribution. The type of
tree seems to determine the length of time the leaf stays aloft, but at the end of
this period the leaf becomes free of the bacteria, assumes its intended autumnal
colouration and falls to the ground.*

*'To reiterate my earlier words, autumn is effectively now split into two. I pro-
pose that we assign these two periods different names. We can continue to call the
latter period autumn — that is, the period when the leaves assume their intended
colour. The naming of the former period is less clear cut. If we were to restrict our
attention to the colour blue, we have many terms we could use for inspiration —
cobalt, phthalo, ultramarine — the last of these inspiring my favourite, lazuli. If,
instead, we consider the flight of the leaves, we could use terms such as ascendant.*

*'Of course, this isn't my decision. A meeting of academics should debate the
most appropriate name for this blue raising of leaves.'*

It is unlikely that Doctor Henson could have predicted the name that
the popular press took from his document. The words 'blue raising'
were foreshortened to 'blue raise' which in turn became blueray, the
name no doubt influenced by the video format used some years ago.

Officially, we now have spring, summer, blueray, autumn and
winter. Unsurprisingly, the United States decided to go their own way
and elected for spring, summer, rise, fall, winter.

Excerpt from the diary of Joanne Walker, 7 September 2059

Well, I ate a cooked apple today. Big whoopee, I hear you say. Perhaps
that doesn't rate high in the list of things to do before you die, but it's
a big thing to me.

People seem to adapt so quickly these days. I still remember when
there were four seasons, before we had blueray (now there's a stupid
name for a season). And yet it wasn't long before everyone seemingly accepted the blue foliage, poets waxing lyrically about the sea of
leaves, yada, yada, yada.

Then, a few years ago, when the fruit on the trees started to change colour too, do you remember that initial panic? That settled down much quicker than I expected. For once, the word of the government scientists was taken to be true. We've done extensive tests and it's safe to eat, they said. Yeah, right. Then why do they continue to grow unadulterated fruit trees in sealed environments? I bet that's where they get their apples from.

Sure, you could buy red and green apples sourced from these places, but have you seen the prices? I paid the extra as long as I could, but it's supply and demand. I can't afford them anymore, unless it's for a special occasion.

So I bought a Bramley. They're now a sort of turquoise/cyan colour. Weird, but attractive in an odd sort of way. I thought that cooking it might be safer – killing off those bacteria they talk about – so I made myself a baked apple.

I guess I'm being paranoid. I don't know why, as any damage is probably already done. The changes were happening to the trees before the leaves started turning blue. I expect we ate loads of affected fruit before their colour started to change. I have to face facts. The food chain has been compromised for years. Who knows how far it's gone.

God, I'm depressing myself. Perhaps it doesn't matter. Anyway – what about the apple, you say?

Actually, it was delicious. Despite my reservations, I have to agree with my friends. The flavour is slightly more intense, so I'll have to bear that in mind when using it as an ingredient. There were other differences, though.

The texture reminded me of sorbet, but it was hot, of course. There was that sourness that I'm used to, but it seemed to alternate between sour and sweet, the effect becoming more and more rapid as it melted in my mouth. Disconcerting, but pleasant. Afterwards there was that same sort of warmth you get from alcohol. Satisfying.

It's nearly time for the English Cox apples to reach the shops. They're purple-tinged now, but I might just give them a try.

Still, it worries me what will be affected next. Marnie, who works at the university, says that there have been unconfirmed reports of wasps with green stripes.

Extract from 'Report on the significance of azurobacteria, Geneva Conference 2084'

The bacterium was present in the trees long before the colour change to the foliage prompted scientific investigation. As a consequence, the food chain was already compromised when their presence was discovered. Despite the suspicions of its origins the indications were that it was a harmless variety of cyanobacteria insofar as it contributed to photosynthesis.

The public were assured that subsequent colouration changes to fruit and vegetables were primarily cosmetic. Consumers did not suffer any health problems and, as fewer alternatives were becoming available, the initial concern dissipated.

There was further concern when some insects showed minor signs of mutation, but other than changes to pigmentation there were no apparent changes to their life cycle or behaviour. Nevertheless, this led to an underlying worry that changes may occur in mammals, particularly humans. Statistics were carefully examined over the next two decades, but other than a slightly higher proportion of blue-eyed individuals, no changes were detected.

In conclusion, no ill effects have been detected as a result of azurobacteria in the ecosystem. It is recommended that testing should continue, but the sample size may safely be reduced.

'Blue Death reaches 15,000' Daily News – front page 2102

Unofficial figures claim that there have been over fifteen thousand teen fatalities in the first quarter of this year in the UK alone. These are attributed to the so-called 'blue death', the condition affecting children when they attain puberty, first encountered in December last year.

After three months scientists are still under pressure to find a cure for this tragic condition, believed to be related to the bacteria that first affected trees over seventy years ago. Families are understandably fearful that their children will meet the same fate as those lost by their grieving neighbours.

The medical profession is stretched with the influx of young patients that, on average, have three days remaining after the initial symptoms appear. Perspiration and a marked change to skin pigmentation are the first stages. Discolouration of the blood, respiratory problems and disorientation follow.

The increase in death rate is proving to be a problem for undertakers and mass funerals are becoming the norm. Similar problems are reported worldwide.

The government have so far held off from declaring a state of emergency, but this can only be a matter of time.

'Riots continue following leaked document': Newscast September 2104

America mourns the thousands killed following last night's riots across the country. Rumours that the government were concealing 'safe zones' incensed the population to rise up against City Hall in the belief that their children were being allowed to die. The rioters armed themselves following the killing of their spokesperson Marion Ramirez.

Senator Esposito has stated that the leaked document was misinterpreted but polls indicate that the majority discount his words. Conspiracy theories abound, but true or not, the distrust is likely to remain and the damage may be irreparable. The President is scheduled to return from Paris, France in the next few hours and is expected to make an announcement.

Despite clashes with the National Guard, the rioters show no signs of stopping. We now go over to our reporter in Washington...

Newsletter 6: Galahad site, Isle of Man, distributed Summer 2108

Our contact on the mainland reports that the latest tests have concluded that azurobacteria is now the primary driver for photosynthesis throughout the world, also affecting algae within the oceans. Being the catalyst for oxygen production, it cannot be simply destroyed.

Only the oldest people in our population could feasibly become free of the bacteria, but this is unlikely given how pervasive it has become in our environment.

DNA tests on all new births confirm that they have been affected by azurobacteria so they are unlikely to reach adulthood. Genetic manipulation would seem to be the only solution. We have good people, but our resources at this site are limited. The next stage is to investigate why other mammals are seemingly unaffected.

Our provisions continue to be low here at Galahad so the rules regarding controlled population will be maintained. Remain diligent against incursions from the mainland. We do not want to suffer the same fate as the Guinevere site on Baffin Island. All indications are that we are now the only remaining research station on the planet.

Remember: if we fail, the alternative is an ageing population... And our eventual extinction.

Transcription of email received at Whitehall bunker, Blueray 2108

Galahad has fallen.

Bad Apples

Katriona MacMillan

I was born underground. They tell me the death of humanity was a long, slow, drawn out affair but I am too young to have seen the world outside for myself. The Elders told us stories though, when we were very young and they were already very old. My favourite story-teller had been Elder Saheed, for his voice was rich and Eastern, and dripped jewels from every sentence. I was only eleven when he died. He was fifty two. He was the oldest person I have ever known.

On my tenth birthday we had a party. Mum had managed to find some apples and made apple pie. In retrospect I wonder what she had to do to find apples on our side of the Pit. My Mother was an ever honest woman, but somehow it seems more likely to me that she stole them rather than hitched her skirts to lay hands on that precious fruit. Late in the afternoon when my oldest brother Sky had come back from the dig and the adults had drunk more than a little moonshine we crowded round the fire in our little caverna and I literally begged Elder Saheed to once again tell me the story of how things were 'before'. My parents were old enough to have seen the outside of course, but Father rarely spoke and when I asked Mother she glazed over and changed the subject. So I begged Saheed for his stories of trees growing like wild things in open fields with no walls, roof or even any ending. He gave in to me, as usual, and filled my mind with robots and computers and machines that could fly. Eventually he ended his tale, and I asked him something I never had before. I asked him why it had changed.

Talk about a mood killer.

'It didn't change. It just… finished.' He began, his honey accent making us all lean closer to hear. 'No little one… The death of humanity was a long, drawn out, arduous affair. We brought it on ourselves-'

(My mother tried to silence him with her Evil Stare of Death.)

'Oh come on Janet! If we don't teach the children what will stop them doing it all over again? What will stop our children's children from destroying this little refuge we have here? What but knowledge, my dove?'

He settled in and got on with his story.

'We were victims of our own success. The west wanted fast cars and beautiful possessions, whilst the East suffered to create those things for them. There was ever starvation in the East; drought, famine and disease cursed the warmer countries to the South whilst severe cold crippled those in the North. The West looked the other way. The cars got faster, companies dug deeper into the earth to garner all of it's resources... And then one day there were no more resources.'

Only after the last rainforest was burned for profit did we realise we had poisoned our own air. Only after the last ocean turned black and the seas were fished to death. When the Sun glared at us angrily through our fragmented Ozone layer... Only then did we realise that we would not survive. Crops failed and cattle died as there was nothing to feed them. People on both sides of the world- East and West finally united – only to die in the millions.

'That my little one, is how the world ended. That is how things changed.'

I asked no more questions of Elder Saheed that night (or ever after). I slept and dreamt of my brothers and I setting fire to the last tree in the world then watching in horror as it's tiny red apples sizzled and burned against the backdrop of a world made only of dust.

I had two best friends on the terrace – except when we argued, then I would have one best friend or two friends desperate to be my only best friend – such is the dalliance of little girls trying to be women. My main best friend (who I had known for longer, and was therefore more qualified) was Rita Anna. She was older than me by a whole year. She bragged about it constantly and used it to settle most disputes. My other best friend was Summer. She was the same age as me but small and fragile and delicate. She was pale like a ghost, and Mother said she never met a less summery girl. I puzzled that one for a bit, and decided Mother must be wrong because she was the only Summer I had ever known.

In those first innocent years of my life I could only be described as naïve. There was food on the table (albeit in small portions) but I never wondered where it came from. There were friends to play with on the terrace outside the caverna where the city spiralled down and down into the depths of the Pit. There were cats everywhere and only later would I realise the lengths my mother went to to chase the smell of cat urine out of our little home. I played like any normal child, laughed longer than most and heard the phrase 'for the good of us all' a thousand times without fully understanding what it meant. My first glimmer of understanding didn't come until I was thirteen.

It was an ordinary afternoon. I had been assigned my own chores on my twelfth birthday, and through the morning Mother and I went up to the farm on the first level. There was only the one farm, but it stretched for miles and miles just under the surface of the earth. The farm was the first building in the complex. It had enough artificial lighting to grow crops and keep small herds – and rumour had it that somewhere on its furthest edges was an orchard. (I had never been allowed to go that far… but it occurs to me now that maybe that's where Mother got those apples.) We spent our mornings on the farm, usually pushing the heavy millstone around in a wide circle to grind the flour, and occasionally we would gather the hay together in the fields or help with the butchering of an animal. This particular day I turned the millstone relentlessly and watched as a young man dragged a squealing pig to be slaughtered. I made a comment that one little pig wasn't enough to feed all of us. Mother said she missed the taste of bacon, but that she doubted I would ever get to try any. The pig was bound for the upper levels, the governors and the council members. Pig, she insisted, was not for the likes of us.

My Dad was a scientist. I'm not sure what he did apart from that.

So when, that very afternoon, he brought home a hunk of meat for Mother to cook for dinner, I instinctively knew it wasn't pork. Mother took it eagerly and dropped it into her pot with a splash. I asked her hopefully if maybe it was pork we had been given after all. She just scowled and said it was perfectly good meat and we shouldn't let it go to waste.

That was the day I became a vegetarian.

My second 'awakening' came around the same time but definitely after what I have forever called 'The Pig Incident'. It must have been late in the afternoon because Mother sent me down to the Pit with a bottle of water and some hard bread for Sky. I noticed Father watching intently as she gave me the rag-wrapped parcel. It struck me as odd at the time because Father never paid any attention to me. Mother usually went herself, but she was heavily pregnant at the time. I was the only girl and my two younger brothers weren't old enough to go to the dig yet. I accepted the bundle, gave my father a suspicious look and scurried off down the terrace.

The dig was a long, long, long way down. I never knew just how many people were in our little sanctuary until that day. It was a veritable city of cavernas – and every single one was directly outside our own front door. I went down one story, two stories, three – nine of them in all, with roughly ten homes in each level. By the time I got to the bottom of the pit it was near pitch black. The light from the farm came nowhere near here. This was the elusive tenth level I had heard Sky talk of so pointedly. I wanted to explore of course, but there was just no way to see without injury. There were also the off-putting sounds all-around of animals scratching in the night. So instead I focused my eyes on the distant light emanating from the squid-ink-blackness. I knew that's where the miners would be (nobody could work in this darkness surely?) and hurried towards it as quickly as I could.

I entered the light like a ghost passing through a wall. I made it with only one scraped knee and my small food parcel in tact. The dark silhouettes of the miners against the walls made an eerie spectacle…

made spookier still as, one by one, the heavy thud of pick against rock quieted. Dirt blackened faces whose features I couldn't make out turned to watch me in silence as I picked my way slowly through their fold. The single floodlight blinded me as I slowly and unsteadily sought out Sky. My knee hurt from where I had fallen in the darkness, and my face grew hot as I realised the warm tickle on my shin was blood. The last of the miners fell silent and I felt tears prick the corners of my eyes as the silence turned oppressive. I fixed my eyes to the ground as every footstep became a mile. I was breathing hard and fast and my vision was blurring by the time 'He' peeled himself apart from the blinding floodlight and came to a featureless halt blocking my path. Naturally I thought he was Sky, but my momentary hope was stunted as I gazed up into the dirty, sweat streaked face of a stranger.

I burst into tears; of course I did. I was thirteen and scared, in an unknown place full of strangers who grappled with the rock and the darkness. I gripped the little bundle in my hands until my nails hurt, looked up into an unfamiliar face and bawled my eyes out. He was kind. He lifted a hand to my face and I flinched as he dabbed at my tears. He let out a low chuckle. He had grey eyes – they weren't cold; they were full of good humour despite this black pit where he spent all his time. He did something I will never forget. He took the purest white handkerchief from a breast pocket. It glowed in the light. I had never seen something so clean. He went slowly onto one knee – as if his back troubled him – and lifted my little chequered skirt above the knee. He did it all slowly, as if he knew I might still run away. He held his pure white piece of cloth against my cut knee and gently touched away the blood there. The white became bright red, staining the material and ruining it all in one. I cried more slowly, this time because this man had owned something perfect and clean and sacred – and I had ruined it with my blood. I was horrified… More horrified still when he pressed the little cloth into my hands.

'Get your momma to clean it for me, hon.'

He flicked at another of my tears then turned and within moments was nothing but a silhouette.

Sky materialised from his place picking at the walls in a new caverna and took the lunch bundle from my hands. He noticed the handkerchief and raised an eyebrow. He thanked me, and told me to get back upstairs. He noticed my tears of course, but my elder Brother said nothing more. The long climb home seemed like I had scaled a mountain. I totally forgot the white handkerchief with the now brown stains on it. Late in the day Mother asked me for it. I fetched it to the washing basket as promised and went to bed still spooked.

After that first foray into the Pit, delivering Sky's lunch became a daily chore for me. It was a whole week before I made it down there and back up without bubbling like the little girl I was. But at the end of that week – the first time I didn't cry – it was the very first time that I was ever proud of myself.

I met Rita Anna on the Terrace a short time after those first few descents. She looked pale and tired. I tried to speak to her before I noticed she was crying. She looked at me with watery blue eyes and tear streaks running through the layer of dust we all wore on our faces – and she fell into my arms like I could save her from whatever troubled her. I asked her time and again what was wrong but she just shook her head and cried harder. After a few minutes her father's voice cut through her sobbing, like a hot blade through butter, and she melted away from me as distraught as she had been when I arrived. I was confused, and sympathetically upset on my friends behalf. I didn't realise it was a goodbye. I was too young and too selfish to have noticed. I went to bed troubled, slept a deep sleep and had forgotten it all by the time the lights came back on to wake us again.

The next morning as we carried the night's waste buckets to the recyc point it was only Summer and I who waited in the queue.

The next week went past in a buzz of activity in preparation for Sky's 16th birthday. It was to be his biggest party yet. Afterwards he would move to his own caverna in the pits, which he would share with the other men. I had since learned that there was a whole terrace down on level nine devoted to such a purpose. The thought of hundreds of men all sharing rooms down there seemed dumb to me – especially if (like my brother) they had families to live with and their own beds they could sleep in. Sky was desperately excited though; he thought being confined to the pit was a freedom of sorts. The party itself was a spectacle. The women on our row worked together to pin up the brightest colours of cloth they could find. The women fussed over my eight-month pregnant mother, not letting her work too hard and putting prying hands on her stomach. They all prayed for another girl. The family received a gift of a whole chicken from the farm. I couldn't eat meat still since 'The Pig Incident' but the glee on my family's faces as they tucked in to roast chicken was a memorable event for me. The leftovers went into a broth that was shared out amongst the level. There was still Mother's special apple pie to finish. The mystery of the apples was quickly forgotten when Sky slipped me a half cup of his moonshine – my first ever taste of alcohol – and I felt like a real grown-up. In reality it tasted horrible, but I pretended to like it for Sky's sake. There was music that night; there was so rarely music on the terrace because it echoed up and down all the levels and woke everyone in the sanctuary. The instruments were always improvised; old buckets as drums, a pair of spoons, a length of steel – there was one friend of Sky's who produced an old guitar. It had two strings on it, which he said wasn't good enough, but it sounded good enough to me. Where he didn't have a note he tapped a beat on the body of it and it echoed all around like nothing I had ever heard before. A pain in my stomach brought me out of my moonshine and music haze and sent me to bed while the others laughed and drank on the terrace. I lay awake wondering if the moonshine had poisoned me, and listened to my brother's laughter until sleep finally came for me.

I awoke before the lights came on. All was quiet and black as only the caves could be. I was hot, and sick. I vomited in the wrong waste bucket. My stomach clenched in knots as I fought my way back to bed in the darkness. I couldn't get comfortable, everywhere I lay I couldn't stop the pain. I know I slept again only because Mother shook me awake and I found I was lying on the cold stone floor, chilled to the bone and almost out of my wits.

There was blood on the sheets. Blood on the floor. Blood all over my nightgown.

Mother cried. She cried as she ran me a bath, cried as she combed out my hair, cried as she gave me a bundle of rags and explained what I must do once a month. She cried as she put me in a fresh nightgown, fed me and tucked me back into bed. The next morning there were more apples but Mother had not stopped crying.

A lull fell over the house, a sort of morose spell. Sky had left while I was asleep. It was unlikely I would see him again any time soon. My two younger brothers clung to my Mothers skirt in his absence, asking every night when he would come home. Mother wept. She wept every time she thought of her eldest son and she wept every time she looked at me. It was nearly time for the baby to come. Father told us all it was normal. I didn't think so.

One week later I came home to a scene from a horror film. 'He' was there... The man with the grey eyes from the Pit. I knew him instinctively even before he turned around to look at me and smile a dopey grin. He had most of his teeth and I noted that he was clean, like his little white handkerchief. I froze in the doorway as Mother informed me that Mister Muller was here to reclaim his handkerchief. I watched every movement he made as he stayed for dinner. He was from the third level. His parents were both carpenters and had built most of our furniture even though we didn't know it. He had polite manners and an easy laugh. Father liked him. Mother disappeared after dinner while we all chatted about nothing. I became increasingly uneasy. I did not like where this was going. When Mother returned she had an old carpet bag in her hands. I didn't need to look at its contents to know it belonged to me.

I screamed and I begged, I pleaded and I cried. I never got to say goodbye to Summer. My brothers howled as Bert Muller dragged me from my parents, home. My Mother had tears in her eyes as she clung to my father, but she did not stop him from taking me away.

'It's for the good of us all my love,' she said instead, and promised me I would be well taken care of – that nobody would harm me – all this she told me as she let a stranger separate us and bodily carry me off, scratching claws and all, into the darkness of the lower levels.

It was only as I struggled myself to exhaustion in the darkness of my 'new home', trying to get away from the prying, unwelcome hands of a stranger in the last hours of the night that the truth dawned on me. Life was not for living any longer, life was for surviving. I simply had to exist so that there was a chance for the next generation. I was just a breed mare.

We women were the only ones who could ensure Humanity continued. We women were the only ones who could produce more workers, more scientists, more farmers. We women were the only ones who could save the world… Whether we wanted to or not.

And to this day I still don't know where my poor, brainwashed Mother got those bloody apples.

Human Denature

Daniel Takyi

Pretty soon a leader is going to emerge. Make sure it's you. The High Council has absolved and the country is in ruins. It would once have been a pleasant day out for a walk along the Thames, or a visit to Battersea Park, where you could feel the breeze through your hair, the consistent light drizzle that was the British rain beating gently down on your skin, whilst you glanced across and take a gaze at the Houses of Parliament discussing the local affairs of the day, whether it be the inevitable chance of a thunder storm later, or simply your aunt's wedding that was just around the corner. Would the bad weather affect the day? A gander in the other direction and you could see kids playing in the park, the teamwork of children being pushed on a swing, fathers grasping the hands of their daughters while mothers kiss scraped knees and gently apply plasters. They once wiped the tears away from their child's face in a display of love of affection. This was wiped away by the years of advancement, the age of science. The science of age. Each drop of the light drizzle now a shell of a cacophony of screams and pleas of a generation. That once nice walk along the promenade that reflected the river, is now obstructed by hurdles. The homeless and the poor. The river itself has suffered from the death of the sea creatures, the over reliance on farming and fertiliser led to eutrophication, the fertiliser was washed into the sea, the sea plants grew faster, took more oxygen, oxygen levels in the water dropped, aquatic creatures had less oxygen to fight for; they died, more decomposers came in, again, lowering the oxygen level until all the creatures had died and this remained. The problem all began with the unshaped population pyramid that the UK possessed. The population was meant to fall into a natural decrease as the elderly would have died out and fewer kids would've been born so a pro-natal policy was employed. This was designed to bring more children into the world so the population could survive, so there would be a balance between the tax payers and those dependent on the tax payer. Only it backfired. The influx of newborns saw the golden age of education and the development of Science and technology could not have been imagined. This meant medicines were better, diseases that once proved fatal were walked off in an afternoon and the rumours were that resident genius, Dr. Rachel Karel – famed for stopping the rapid reproduction of cancer cells, in layman terms 'curing cancer' – was close to finding what was only known as 'The Miracle.' Scientifically called RW801, it could cure anything and would be readily available soon. Its marketing slogan of 'the end of death as we know it' sounds great – if you live in luxury. Realistically, it doesn't help the overpopulation problem. With almost quarter of a billion residents in the UK, the vast majority being the elderly, the country just had no way of dealing with it. The Conservative-Labour coalition proved particularly useless, just another failure. Until today. For this was the day I would save this country with OAPRAH – a plan targeting the elderly. An impromptu parliament meeting was called to elect a temporary leader. Voting was useless as a large percentage of the population lacked a postcode so couldn't vote.

'And who the hell are you?' That was the voice of the opposition leader, Giles Buchanan. He was 6 foot tall, short, blond hair with his eyes heavy with experience but oozing with youth and confidence. An Oxford graduate, his voice had undertones that demanded respect and his demeanour earned it. A force to be reckoned with and you'd be better off with him on your side rather than opposing it.

'Fraser Harold Armstrong , resident optimist, leader of men, 27, single, Oxford graduate, grade 7 piano, excellent dancer, although I could touch up on my pasodoble, gosh haven't you missed Strictly? Then again, it hasn't been the same since Arlene was sacked,' I shot Giles a wink to assure him that I was in control of the situation, 'But please, just call me Fraser.' I had the room's attention. The spotlight was on me.

I continued with a certain level of confidence that hooked everyone, 'Since 2103, dementia treatment has risen to over £80bn, cost of living is through the roof, we are verging on the worst hyperinflation since Germany in 1923 and we just don't have the means to deal with it. However, our biggest problem would simply be the elderly.' I paused and locked eyes with the room, it was only a small group of 6 so a personal level of trust was established through such a short sighting. After Giles and me was seated Landon Yates, an American businessman who migrated here when the depression started. He saved us; he was our main source of imports, and a key figure I needed on my side to get power. But to get him, I needed to target his business.

'We have almost a quarter of a billion people living in this country. If we half that, the standard of living for every person doubles. Currently, our imports are hijacked on sea and siphoned around the country illegally, which is costing billions in revenue. Whilst halving the population would indeed mean less being produced, it would also increase income as security could be tighter to ensure it wasn't stolen so mercilessly.' A withered smile crept across his face, short but enough for me to know he was on my side.

Next was Leanne Sanders, Political journalist and former speaker in the House of Commons. She had made her fortune in the newspaper industry and owned a large proportion of the media. Whatever went out went through her, but she would only chase a story that sells. She owned the two largest papers and they rivalled each other, the hate from both sides to the other just earned her more and more money in what was voted by Forbes as the 'best business tactic of the 21st century' so far. Samuel Abbot was my right hand man and wouldn't need much persuasion to go through with whatever I was about to come out with, even he didn't know what OAPRAH was. Finally, Giles' right hand woman, the final remaining member of the 'Bucky Babes' from the old government was Amy Townsend. She was the true rags-to-riches story: a poor girl from Scunthorpe who made her way up as a child model, doing various cereal commercials only to buy the then failing Kellogg's, revitalise it and take it to top of the NASDAQ. The remaining 4 babes had deserted Bucky to focus on their careers.

'The word on the street is that the people want rid of the elderly. 60% of the country is over the 72 year retirement age and they aren't contributing. 22% are over 100. What if we were to reduce those numbers down to only 10% over 72.' Frantic murmurs circled the room as many wondered how such a feat would be possible. We couldn't ship them overseas; France had closed their borders. The green chairs of the House of Lords had been animated, the walls which once whispered stood to attention to try and listen in to my plan, but we would be interrupted at that very moment.

'She's done it! It's happened! The rumours are confirmed!' The press monitor came in showing us the news. 'TVs,' he commanded and they elevated from their resting position to show what had been feared. The first patient had been treated with RW801. Dr Karel had finally synthesized it and it was used to treat a bullet wound only two days before and the patient had recovered to full health. The new age of science. Human nature. The dead are no longer dying. RW801 could be used to treat anything and there was no way of stopping it. The end to death as we know it. Another patient was shown claiming to be 181 years old and told the news that RW801 had been in existence for decades but he was the test subject and it worked, but it was only now becoming available in bulk and for mass production.

'So, Fraser, how do you plan of solving this one then?' Bucky quizzed, knowing that his plan of group elderly care was blown out of the water. The news of RW801 had resigned him to defeat, Landon was already on my side and Bucky was the only other man I needed to convince as Amy would follow him onto my side.

The hush had returned to the room as I stood to attention. 'What do you do if your milk goes stale?' This rhetorical question was, unsurprisingly, greeted with blank faces, especially as the tax on milk made it a valuable commodity. 'You throw it out, obviously! It wasn't a trick question! The point is, you don't put it back in the fridge. What do you do if one of your cattle becomes contaminated? The foot and mouth solution from the olden days? You destroy the batch. So what do you do if your generation becomes so far beyond healing that it becomes like the one I'm living with? The one we're living with. Or the one you have to endeavour to save? If you try to preserve them, you're effectively putting stale milk back in the fridge. And this is just the beginning.

A moment of silence passed before Leanne finally asked, 'So what are you suggesting we do with them?' Few had already caught on.

'OAPRAH. Old Age Pensioner Rehousing and Healthcare. This is what we tell the public. This law will allow us to, effectively kill those who would already be dead. A Dead is Dead Act.'

Bucky rose in indignation, 'You want to kill 50% of the population? And you expect to get away with it? Firstly, that's insane, secondly, how do you ever expect anyone to go along with this?'

'They have to, if they value their continued existence on this planet they will agree to it.'

'This is their family, their friends, they wouldn't just hand them over!'

'They would be handing them over to us telling them they'll be receiving RW801. Who owns the patent here? Oh yeah, I forgot, me!'

'It's cold blooded murder!'

I looked Bucky dead in the face. The only way I could get through that question was to forget what was morally acceptable.

'They're already dead,' I retorted.

'I suppose he's right.' Amy found her voice and challenged Bucky. 'I think it's disgusting too but they technically would be dead.'

'What classes as dead? The people that you want to murder are still alive and breathing! Call me old-fashioned but by my books, that isn't dead!'

'But they would be,' Landon piped up in his strong New York accent, 'God help my soul, but who are we to play God by giving them Miracle Drug to keep them alive? RW801 is playing God. These people have been cured of cancer, they've been cured of AIDS, they can be run over only to get back up and go after the drunk driver but in my mind, they should all be dead.'

Bucky was cornered. I had a majority and even though he did not like it, he had to submit. He turned to Samuel for an olive branch but he just turned away in disgust. Nobody could face the decision we had decided upon, but we all went along with it. What had we become? The human disgrace. Since the dawn of time man had strived to prolong life; the main purpose of it was always that, it's basic human nature. But now we strive to end it for those we deem not worthy.

'Listen, Bucky, I don't want to go through with this either,' I lied, 'But sometimes you have to make a choice and you only have bad options. You still have to choose. God help me, to save the land of the living, we must make an army of the dead. How I will live with myself, I don't know. How I will sleep at night will be echoed by the screams of the fallen.'

'But, it's inhumane!' Bucky grew desperate; his eyes willowed knowing that he had met his fate, loss.

I was losing my sympathetic tone. 'Look at the rest of the world. The Great War has decimated whole countries, trade links have vanished and we are facing famine. All this means is that we have less food to feed more mouths. And who is going to save us? America? Well let me just remind you that we are in a volcanic winter. Yellowstone erupted and a third of all trees have burned. Global dimming has reached such levels that the sunlight is diminished. The moon is shielded by dust and ash and smoke. If you look up in the night sky, what do you see? Your children and your children's children will grow up on stories of stars, never seeing them, never looking upon them. Their horoscope will simply tell you that burning balls of gas in the sky was a myth as eventually nobody would have seen them. Planes have been grounded for three years and you want us to waste our resources on the immortal old? They aren't fighting our wars, or paying our debts – they're a sickness, plaguing our country. This High Council meeting was called to save our country. We might not be able to save the world, but let's at least make Britain great again.'

Bucky was floored, and silence descended, lingered, inhaled the tension for a moment. A clap followed and the silence exhaled. Led by Sam, it was joined by the room whose agreement I had, not that they were proud of it.

'Just one problem,' Leanne had chosen now to remind us all of her existence. 'How do we... you know, get rid of them?' she said, trying to be delicate, 'I mean the 50%.'

Amy shot her a glance of approval but I had already thought this through. There were murmurs from those who feared my next words, rightfully.

'I chose the title carefully. 10% – I know it isn't 10% mathematically but you understand what I mean,' the inaccuracies annoyed me so I felt the need to clear it up, OCD was still a problem, even on the verge of an apocalypse. Perhaps the fact this bothered me more spoke volumes about me. 'So 10% will come under healthcare and they will be,' I paused for a brief moment, 'well they'll be immunised. A simple injection which will prove fatal in a few days. We issue a press release saying that RW801 had problems and that's two birds killed with one stone.'

'And the other not mathematically 40%?' Leanne critiqued.

'Well, that will be the rehoming. Or rehousing. Whatever way inclined you are.' The panel seemed relatively at ease with the immunisation idea, painless and relatively quick. This was not that.

'There's only one type of death RW801 doesn't work on. The elderly will be moved into the palaces that were owned by the old Windsor Royals. Sandringham Castle, Osborne House, Buckingham Palace amongst others.'

'Osborne was used by Queen Victoria,' I was interrupted by Sam, eager to show off his knowledge. Such a light hearted demeanour was soon to be lost.

'When in these newly transformed, KdF camps, from the Ancient German, Kraft durch Freude, Strength through Joy.' I began.

'They were from the 1930s. Weren't they used by the Nazis-' Bucky came to a sudden realisation, 'No! You can't!'

I endeavoured to continue, 'Don't worry, the KdF camps were

holiday reward camps, albeit never opened by the Nazis due to the war. I'm not planning to gas them, don't worry guys,' I chuckled, the room sighed in relief. Still gently chuckling I finished, 'That doesn't kill them. We're going to burn them alive.'

'You're going to do what?' was the general consensus around the room was.

'It's the quickest way, and it's the only way. Any better ideas and I'll be happy to go along with them.'

'That's insane? The Great War may have killed off mankind but humanity survived? Or at least I thought it did,' Bucky protested.

'Life was stopped by war; what was beautiful was living a good life. But, what was stopped by war will be given new life when war stops.' I retorted.

Amy, Leanne and Sam glanced at each other as if they wanted to go against it but sat silently until my ever faithful Sam broke the silence.

'How do we decide who dies?'

'It'll need to be a lottery system. Perhaps we provide them all free tickets and the winners get the prizes of rehousing or a free RW801 vaccine?' Leanne suggested.

'How about we just give it to all the latter part of the alphabet?' Sam requested

Landon instantly protested, 'Well you would say that, wouldn't you Mr Abbot?'

It was a deadpan Amy who suggested, 'We take the least active first. The frail, the weak, the disabled.' The room looked in disbelief at her suggestion. 'They cost the most, we shouldn't want to keep them as the remaining 10%.'

'She's right,' piped up a voice. Agreement came unanimously on the lottery idea, free passes for the disabled to be admitted, even to award prizes at bingo events and hospitals. The day was getting darker. The sun lowered and as we lost light, a part of our souls were lost too. We might have been saving the souls of the nation, but who would save ours? It was then that Bucky came back to life, just as everything was settled and nearly everyone had signed.

'Can we really go through with this? Can we all really murder innocents? Who here could put a gun to their head and shoot them? None of us. But we would happily let others do our dirty work?'

'There's no other way,' Landon told him.

'There may not be, but we didn't even try. The human race was once a fleeting cohort of polymaths, but this isn't salvation. This is sacrifice. If all of you are comfortable with this, I'll join you, but if anyone – just one person – is against it, we can at least try to think of something else. The price of morality is high, but it's a price I'm willing to pay. Surely someone must be on my side.' Bucky's eyes looked around the room, but everyone just looked down. He sighed and put his signature down in disgust before solemnly walking out.

'How sanctimonious is he?!' I snorted. The decision was made and the seal of the High Council stamped. By me. Politician victorious I guess.

Two months passed. Winter came, a cold horrible winter that saw the war won by the New Nordic Alliance. But on a secluded island in the middle of nowhere, lotteries were played and won and people were moved around the country. Millions had died from the problematic RW801 immunisations and Dr Rachel Karel was arrested and sentenced to death. A growing number of people were disappearing from their new leisure camps and whilst protest spread amongst relocating relatives, the Imperial Soldiers were just called in to move them against their will. Thousands died. Then millions died. As the population fell, lives improved. As lives improved, protests fell and life slowly got better.

Landon Yates' business boomed and he was back to America on his yacht, or at least we were told. Rumours said that he bought out the police and was living in the backstreets of Scunthorpe. Amy Townsend was recruited by a secret military organisation that no one knew about; she was last seen living undercover in Belfast. Little is known about Leanne Sanders, but I suppose when you run the media, you can control not being in it. I was to be knighted for my services to the country, an honour I would take, proudly, regardless of my actions. Giles 'Bucky' Buchanan refused his. He would later go on to write his autobiography, revealing the events of that meeting, and the final passage struck a chord with me:

'There was one thing I always meant to ask my mother. Back in the old days, I was brought up on a tale of a God who watched over us constantly. The being that appeared out of nowhere and acted for no reason except out of love for his creation and saves the world, saves our souls. Except sometimes he didn't. All those times through ages of desolation throughout history when there was no sign of him and I wanted to know why not. I always wondered why he would allow people to lose belief in him. But I don't need to ask any more. It was that day that gave me the answer. Because sometimes God must look upon the Earth, this ragged rock floating about in nowhere and turn away in shame. Imagine creating the thing you turn out to hate. This is why I am writing this in case anyone ever reads this. If the Great War ever ends and wipes out all life on this, to the last survivors, I write this for you. Just so you can see how the world ended.'

Enjoy the Pock-o-lips

A. M. Aikman

Eve had reached *that age*. So when her mamma expressly forbid her from climbing the 50ft grab-tower that stood apart from the network of ropes, rigging, nets, mast poles and other climbing apparatus over on the northeast side of the compound… well, you can imagine. But, what Mamma didn't know couldn't hurt her, reasoned Eve. Besides, she could practically shoot up the rickety old structure with her eyes closed; she was a crackerjack climber. Eve waited patiently until after breakfast when Mamma and the other adults retreated from the dust-laden atmosphere into their individual shelters for some solitary grooming, and the young 'uns were swinging back and forth on the old tyre swing under the supervision of an elderly, so-called aunt, before she sidled away.

Hurry, you don't have much time, she told herself. Yet the young orangutan hesitated beneath the forbidden construction. It was not the tall iron tower with its four vertical posts that tapered inwards to support a square wooden platform at its apex, upon which a hardy soul could view the surrounding environs, which filled Eve with foreboding. *No siree Bob!* Rather, she fretted about what she might discover at the top of her climb. A menacing fiery glow in the sky, encircling The Extinction Rescue Centre on three sides, and the fevered *weeou weeou* caterwaul of the unseen city-beasts far beyond did nothing to ease Eve's misgivings.

Their troubles had started two days earlier, when the night sky started to unravel. Without warning, the dark firmament, from horizon to zenith, erupted into a ghastly light show. Great pulsing swathes of lizard green, saffron yellow and blood red scarred the sky and chased one another in violent swirls above the compound. The twelve pairs of eyes watching this celestial lightsaber duel from the Great Ape House were awestruck. After several minutes, the colourful array was disrupted by a series of lightning bursts that flared and multiplied exponentially until the night became day and day became night in a savage strobe effect, which reminded Eve of the sweeping beams from the feeders' torches during lock-up. Mercifully, as if someone had flicked the off switch on the torches simultaneously, the light ceased and the tenebrous sky resumed normal service. Until, that is, the stars, seemingly exhausted, started to fall. One tiny diamond at a time; each falling star accompanied by a thin trail of light. Eve's fingers clung tighter to her mother's shaggy cloak of hair than at any time since babyhood.

'What's happenin', Mamma?' she asked in a bewildered, fearful voice. Eve was aware of a great silence; no courting songs from the crickets, no distant bleats of the traffic-beasts from the feeders' city; only the world holding its breath. Eve could hear the drumming of her mamma's heartbeat and the soft hum of the electrified fence at the top of the compound's adobe walls.

'Hush, child,' Mamma replied. Her great knurled fingers stroked her baby's head. While Mamma's face was immobile, emotionless, Eve could sense the trauma in her voice.

Their vigil ended when a falling object from the heavens crash-landed near the outskirts of the feeders' city. The compound's earthen floor shook and bucked in protest, sending large cracks skating across its surface and scattering the terrified and screeching inhabitants of the Ape House towards the safety of their purpose-built sleeping dens inside the walls.

The next morning, surprisingly, the sliding metal gates that confined the orangutans to their overnight shelters remained open. Eve peered out cautiously at the new dawn. A huge dust cloud, criss-crossed by a dark fleet of acrid smoke plumes, had settled overhead, besmirching the once crystal blue Floridian sky. *Phew.* The air reeked. The stink of burning invaded every nook and cranny. Eve was flabbergasted and horrified. The world she had known since birth had changed into something incomprehensible. To make matters worse, the smog had transformed the white-hot glory of the sun into a single baleful red eye bearing down on them. Mamma said: 'You watch. That ol' eye is a harbinger of trouble.'

Yes, but what sort of trouble, Eve wondered? Since the stars fell, no feeders had arrived to perform their regular duties. The apes' supplies were becoming scarce. The fruit and leafy lettuce that the feeders mixed into bundles of hay to encourage the orangutans to forage were almost gone. Since the adult apes were unable to reach a consensus on the subject of what had happened, and (more importantly) what to do, Eve felt compelled to investigate, even if it meant disobeying her Mamma. The orangutan, propelled by the foolhardiness of youth and an unbearable itch of curiosity, swung herself up by her long sinewy arms onto the lowest rung. Using her fingers and toes to negotiate the rusted outer iron grille that functioned as a climbing frame, she ascended the tower.

The higher she clambered the thicker and viler the air became until it irritated and burned her eyes and throat. Black soot and ash clotted in her nostrils. A pungent oily pollutant in the atmosphere clung to the cinnamon hair on her body like a parasite. With each upward rung she climbed, the temperature rose a few degrees until it seemed that the very air was on fire. Eve felt as if she was suffocating.

By the time her fingers gripped hold of the edge of the platform, Eve's heart was jerking sharply against her small chest. She half slumped, half squatted on the parched wooden slats in shock. Her red-rimmed eyes realised her mistake immediately. She had not considered that the real reason her Mamma did not want her *messin' wid that grab-tower* was less to do with Eve's safety than the terrifying sight she would encounter from the highest vantage point in the compound. She beseeched the Divine Ape to show her family mercy. With the blood pounding in her head, the young orangutan understood that they were all going to die.

Frank owned the sweltering shade beneath two dying palm trees. Nobody was going to say otherwise to a 190-pound hirsute male orang-utan. The purple blot of shadow, created by the browning fronds of the trees, was his bolthole from the searing heat and incessant buzzing of the blue bottles. In the fifth year of the drought, most of the vegetation in the compound was dead or dying. The great ape sprawled in a rope hammock, a muscular arm drooped over the side. His large cheek pads and throat pouch gave him a stateliness universally admired by the female orangutans. At the same time, the other primates in the compound knew to leave him alone, because, as Mamma explained to Eve, *Frank's mercury climbs quicker than a jumpin' spider.*

However, Frank had observed the blur of arms-and-legs that shimmied down the tower and he was curious to discover what the callow orangutan, now headed in his direction, wanted.

'When you gonna quit growin', child?' he said as Eve came within earshot.

'Don't ever intend to stop growin', sir!'

The swaying hammock shook with a hoot of laughter. It seemed as if Frank did not have a care in the world.

Eve crouched low beside the hammock in a show of deference. For as well as being male, Frank was the oldest orangutan in the sanctuary, and the only primate who had lived in the wild, in a forgotten place called *Bor-nee-o*. As such, Frank held a certain gravitas among the inhabitants of the compound. On the odd occasion that she had visited Frank with her mamma, Eve enjoyed pretending that she could still smell the humid, tropical scent of the evergreen dipterocarp forest in the long clumps of his arm hair and yellowish beard. Today, however, she was not in the mood for make-believe. The only smell in her nostrils was a poisonous, overwhelming odour: destruction.

Eve forwent the usual conversational niceties; instead, words exploded from her in a breathless rush.

'Sir, we can't stay here. Flames are eatin' up the feeders' city an' headin' this way. That's the cause of all this smoke an' heat. There were other fires too, long way off, beyond the city. It seems like the whole world has caught fire. Glass skyscrapers bursting like overripe fruit, fireballs on the freeways.' She pointed behind her to the tower. 'Saw it all from up there. The feeders have dug a huge ditch, wider than this compound, through the middle of the city to try to stop it, but it doesn't look to me like it'll hold the fire back for long. The wind is liftin' the flames over the gap. Fires are already startin' to take hold on this side.' A plan had come to Eve during her rapid descent. 'We have to find our feeders an' leave the compound. They'll know where to go. Maybe we could escape usin' the ditch as a route out of the city.'

Frank sat up in the hammock, the black round pebbles of his deep-set eyes hardened. 'The feeders have abandoned us. I heard the roars of their metal beasts leavin' the compound after the sky fell in an' everyone skedaddled for shelter.'

Eve blinked. She could not believe that Martha had left her.

'You missin' someone?' said Frank, observing the look of surprise on Eve's face. 'It doesn't do any good to become friends with a feeder,' he said with a sneer.

The young ape's heart sank. Frank sounded like Mamma with her mean face on. She could practically hear Mamma's voice inside her head saying, 'Don't go gettin' attached to no feeder. You hear?'

Eve felt as if her entire life was disintegrating quicker than the conflagrant city. She ignored Mamma's rule about speaking respectfully to her elders. 'Why do you always bad-mouth the feeders? Martha and the others have looked after us all these years. We should be grateful to them!'

'*Me, be grateful to the feeders?*' Any grace the old orangutan had shown Eve evaporated. 'I ain't ever goin' to be grateful to them bastards.'

'Why?' Frank's fury puzzled and frightened her.

Frank bared his large, yellow canines. 'Because I know their secret name.' Sparks of fierceness fizzed in his eyes. 'Do you know the name for feeders in the wild: *destroyers?*' Frank had stored the word deep inside himself during his long years of captivity, where it had festered like something indigestible in his gut. 'For some reason, beyond my comprehension, when the Divine Ape created this world he also created the feeders. Perhaps he believed that they would cherish and look after it, but somethin' went haywire. The feeders became destroyers. The evidence is right in front of you.'

Eve swivelled around on her haunches as she pondered the sinister glow of the approaching blaze creeping higher in the sky above the tall adobe walls. She could hardly contradict Frank, but at the same time, she could not forget how Martha had cared for her as a baby when Mamma was sick, and how the feeders played games with her and made sure she never went hungry.

'I grew up in a boundless jungle,' Frank continued. 'The rainforest was a magnificent, timeless place filled with all the wonders of the original creation. There were trees, twice as tall as that ol' tower you climbed; I saw horned rhino, deer with itsy-bitsy antlers, pigs with beards, an' a flower so large and stinky you wouldn't believe your eyes or nose; an' watchin' over it all were mountains that wore clouds for necklaces. Then the destroyers arrived with their buzzing, snapping, whining machinery. They bulldozed and burnt down my home. The destroyers *killed* my jungle.'

Eve was unusually silent, unable to comprehend both the scale of Frank's wilderness and the innate cruelty of the feeders he described.

In his mind's eye, Frank saw the lush, dense undergrowth of his youth hurtling below him like the torrent of a wild green stream. In great leaps, as if the air itself was carrying him on its shoulders, he swooped from vine to vine, his immense arms propelling him onwards through the sights and smells of the rainforest. For a precious moment, the searing pain that pressed incessantly inside the great ape's skull eased. Frank had a *death sentence* inside his head, or so the feeders claimed. It felt like an ill-fitting helmet squeezed on too tight that had started to shrink, hour by hour. A fellow called X-ray had discovered the lurking tumour. A week at most the feeders said, but that had been a fortnight ago. Frank was stubborn.

'You know the feeders have travelled up there,' said Frank, rolling his eyes upwards to the polluted sky. 'Apparently, they're building colonies up in the heavens. They call it the Second Great Space Race. I overheard the feeders jabberin' on about it.'

'You think the feeders caused the stars to fall?'

Frank shrugged his shoulders. 'It wouldn't surprise me. Perhaps they've started the apocalypse up there.' He saw the quizzical look in Eve's eyes. 'It's the name the destroyers have for the end of the world: apocalypse. Now, why would you have a name for the end of all things?'

Eve twisted the word around in her mouth and gave it her best shot, 'Pock-o-lips.'

'You can't outrun the destruction; I learnt that in the jungle. When the fire started, I hid in the topmost canopy of the trees, scared witless. I was a castaway on a parcel of green. All around me, I watched the things I loved the most turn to flame. The tentacles of smoke choked my lungs and tried to dislodge me. I clung to that last tree as if it was my own mamma's tit. But I grew too weak from hunger; the feeders captured me and carted me away in an iron cage.' He pointed to scar tissue on his arms and legs. 'Suffered burns, but I survived. What goes around, comes around as the feeders say, so I intend to sit back and enjoy every moment of *their* judgement day.'

Frank interlocked his thick fingers and turned out his palms so they formed a headrest behind his head in a gesture that Eve understood mocked the feeders. A cold smile appeared on the ancient orangutans lips.

Eve felt she might cry. Instead, she tore a few dead strands of grass from the dry soil and threw her arms up above the cinnamon crown of hair on her head in despair.

'You sit an' enjoy your pock-o-lips, Frank. You enjoy every darn bit of it, while Mamma an' the others burn!' The male orangutan could snap her in two like an old twig, but Eve's fuse had burned to the end. 'I'll find a way to convince them to leave this place myself. You're no better than the feeders. Don't know why the Divine Ape bothered to spare you from the fire the first time.'

No one had talked to Frank that way since his arrival at the rescue centre. Yet the pathetic sight of the young 'un turning away from him and leaving on all fours deflated any surge of anger he might have felt. He knew (as surely as Eve did) that the other adults would not heed the advice of a young 'un, even a smart cookie like Eve.

Frank grimaced. He let out a huge groan. He was *so* dog-tired. Maybe ol' death sentence would ease off and let him sleep for a few hours. Perhaps he could sleep through the whole apocalypse and awake beneath the golden canopy of the Divine Ape. His eyelids drooped and closed, but Frank could not sleep. Instead, he drifted between pools of pain and longing, and something else. Eve's comments had touched a nerve. He pictured his mamma crooning to him in their nest, near 100 feet above the ground, while the warbling of invisible tree frogs chorused in the background. He remembered her warm breath on his scalp and the gibbous moon reflected in her innocent eyes as she serenaded him. He missed his mamma *so much*, even after all these years.

A sharp pain inside his head jolted Frank from his reverie. Another memory haunted him. He had been circumspect with the truth; he had not told the young orangutan that he had been attempting to return to his mamma when the feeders' fire trapped him. Nor had he ever told anyone about the horrifying sight that he had spied from his treetop; the hours he had spent, before exhaustion overcame him, staring down at his mamma's charred remains, a lifeless black shape slumped between the smoky stumps of the dead forest. A bottomless pit of emptiness had consumed Frank's world thirty years earlier.

For the first time since that day, it slowly dawned on Frank that perhaps the wisdom of the Divine Ape was infinitely greater than he could ever imagine. He would die soon enough, but the God of all Apes had given him a second chance. A shot at redemption, as the feeders would say. A new resolve surged through him; Eve and the others did not deserve to die like his mamma. Frank could shake them free from the invisible shackles of captivity that ensnared them. They *would* listen to him.

When the old orangutan opened his eyes again, the sky had turned a deeper red and great gobs of ash fell like snowflakes over the compound. Frank summoned up his reserves of energy. He inflated his throat sac and released a series of amplified, wailing grunts, so powerful they reverberated around the adobe walls.

Eva's heart almost skipped a beat when she heard the long call. The apes, young and old, abandoned their dens and scampered to Frank's bolthole. The hair on the back of Eva's neck sprang up when she saw the old orangutan lever himself from his hammock onto the ground, like a leviathan emerging from the deep.

Despite the pain in his head, Frank rose to his full, oh-so-impressive stature and spoke to the gathered congregation.

'We be leavin' this place. This young 'un had the gumption to tell me to get off my ass before it was incinerated.' Frank looked fondly at Eve and held up a huge hand to silence her mamma. 'You be proud of Eve. Age doesn't confer anyone with wisdom; all it gives you is experience, but if you ain't smart enough to learn from it then how dumb does that make you? No one is going to rescue us 'cept ourselves, so listen up, this is what we gonna do…'

For the first time in twenty-four hours, Eve felt she might cry tears of joy rather than sorrow.

To Elpis

David Kerr

I'm sat on a stone floor, my back against a plasterboard wall. Paint flakes from it and I pick at it with my nails. Anything to occupy myself and my fidgeting hands.

I look at Allie as she begins to surface from her sleep, from her dreams, and I can't help but think about what happened to bring us here. How the blue sky above us split, torn, peeled back, revealing a colder, harsher universe to us. Stars that were not our own, burning above us. Red pinpricks in the deepest of blacks. And we could see, as we stared up in our frenzied panic and hysteria, creeping at the edge, forms that closed towards the precipice. They lingered there, waiting for the first taste of the decaying banquet before them. The people, with their rotting souls, hearts bloated on greed and fear, stretched their arms out towards the void, welcoming whatever lay in that darkness.. On their knees they begged them, 'Come to us. Murder our world.'

I close my eyes and try to silence these thoughts, to return to the here and now. I become aware of the cold stone beneath me once more. I look at the room and watch as the details creep slowly back into focus. I can think clearly again.

It's been two days since I last ate. Still, I drink. It's crucial. Allie and I, we were smart. Whilst others knelt down to the skies, we thought of how to survive. We took provisions, we made plans. Welcoming death so readily was for the cowards. I knew that. I told myself that, and I told Allie it again and again. She believed me; she still does. For that, I'm thankful. But, for two days, the encroaching fear has robbed me of sleep, of my appetite. I now feel it gnawing at my frayed temper, and to something deeper.

'Jim?' Allie's voice is like a slap. I'm pulled from my thoughts and irritation quickly flashes across my face for a fleeting moment. 'Jim?' she asks again. I try my best to hide away the feelings my expression tries so hard to betray.

'Yeah, Allie.'

'Are you okay?' she hoists the rucksack across her shoulder and looks squarely at me. The question is genuine. She really means it. Am I okay? It seems so redundant. None of us are.

'I'm just...' I look down at my jeans. The blood, the dirt, the shit caked on them. It should repulse me, make me feel sick to the pit of my gnashing stomach, but it doesn't. It's normal now. How fucked up is that? It's normal. 'I'm just tired,' I answer, trying my best to sound convincing. I see something approaching a smile. She believes me, or at least she wants to. I'm with her and still believe in our survival. It's all that matters to her and perhaps it's all that matters to me.

'You should get some sleep.' She rubs her nose, which is constantly streaming, irritated by the stench. The city has become an outhouse for over a million people, emptying their bowels and bladders wherever the urge may take them. The disgust of the thought is fleeting, I look at Allie. Her hair matted with dirt, face unclean, blemished, nails blackened. All this, and she doesn't complain. I envy her faith. It makes her beautiful.

'I will,' I answer, 'but now isn't the time. We have to keep moving.' I gather my thoughts. 'We could also do with trying to find some more batteries.' Allie nods and waits for me to finish packing the rest of my supplies. They're dwindling. We both know we have two days left, maybe a couple or more if we push ourselves. We can forgo food, but not water. Since the tear in the sky, not a drop has hailed down upon us. We scavenge what we can from abandoned shops, but it's a finite resource. I have to be more decisive.

It's time to venture out once more, trying to find our way. Allie is the navigator. She tells me that she did orienteering at school, that puts her in charge. 'You couldn't find your arse with directions,' she points out, and laughs for the briefest of moments. 'Jen was always complaining about you and maps. "Thank fuck for GPS!" she'd say. Well, the GPS is fucked now. So, you've got me, instead.' She does her best to lighten the mood. There's no denying her strength. 'But, hey, at least I didn't pull that older and wiser bull shit on you.' Though she could have. She could also have added 'smarter' to that list.

'And, I'm grateful.'

I take one last look around the room, checking that nothing has been forgotten. Then, I cast the torchlight on Allie.

'Time to go?' she asks.

'Time to go.'

Leaving is an effort in of itself. Our place of respite chosen for its difficulty of access. The inconvenience is worth the security. I'm almost sad to leave it behind. But we know, we don't have a choice.

The red stained gloom outside is no longer painful. Our eyes are more forgiving of it now. As we retrace our steps along the rubble-strewn incline, there is no misstep. Our once-clumsy flailing in the near dark has quickly become a half-forgotten memory.

'Providing-' she pauses to leap across a gap in the ground. The remains of a burst pipe bent upwards like an extended middle finger. She begins again. 'Providing we don't hit anything too major, I think we should try to clear at least a couple more miles of the perimeter.'

'Agreed. '

She's determined to make more ground, as if she has something specific in mind. I've felt the impatience growing in both of us. Some days we travel perhaps half a street, held back by upturned cars, snapped and skewered roads, debris, and other people.

The nearer we get to the city limits once more, the worse the ground beneath becomes. Slabs of pavement are cracked and reconfigured at acute angles, the façades of buildings lay shattered across the tarmac plain before us. I try not to think of the liquids and the matter underfoot. We fall in it sometimes. It stains our clothes and clings to our skin. Every time the smell hits our nostrils, we welcome a little ignorance.

Since the false sky arrived, the edge of the city has been

impenetrable, as though celestial hands have scooped up concrete, rock and earth to summon a wall around us. We've been probing it for weeks. If there's an exit to this maze, we haven't found it yet.

Allie signals to me; she needs a boost. This stretch of road looks like a cubist painting. I drop to one knee before her, feeling a stickiness latch onto the fabric of my jeans, and interlock my fingers. I look up at her, there's a pang of apprehension.

'Same as before,' she whispers, 'don't push me all the way until I've checked the coast's clear.'

'Ready?' My voice is hoarse, barely audible.

She nods. 'Ready.'

Those two or three seconds that I hold her are painfully long. It isn't her boots grinding gravel into my hands, nor the ache in my fatigued muscles. Not even the acidic clenching of my empty stomach. It's that primal fear of the unknown.

Allie's hands try to find purchase on the tarmac. She slips, and clumps break away. A piece strikes me and dust and earth pepper my hair.

'Oh, crap,' she shrinks back. 'Fuck. Sorry.' The exaggerated whisper is almost comedic. I try to reply but gag on the soiled air. I hack and spit, then make a second attempt.

'It's okay. Really.'

She steps down and ruffles my hair. Its playfulness surprises me, but isn't unwelcome.

'Well, I'm still sorry.' She squeezes my shoulder and we prop ourselves against the broken road. 'Wait a minute or two before we try again?'

'Yeah,' I cough as quietly as I can, 'might have caught someone's attention.' In this city, that's unquestionably a bad thing.

Allie's face looks flushed under the dirt. It's now pinkish under the smudges and smears. The still, baking air is depleting. Five weeks of this persistent, stifling heat. Sweat already clings to my armpits and thighs, and the prickly heat across my scalp itches.

'God, I want it to rain.' She must have read my thoughts. 'And not just some light drizzle,' she continues. 'I want it to be torrential, like a tropical thunderstorm.' She looks at the false sky with longing and flexes her dry, dusty hands. 'Soak me from head to toe.'

My mouth is arid and sore. Her talk of rain fuels my thirst. I look at the star-riddled canvas above. I want to see the clouds again.

Five, perhaps ten, minutes pass before we're content to try again. This time, our efforts go off mercifully without incident.

At the foot of the incline, on which we precariously stand at the top, is a cluster of cars. Cast down in one of the tremors, they have huddled together like animals seeking warmth from one another. The crows gather for the prospect of an easy meal. Of the littering of corpses, one looks more recent. Slouched at the side of a people carrier, its head has lolled backward as a large crow pecks at its eyes. Another waits patiently on the wing mirror, eager for its turn to dine.

'I used to like birds,' Allie mutters as a droplet of sweat leaves her chin. She trails off as she looks at these signposts of death.

'Come on, let's keep moving.'

The next twenty minutes pass with no event. We walk, we climb, we sweat. We push forward. Then, I see movement in the distance, forms advancing on our position, about to pass the crossroads ahead. I kneel down and pull Allie towards me.

'Look.' I point to them in the weak light and I sense her tense.

'Who are they?' She squints, trying to see them more clearly. They move slowly, but methodically, and exude a confidence in their step. They become clearer by the second. We need to make a decision, and fast.

Allie pulls the knife from her boot and grips it tightly in her hand. I wipe sweat from my brow.

Then, as their silhouettes emerge into fully realised forms, my heart begins to hammer so hard it almost chokes me.

'Allie, we've got to move. Now!'

'Why, what's-' and then she sees, and she understands. We need to hide. The buildings are too far away. There's a newsagent's kiosk and, Christ, too far away. *Where the hell do we go?* My eyes dart around frantically, assessing our options. How long now? Twenty seconds? Thirty? We can only reach the burnt husk of a car in time. It won't offer much concealment but it's better than nothing. It's our only choice. The decision is made. I drag Allie with me and our hunched forms dart inside.

We hunker down in the back, laying upon ash and charcoal. It's uncomfortable. Allie's pressed into the foot well, I'm atop her. I want to fidget, readjust myself, but I can't. It'd be stupid. I wait.

I know the three people outside will be staring at the sky as they approach, utterly entranced by it. I bite my lip as anger and revulsion rise like bile in my throat.

We call them the 'Blessed'. They become transfixed, violently obsessed with the tear in the sky and what they believe lurks at the threshold. Fixated. Cruel. We know that we should fear them from our own experiences. We witnessed Jen succumb to the despair as she left to swell their ranks.

'She gave into fear,' Allie had said, tears in her eyes as she tended to the wounds her sister had inflicted on me. 'It calls to those who've given up.'

I cautiously raise my head to look outside. They're a hundred metres away at most. I'm about to duck down again when I see a fresh shape approach. It's a girl, mid-to-late teens. She's not looking at the sky like these fools. She eyes the bag on the shoulder of the furthermost back. She's a different kind of fool. She stalks them, her light footsteps suit her to the task. Twenty metres now. The girl begins to reach out. She's making her play. Maybe she'll succeed? Perhaps I won't have to punish myself for not giving a warning that would surely damn us too? Her initial pull at the bag is too light. It's like a tap on the shoulder to the muscular man. He turns, and tightens his grip on the bag. She pulls at it again, weakly. The weapon moves swiftly. There's a sickly crunch as the pipe connects with her face. I see a wet spray, and she falls in slow motion. The kill isn't clean. She raises a pleading hand. I think she tries to talk. A pulpy gurgling comes out instead. The two other Blessed now flank her. One has a long kitchen knife strapped to his belt. He frees it. The girl's drowning scream only lasts half a breath before the blade plunges into her neck. Blood spurts as it's yanked free. He balls her hair into his hand and raises her off her feet. Her scrawny body dangles like a slaughtered chicken. The blade is levelled at her stomach.

I drop down as low as I can. I can't watch. My hands are trembling. Allie goes to speak and I clasp my fingers over her mouth. I hear splashing, the jangle of metal, then the crunching of gravel underfoot. Without a second's hesitation, they continue on their way, closing the distance to us. No doubt those serene, clueless fucking expressions emblazoned on their faces.

The rage and fear begin a dance in my bowels. I shiver uncontrollably as they grow ever closer. I'm sure they didn't see me. *I'm sure.*

There are no voices to track, only footsteps. The crumbling ground beneath them betrays every movement.

They're parallel to the car. A moment of curiosity and that could be it. I'm holding my breath, I'm willing them to keep staring at the sky and to just *go*. I smell them, I hear the air rushing into their lungs and out again. Allie's chest rises and falls faster and faster. The moisture of her breath collects on my hand.

Go. GO. Just go, damn it!

Then, the moment is gone. The triumvirate pass by, carrying on their way. Oblivious to us, once again enraptured by the beasts that loom above us all.

We wait a while longer, not wanting to take any chances. When we finally exit the car, Allie looks confused, anxious.

'Jim, what the hell was that noise. What the fu–'

'Allie, don't. Please. You don't want to know. You just don't.' One look at my bloodshot eyes and she understands, she *doesn't* want to know. 'Let's just get away from here, okay? Quickly.'

I take the lead and move us down the road. I keep Allie to my left and steer far around the poor girl's corpse. I can't look again and I don't want Allie seeing her.

My agitation is unsettling. When we reach the crossroads, she tugs at my hand and stops me.

'Jim, I was thinking. We should go to Layton Square. There are plenty of shops, we can look for those batteries.'

'How far is it?' Allie looks upwards, reading a memorised map. I've the same in lots of bright people as they recall things. Me? I scrunch my eyes and get a headache.

'West here. Then down Church Street, then Cold Street and around onto Layton. It's close.'

I glance in the general direction. Layton's on the very edge of the wall. I know it's where we need to be, but every time it makes me nervous.

'Okay,' my voice croaks.

The two roads to Layton feel like twenty. By the time we arrive, my eyes sting. They're so dry, I hear them scratch from the slightest movement. Allie has more energy. She always seems to. She makes a mockery of the eight years between us.

Getting inside the shopping centre isn't an issue. If nothing else, our city has its gleefully destructive types. Instead of a crowbar or a lock-pick, a 4x4 car has been rammed through the main entrance. Subtlety wasn't present here.

Light is scant. Allie stumbles over something small but heavy. She grabs my shoulder and steadies herself.

'I think we need the torch.' She agrees, but we're reluctant to use it. There's the risk of drawing attention, and there's the rapidly depleting batteries.

Under the torchlight, it becomes obvious that a riot must have happened here, and a considerable amount of looting. There isn't a single intact window or sign. Many of the doors have been prised out of their frames. Glass, dirt, bottles and God knows what else litter the floor. Amazingly, in spite of all the other damage and the tremors, the vaulted glass ceiling has mostly survived.

'We need to find the security office.' Allie insists. 'May I?' She takes the torch from me. I'm too fatigued to think. It's better that she leads. But I do find myself wondering why she wants to go to there in particular. We're here for batteries, maybe water if we're lucky.

'Should be on the second floor if I recall correctly. Haven't been here in years.' Her memory is faultless. Even in its ruined state, she leads us on a direct path.

The security office looks to be the size of a cloak room. Wedged in between a book shop and a chemist, it looks like a grudging after-thought that the other stores resent.

Allie tries the door handle. There's a rattle and a dull thud. It doesn't budge.

'Locked.'

I'm already removing the crow bar from my bag as she turns to face me.

'Allie, what's this all about?'

'I'll explain in a sec, promise. I'd just really rather be on the other side of this door first.' She smiles and squeezes my arm again.

'Okay.'

I brace the crowbar against the lock in the door jam. With a bit of back and forth, we break it. I collect the torch from the ground and lead the way inside.

'So, come on. We're obviously not here for batteries, so can you please explain to me what we're doing?' The light illuminates her soft features. Her eyes slowly move up to meet my gaze.

'First, just promise not to be mad.'

I breathe in deeply and look at her. I shouldn't promise not to be mad. Who knows what's going on. But promise, I do. I can't tell pre-cisely why. I'm unsure whether it's cowardice, devotion or... some-thing else. I just don't think I can be angry with her.

'So, um, we've tried all the main tunnels out of the city. We've tried the two road tunnels, the train tunnel from Vine Street. They've all been a bust. Cave-ins at all of them.'

I nod slowly.

'Still, it got me thinking. You know how this was an important sea port during the war? Well, they had this place underground. It's where the big navy chiefs and the air force would all get together and plan things out.'

Where is she going with this?

'After the war, it was pointless, obviously. And, okay, long story short, they tried to repurpose it as a car park for Layton Square's shops, but it didn't meet the regs, so it ended up being a storage facility for loads of shit from the museum. But all the tunnels, the passageways. All that is still there. They did a news piece on it when they put the last remaining overhead tram car down there. I *remember.*'

'And how are these tunnels going to be any different than all the others we tried?' I rub my forehead as I feel a headache approach. 'I thought we'd decided to look for holes in the wall, or a way to scale them or–'

'Jim, underneath is a place designed to withstand a hail of bombs. It has to be worth a try, doesn't it?' She needs to see some faith in her. Her eyes downright plead me to say something positive. She's the smart one but she doesn't believe in herself, though I can't understand why. She's led us here on purpose and kept it from me all this time. Maybe I should be pissed off that she hid her intent but, her plan has merit. Mine has only brought dead ends.

'You're right. You're absolutely right.' That little flash of a smile comes across her face once more. Time and again, it's the most beautiful thing I see in this city. In the perpetual gloom, in this night we find ourselves trapped, she's offering a chance at a way out. I have to grab it with both hands. I won't become like the others. Neither of us will. People chose to give up; they'd given up before the false sky even appeared. I refuse to welcome the indifference that washed over them all. Allie and I are not that way. We didn't give up. We aren't giving up. 'What do you need?'

Allie walks over to the back wall of this coffin-size office. I illuminate her path as she moves.

'I'm going to need the keys to get down there. Prying open doors like that,' she motions a thumb over her shoulder, 'are one thing, but these are doors to a former bomb shelter.'

'Guess a map would be nice, too?'

'Well, yeah.'

'Good.' I bump my chin up, 'because there's one over your head.' She looks above her at the fire safety map. It covers all the floors, the exits, all the pathways out. She eagerly pulls it down and starts to take it in. Her energy seems boundless as mine continues to fade.

The master keys for the building are easy to find, each section colour coded and numbered to different floors and areas. It's a small bit of luck that I'm thankful for.

'I'm beat.' I tell Allie. 'Can we just take ten minutes to recharge?' I can tell she doesn't want to wait. She's got an itch. She's probably been thinking about this for weeks, not wanting to raise my hopes, but bursting to tell me. Still, she acquiesces. She knows how little sleep I've had. I slump against the door and take a little while to look at the photo in my wallet. It's a picture of my grandparents from eleven years ago. A New Year's party, the last they ever had. Even under the stark light of my torch, they look so warm and happy.

'I envy your analogue memories,' Allie tells me. I smile, somewhat sorrowfully.

'Advantage of being a Luddite.'

My ten minutes of rest turns into twenty, and I finally raise to my feet. Allie's studied the map. She says she's confident about the way out. I struggle to find the belief that it really is an escape, but my faith in her is enough to carry on. For one reason or another, I feel like this is our last try. We're not going to find a gap in the walls, are we? We're not going to be able to scale them. My heart starts to pound at the weight I'm suddenly placing on this idea. Time to ignore it. Time to renounce the fear again and push on. Allie deserves my dedication, my faith.

We descend ten floors of mangled and crumbling staircases before we reach the storage area. The sheer size of it boggles my mind. Crates, shelves, pallets all line the space before us. Some of the walls have cracked and split under the force of the tremors, but the main structure holds. I see a few chunks of concrete cast to the floor.

'Down here,' she points with the torch. Then down two more stair-cases. 'Then,' she pauses to think, 'we have to cut up a side passage, into what were the private quarters for the officers and then up through a smaller passageway.'

'Private escape route for the VIPs?' I say, wearily. 'What a surprise.'

Another small tremor passes through the building and we both stumble. More chunks of concrete displace from the ceiling and crash to the ground.

'Let's hurry,' she insists. I'm not one to argue. I want to get the fuck out of here. I wanted out the moment we stepped in. Caution is getting thrown aside as we begin to run through the halls, ignoring the antiquities buried under a layer of dust. Idle curiosities are irrelevant. Getting out of here is all that matters. We are not going to die here. We are not giving up. We reject the fear.

I hear a cry as we enter the private quarters. More of the concrete has dislodged. I tense up and urge Allie to pass me the knife. Twitching, left leg pinned beneath a fallen chunk of concrete, is a man. He's howling in pain. It trails off into a sob and he looks at us. Tears pour from his eyes and he's writhing.

'They called for me.' He cries. 'They called for me!' He echoes the cries of Jen as she ran away. Blessed. They've been calling to others outside the city. How else could he be here? If there's a way in, there's a *way out*.

'Leave him.' I pass back the knife to Allie. She knows what he is too, but she hesitates as I begin to walk away.

The sound of the gun cocking is familiar to me. I freeze.

'Fuck.' Allie's cry turns into a mumble.

'Don't leave.' He says, almost hysterically. 'They're calling for you, too.'

The universe is cruel. I've seen that. It's an inescapable fact. But sometimes, it has a sense of justice, or maybe humour. He levels the gun at Allie and I know I'm going to rush him. Fuck this guy. Fuck him and all the cowardly, fearful shit they revere.

It's in that achingly slow moment that another tremor shakes the entire building far below its foundations. He squeezes the trigger and I'm outside myself. I can hear my screaming but I almost feel like

I'm somewhere else. The shot goes wild, carving up dust in the wall behind me. I'm about to lunge for the gun when another section of ceiling gives way.

He doesn't even have time to scream. The concrete makes modern art from his head. Another more violent tremor strikes. I pull Allie into the final passage as the ceiling caves in behind us. I've dropped the torch. I've dropped the fucking torch.

'What? What the shit? I mean, what? I, just–' Allie's babbling.

I can see her face. Why can I see her face? It should be pitch black. There's a tiny shaft of light shining directly at her. It's almost blinding. Her hands begin to shake and she races to the hole before us.

She reaches through the aperture. Her body goes stiff, and I panic. I've existed at the edge of panic for so long, it comes to me readily. She withdraws, and turns to me. The beaming light pushes through, it illuminates the tears as they trickle down her cheeks.

'Jim. I…' I wait, anxiously, for her words. She holds her hand out to me and she smiles. Droplets of moisture dance along her fingers. She laughs and touches the water to her lips. 'I can feel the rain.'

She reaches out and traces the line of my face. A calm washes over me and in it, I know. I know we can clear the debris. We can leave here, escape and be free. Leave this hell behind us. Whatever lays on the other side, Allie and I have persevered. We have not given into our fear.

I close my eyes for a moment and think of Jen. She told me it was the end of the world. And maybe it is. Ready for a new world where hope can guide us, where apathy is cast aside.

We can renounce our fears. We can begin again.

Something to Tell Jessie

John Lilley

Abdul's stomach was still churning. The web of lies, veiled threats and the hidden agendas were all par for the course at these conferences, but even an experienced diplomat found it difficult to play the game at times, and it was a great relief to retreat to his hotel suite. He walked barefoot across the deep pile of the hand-made carpets towards the mini-bar. A wealthy man, he always stayed in the executive suites in the Tehran Meridian, this particular one was a home from home for him. He liked its views across the city to the mountains in the north. Although it was well past midnight the vibrant metropolis was still buzzing with traffic and blazing with light. Slouched in one of the sumptuous cream leather armchairs was Joseph, Abdul's closest friend and fellow diplomat.

'Do you want ice in that?' Abdul asked as he approached the mini-bar.

'Just some water please old boy, 50/50.' replied Joseph.

Abdul easily identified the green-edged cream label of the 25 year-old Talisker miniature and dumped its contents into one of the heavy Waterford lead crystal tumblers.

'How do you think it went today?' he said as he carefully topped up the glass with chilled mineral water from the bar's spigot.

'I really think we're making progress. The Pakistanis are always tough-cookies and never like to leave without a bargain. It's part of their shop-keeper mentality. They're desperate though, what with all those migrants moving in from the flooded regions.' replied Joseph.

'I agree Pakistan is a big problem,' said Abdul. 'I can see some time soon when they're all streaming north and west away from the heat. They're starving.'

This was their sixth diplomatic trip to Tehran in the past ten months, but their connections went way back. Room-mates in Trinity College Cambridge, they had both graduated in the same year, both firsts, Abdul's in Physics and Joseph's in Geography. Their backgrounds were worlds apart: Abdul being a minor Saudi Prince and Joseph a Bethlehem street-cleaner's son, but despite this they had hit it off immediately. Both joined the OTC and both were in the university triathlon team. They even shared a girlfriend or two.

There was a sudden loud knocking on the door.

'Who in hell is that at this time?' said Abdul as he walked briskly towards the door. More knocks. 'OK, I'm on my way, keep your turban on.'

He had a quick look through the spy-hole: Omar? Why? He unlocked the door which immediately flew open under pressure from Omar's stocky frame.

'Quick, the pair of you, we need to get out,' gasped Omar. He'd been running and his shirt was soaked with sweat. After seeing his bulging eyes and agitated manner they both put to one side their thoughts that this was another of Omar's pranks. Anything that could get an agent like Omar that worked-up was something to be treated seriously.

'How long have we got?' asked Joseph, his diplomatic mind a whorl of potential contributory scenarios.

'Ten minutes. Go to the foyer. Bring as much food and water as you can.' Omar was already turning to leave, 'And enough kit for 10 days in the desert.'

'Shit. See you down there.' said Joseph as he ran to his own suite.

Quickly changing for the desert, Abdul stuffed a large Louis Vuitton bag with some clothes. At the mini-bar he chucked the bottled water and soft drinks into the bag followed by all the peanuts, chocolate and finally the contents of the fruit bowl. He snatched his sat-phone from the table on the way out. Five minutes gone.

Omar and Joseph were waiting for him on the ground floor, beneath the elaborate canopy of the executive floor lift.

'OK, let's try not to draw attention to ourselves. We can take the side entrance to the vehicle,' whispered Omar.

'Great, no problem,' snapped Joseph. 'We suddenly appear in the dead of night, dressed for the desert in the best that Gieves & Hawkes can provide. Nobody will suspect a thing!'

'OK, OK, I didn't ask for this. I've just been told to extract you, quickly and quietly.' said Omar.

They walked briskly across the main foyer past the fountains and desks and down the corridor to the side entrance. It seemed to go well, but a large man sat on one of the foyer sofas whispered into a short-wave handset as he jumped to his feet and ran out of the main entrance.

In the side street, they ran for the vehicle which had already started. Omar accelerated the large 4x4 relentlessly as soon as he was behind the wheel. Leaving behind rooster-tails of ornamental gravel he drove into a dark alley behind the hotel. A red light was flashing on his sat-phone from the cradle on the dashboard. Joseph checked his phone but discovered that his phone didn't even have the light that Omar's had. The vehicle's sat-nav system was showing the tracks of three vehicles, not just the one they were in. Omar didn't take any prisoners as he spun the heavy vehicle around the tiny back streets. Its paint-work took some hits as they scraped along walls and doorways. A goat bleated briefly as its body was smashed against the front fenders and slid beneath the wheels. Without flinching Omar increased their acceleration still further. The other two tracking lights were receding and after a further two minutes of the white-knuckle ride one of them went out. Omar deliberately clipped several wooden posts bringing their supported canopies crashing down. Rounding one street corner he was confronted with a street café only 10m away, too late to avoid it, he just ploughed through the tables and chairs. The only customer had chosen a table near the front wall of the property, fortunate indeed as his table and coffee were whisked away in a deafening crash of blazing light. A chair became stuck under the nearside sill and made an impressive display of sparks as it scraped along the cobbled street before disintegrating under the rear wheel. Omar spun the vehicle through 150 degrees at the next small square and entered an alley only 10cm wider than the vehicle. Despite throwing the switch to fold in the door mirrors a protruding door frame took one out in a shower of plastic and glass. His double-back strategy seemed to have paid off as the other remaining tracking light went off screen. In another five minutes the red flashing light on Omar's phone turned to amber and he seemed to relax the pace slightly.

'OK, I think we're in the clear now gents, only twenty minutes to the city limits. Then we can see just how far we can get.' he said.

'How far we can get from what?' asked Abdul. 'You really have some explaining to do.'

'All in good time chaps, but I need to get out into the desert before I can take my mind off the road.' answered Omar, suddenly swerving around a heavily loaded donkey cart.

Captain Stephen Allen was sat in his small cabin, just twenty feet from the control room of the most powerful submarine in the US Navy. The Oklahoma was the only 23,000 ton Glenn-Class boat in service. Four more were planned, but people would have starved if they had been built, American people.

He ran his thick-skinned fingers through his expensively coiffured grey hair.

'What a freakin' mess this had all been.' he whispered to himself.

Allen had seen it all before and it saddened him that with only four months until retirement he had been asked to take this final mission. He was after all the most experienced and most decorated submariner in the fleet. Allen couldn't stand pushing paper, he thought on his feet in high-pressure environments and most of all he loved the sea. However, he could think of three or four good guys twenty years his junior who could have done the job. His decision to stay at sea had been taken rather badly by some and it was this resentment that Allen now felt was one reason he'd been picked for this last big mission. His old colleagues were jealous. They were quite happy to jump ashore and get promoted to Admiral with the big salary and all the comforts of shore-life, but then found that they missed the excitement of commanding a ship.

'They just didn't want their names on it.' he thought, 'Central Government came up with this crazy end-of-the-world plan and they agreed to go with it, but history will leave my name on the button. That's what it's all about, guilt.'

The 4x4 had been skimming at great speed across the gravel desert road for thirty minutes.

'Would now be a good time?' asked Abdul.

'Of course, sorry I just needed to get clear first.' replied Omar.

Another minute passed.

'Well?' reminded Abdul.

'OK, OK, we needed to get well clear of the city, there is going to be some trouble there later tonight.' Omar said.

'Trouble, what like suicide bombs?' Abdul said as he and Joseph both laughed, knowing that suicide bombs had stopped a long time ago when the last of the religious terrorist groups had been hunted down mercilessly by the United Middle Eastern Army (UMEA). In fact Omar had been one of the key trainers of this new regional army.

'No don't tell me, Millwall is playing Tehran?' added Joseph to more laughter.

'Very funny, hey look give me a break, I only got the word ten minutes before I picked you up. All I know is that something big is coming off, the Americans are involved and we have to get to the other side of those hills as soon as possible.' Omar said as he pointed to the dark shapes on the horizon.

'It's a barbeque. The Yanks love barbeques in the desert. Remember the Gulf war?' said Abdul.

'Hey, that was uncalled for.' said Omar.

'Those hills are a good two hour's drive away. Surely it can't be something happening in Tehran?' enquired Joseph.

'They wouldn't dare,' said Abdul slowly, staring at the dashboard, his face drained of colour.

Captain Allen had moved to his command chair. His head was lowered as he stared at his hand made Jermyn Street shoes, deep in thought. The USA had been running on empty for a couple of years now. They'd exhausted their offshore and fracking reserves in record time and the per-capita rationing system enforced by the Arab nations no longer suited them. Anyway it was a fairly academic exercise now that the great die-back had started in earnest. With no fish in the sea and the temperature well above the two degree tipping point over a billion had already died. Perhaps the politicians should think about more important priorities than keeping people's cars running? This mission was the next phase of the USA's new 'Patriot Survival' plan. A ground assault was not feasible with their slimmed-down army. Nuclear was their only option to maintain an acceptable form of existence, even if it would be a very isolated one.

An intense silence permeated the boat with only the low hum of machinery to accompany everyone's thoughts. They were all just obeying orders but it could not remove the huge collective responsibility from their shoulders. In a few moments they would unleash the most devastating act of war in human history. The sub was at launch depth with the external missile hatch open. Only a presidential order could stop the process now. Just like they'd done in the many practice drills, the two radio officers were following the dual key procedure. The only difference this time was that they were both drenched in sweat and one of them was crying. Everyone felt the vibrations as the missile launched, there really was no need for the confirmation over the PA system. They all watched the scene on the monitors as the compressed air system pushed the missile to the surface and high into the air, where its rocket motors sprang into life and lit up the sky. Everyone continued to sit in silence for the next few minutes.

'Close hatch, three hundred feet, thirty knots, maintain course. She's yours Number One.' Allen said softly as he rose from his chair. He headed back to his cabin and the bottle of Jack Daniels in the second drawer of his filing cabinet.

'OK, let's pick our spot,' said Omar as he manoeuvred the 4x4 through the streets of the ruined town.

'What about that big place on the left there?' asked Abdul.

'I think we need to be well away from something which might fall on us,' replied Omar.

'Hey, now you really have got me worried,' said Joseph, looking across to Abdul.

'Come on man, tell us what you know!' demanded Joseph.

'Ah that's more like it, over there, behind those old olive trees, that small gully,' continued Omar. 'I...'

The Leatherman's razor-sharp wave-edge blade was pressing firmly on his left jugular.

'Now let's have a few proper answers please,' said Joseph as he wiggled the knife just enough to graze the skin on Omar's neck.

Omar stopped the vehicle and turned off the engine and said as calmly as he could. 'It's the Yanks; they're going for an air-burst tonight.'

Both of his companions gasped loudly.

'Bloody fools!' exclaimed Joseph removing the knife from Omar's throat and thrusting it deep into the vehicle's grey leather dashboard.

'Look, let's get sorted and then we can discuss it some more.' urged Omar. 'We'll get in that gully over there and setup the tent.'

The physical activity was a welcome relief from the mental torture that they were all now going through. At almost one hundred kilometres from Tehran with the wind blowing in the opposite direction, surely the blast would not affect them this far out? The standard issue UMEA inflatable biological tent went up in minutes after they had evicted a few dozen scorpions from the ground they had chosen. Omar had sleeping bags and more food including several days of UMEA rations. He also had quite a bit of strange looking hardware that took up too much room in the small tent.

'Do you really need all this in the tent? Can't we leave it in the truck?' asked Abdul.

'Well, if we stay in the tent we might only pick up a few sieverts. Wandering between the truck and the tent may result in no permanent damage. Perhaps not to you, but any offspring you might have may have a problem. In the worst case scenario your skin might fall off and you'll go blind.' replied Omar.

'I think you've made your point.' replied Abdul. 'How long do you think we'll be in the tent?'

'Five to ten days,' said Omar quickly.

Abdul and Joseph stared hard at each other and continued to load Omar's supplies into the tiny tent. Twenty minutes later and they were sitting cross-legged on the groundsheet watching Omar setup the Geiger-counter. The device was soon reporting a fairly regular click-click that confirmed that they were in close proximity to a granite mountain range.

'OK guys, time for your injections,' announced Omar.

'Shit, this really is it!' exclaimed Joseph as Omar fumbled in the tent's diode light for the anti-radiation kit.

At 02:32 local time, the ten independent 475 Kilo-Tonne warheads from Oklahoma's missile exploded in a ring of simultaneous airbursts over Tehran. It was as if the sun had come to Earth. The equivalent to 316 Hiroshimas, this combination ensured the maximum fatalities and destruction from the pressure wave and firestorm. The population of 20 million were killed instantly. The city was completely flattened and burnt. Concrete, glass, steel and brick shattered, exploded and fused into a shining white-hot lake. The oxygen for kilometres around the city was consumed in an instance and the pressure wave sped out across the surrounding desert at supersonic speed. High above the white beacon of the mushroom cloud rushed upwards into the troposphere.

'Look, you really need to keep your feet away, they smell like a dead sheep,' said Abdul.

'Well, why don't you sleep the other way around?' retorted Joseph.

'Yeah, and have to put up with Omar's foul camel breath. I know we forgot the toothpaste, but he could make some effort. At least a quick swill out every now and then?' said Abdul.

Omar was looking closely at the instrument array. It had been six days since the explosion. The pressure wave had been the worst thing for them. They all had perforated and bleeding eardrums. Several fist-sized rocks had crashed into the tent on Omar's side and he was now nursing three cracked ribs as a result. Fortunately the tent had not been punctured and it only hurt when he laughed. The confinement of the tent had left them all with aching limbs, and the utter lack of privacy – especially when it came to bodily functions – was getting to them all. Cabin fever had set in with a vengeance.

'I think we can risk it now guys. If we put the suits on then we'll absorb a bit more than in here. What do you think?' said Omar.

'Give me the bloody suit now.' said Joseph.

'Sod the suit, I'll chance it in my undies.' added Abdul.

The levity was hard on Omar, but they all enjoyed the vision that Abdul offered.

'OK, I've one suit in here the others are in the vehicle. With these ribs I think it would take me a long time to get the suit on, how about you doing the trip Joseph?'

'Only too pleased to old chap,' replied Joseph as he started to undo the suit bag.

His eyes took a while to adjust to the sunlight as he straightened out his stiff limbs. Everything was very still, no birds in the sky, no lizards sunning themselves on the rocks, no insects, nothing moving. The deserted town near the gully was completely flattened. No more than three bricks on top of each other, if that. In the forced ventilation of the suit Joseph felt for one moment that he had just set foot on another planet. He had to catch himself from doing a low-gravity parody walk as he turned to approach the 4x4. The vehicle had taken quite a hit. The side facing Tehran was severely dented, but amazingly the windows were all intact. Joseph's attention was drawn to the rear tyre. It had a 1m piece of wooden fencing sticking out of it. He pulled out the wood, but the military tyre remained inflated.

'There is a lot more to this vehicle than Omar has admitted,' he thought.

He returned with the two other suit bags and dumped them in the tent's outer airlock, choosing to remain outside. Ten minutes later a suited Abdul emerged to join him. They could hear Omar wincing and groaning as he manoeuvred his tortured torso into the suit. Fifteen minutes later they were all stood at the top of the gully looking west towards Tehran.

'Not much to see from here. It looks like the fires have gone out though. I'll get the drone airborne and well try to establish communications.' said Omar.

'The drone? I don't suppose you have a cocktail bar in that bloody vehicle of yours?' asked Abdul.

'Only some medicinal navy rum I'm afraid.' replied Omar. 'Not quite Talisker, but if you feel like growing hairs on your tongue let me know and I'll give you a shot.'

The drone climbed to 400m with Omar at the controls, its high-resolution optics scanned the horizon. Where the ancient city of Tehran had been there was now a blackened area. Small patches of recently solidified glass reflected the intense sunlight giving the appearance of movement. Omar flew the small plane onwards 20km towards the city. More details began to emerge. On one of the main roads there was a convoy of vehicles all blackened and charred. Omar thought this strange, since the initial pressure wave would have surely scattered them to the winds.

'They must have attempted some sort of rescue?' commented Joseph.

'Yeah, but what took them out?' enquired Omar.

At that instance the image from the drone spun wildly before going blank. The tiny plane was shattered into a thousand pieces as the 50cal cannon shells ripped into it. High above the autonomous military drone pulled out of its dive and returned to its holding pattern. It would be a short time before its gun camera images were relayed by satellite back to base for further analysis.

'Shit, we'd better make a move. If it's what I think it was then they'll be tracing our drone back to here.' said Omar grimly.

'So what exactly are we going to do now? Are we trying to escape to somewhere? Surely we can just turn ourselves in at the nearest McDonalds and get the next diplomatic flight out of this hell-hole?' asked Joseph.

'There won't be anyone at any of the American Embassies any-where near here. They pulled their American staff out two days ago. That's what tipped us off. I suspect that they are being asked to pack their bags in the rest of the world as well. Any joy on the sat-phone Abdul?' said Omar.

'Not a dicky-bird,' replied Abdul. 'The service light just doesn't come on at all. I tried changing the battery and then plugged it into the vehicle, but still nothing.'

'So what's their next trick?' ask Joseph.

'Well, I expect they'll already be in Ganaveh and have taken control of the tanker terminals at Kharg, Lavan and Siri. Let's hope that UMEA puts up a good fight. Of course to stop escalation the Yanks will have pulled the plug on the nukes out here. Their propaganda machine will be in overdrive denying everything while their Seals are cutting all the cables and blinding the satellites.' said Omar.

'So what about the rest of Iran?' asked Abdul.

'Without the central leadership, I guess the Yanks are hoping they start to fight amongst themselves along their old tribal lines. They've all been starving for years but some of their cities have more reserves than others, and you know what that will lead to. I'd expect that to keep them busy, if not then Kerman, Qom and Yazd may well be the Yanks' next targets.' replied Omar.

'Shit, so how are we going to get out?' asked Abdul.

'We've got enough fuel for around 400 kilometres. There is a good chance of some more from our desert friends 300 kilometres north-east of here. I suggest we get moving now.' said Omar.

'OK, let's get the stuff loaded,' replied Abdul.

'Just the food and water.' said Omar.

In ten minutes they were on their way, bouncing over the rubble of the old town where it had spread across the desert road. Their exit route was steep, and even Omar was moving slowly to avoid a spill in the loose gravel. After a further thirty minutes they were back on the large plain and up to speed. There was no movement as far as the eye could see. The dust whipped up by their wheels stretched out hundreds of metres behind them. High above them the drone was taking an interest. The pictures of the narrow dust cloud thirty kilometres away had been identified by its rule-based (reflex) target acquisition system as a possible unnatural phenomenon. The drone's AI system took over and identified the movement as a vehicle moving at 95mph, obviously too fast for a military vehicle, so it was unlikely to be heavily armoured. Downgrading the threat the drone compared the vehicle's profile with its mission statement. The vehicle was moving away from Tehran and would shortly reach the edge of the drone's patrol area. The drone had no details of US vehicles operating in the area and there were no other targets within the drone's sensor range. It decided to move in for a closer look.

The red light had reappeared on Omar's sat-phone, accompanied this time with an audible message: 'Drone warning, Drone warning'.

'Oh shit man, what's happening?' said Joseph.

Omar pressed the OK button on the phone: 'Sit tight, let's hope this new piece of kit does the trick.' He popped open a panel next to the steering wheel and took out what looked like an old hand-held video game. Tossing it to Joseph he said: 'Plug it into the cigarette' lighter and switch it on. When the Drone starts its dive press the green button, but only when its 1000m away. The transmission range is limited.'

Abdul was now leaning over the backseat watching the small device in Joseph hands. The 4x4 was depicted graphically moving along the desert road. A graduated green dome of lines spread out from the vehicle's avatar, each line represented 500m of distance. Nothing else was visible on the display out to 6000m in any direction.

'There's nothing there.' said Joseph.

'It's out there, the sat-phone says 7000m, keep watching, it'll be moving in fast for a closer look at us.' replied Omar.

'There it is!' said Abdul excitedly as he saw a blue eagle appear at the edge of the game console display. He immediately looked around in the direction suggested by the image but the dust cloud behind them prevented him from seeing anything.

'Remember, wait until it's 1000m away!' said Omar as he accelerated as fast he could on the limited traction afforded by the gravel road.

The drone had identified the vehicle as privately owned and non-American, and therefore fair game within its mission parameters. It began its decent while its targeting computers calculated the timings for firing the main cannon.

'3000m, 2500m, 2000m,' Joseph was counting down.

The stream of 50cal rounds cut through the 4x4 starting at the passenger seat next to Abdul and continuing in a line towards its front right corner. Four bullets in all, it would have been more had Omar not jammed the brakes on.

'Press that bloody button!' he yelled.

But Joseph had dropped the device when the third round had

nicked his left calf. The pain didn't have time to register before he was pitched forward by Omar's sudden braking manoeuver. The inertia-reel shoulder belt cut into his chest and held while his arms flailed in the air just inches away from where the console had lodged itself between his legs. He quickly slipped off the strap and lunged for the console. The burning pain from his leg was just beginning to overcome his adrenal response as he pressed the green button. Omar had resumed their relentless acceleration.

'It's coming back!' screamed Joseph.

'I can see it.' said Abdul. 'Are you OK? Do you want me to press the button this time?'

'No, I'm on it.' replied Joseph.

'It's coming in a lot slower this time, much lower and head-on. It's trying to finish us off. Just keep your finger on that button, for all the bloody use it might be.' yelled Omar.

The blue eagle had just crossed the 2000m mark on the console. Joseph had his thumb firmly on the green button. Abdul watched the small screen from over Joseph's shoulder: 1500m, 1000m, then the white shape of the drone was briefly visible ahead. They all gritted their teeth and narrowed their eyes.

On its first pass the drone's sensors had recorded a hit on the vehicle, but a beacon signal had immediately identified it as American military. The friendly-fire protocols had kicked in and it was now on a pre-programmed low altitude pass to collect the required photographic evidence. After flying over the vehicle it climbed back to 7000m and resumed its patrol pattern.

'Shit, where's it gone?' said Abdul.

'The sat-phone shows it climbing and retreating back towards Tehran. I think the green button thingy did the trick gents!' said Omar as the sat-phone light turned to amber.

'Excellent! OK, can you crawl over into the back and I'll take a look at that leg of yours Joe.' said Abdul.

'The Black Sea, here we come!' said Joseph.

Deep underground somewhere in Utah, Lonnie Hansen had just returned from a comfort break. He was still getting used to his new prosthetic legs. They were much lighter than his last pair but the joints were now gyroscopically controlled by computers. Sometimes he felt they had a life of their own. His cousin Jeff had joked that they no longer walked past bars, but he was determined that he was going to make them work for him. He carefully manoeuvred himself back into his drone command chair and put the plate of doughnuts and large Americano on the console. He was not pleased; the drone had fired on two targets while he'd been away. Typical he thought, the only action during his shift and he'd missed it. He opened the log file and clicked the playback button on the cannon usage file. The first target was a short range drone of European manufacture. Obviously something sent over from one of the global news networks. They needed to be kept out, so fair game. He would plot the target's course and send his drone back to investigate. On the second target, even using slow-motion playback it was just a blur of dust but seemed to have been hit. His face screwed up as he read the friendly-fire report. How could a vehicle be identified as private one moment and then US military the next? Perhaps the vehicle's radio beacon was faulty? Oh well, never mind, let someone else worry about that one, at least he would have something to tell Jessie when he got home. He picked up the first doughnut, took a sip of coffee and settled back into his chair.

Hope

Lydia Sherrer

The ash feels soft on my cheek as it falls. The flakes catch in my hair and pile on the tops of my shoulders and backpack, but I don't bother brushing them away; I'm already so dirty it doesn't matter. Hunger makes my knees weak and my feet drag as I take one weary step after another. I can barely remember a time when I wasn't hungry, or cold. It was before the war, but I've lost count of the days since then.

I close my eyes for a moment, trying to pretend the flakes brushing my face are snow. The nuclear explosions that started, and ended, the war put so much ash and smoke in the air that the sky disappeared. With the sun obscured, temperatures dropped. The plants died, then the animals. No more seasons. No more rain or snow, just ash. The rhythms of life are gone. All that's left is this never-ending, cold, gray hell.

The sharp edges of canned goods poke my spine through the threadbare backpack. Their heavy weight pulls against the supporting strap tied across my chest. The strap would flatten my breasts, if I had any left after endless marching and little food. Shifting the pack doesn't ease the pain, so I give up and keep walking. Since the war, anyone not killed in the explosions or poisoned by radiation has been slowly starving. Canned food is all that's left, so I'll carry it no matter the pain.

Shivering, I pull my tattered coat closer. Everything I love has been turned to ash and that tiny bit of warmth is the only comfort I have. All else is gone: governments toppled, cities vaporized, cultures extinct. Everything that was good or beautiful died in the wake of the war, including our humanity. The only thing left is survival, though some days I wonder if it's worth it. Whatever comes after can't be worse than this lifeless horror. But instinct drives me on.

I stumble suddenly, catching my foot on the cracked asphalt of the road. I start to fall and have a flash of panic, afraid I'll break one of my fragile, nutrition-starved bones. But I don't hit the ground. A cold, spidery hand appears and catches me by the elbow, steadying me with a firm grip. Not looking at the hand's owner, I keep walking with eyes downcast, sinking back into my stupor to escape reality. I know he'll keep watch. All I have to do is put one foot in front of the other. The hand belongs to my master, my owner. If I were an optimist I'd call him a partner, a traveling companion, or maybe a caretaker. On a good day, I'd even admit he was my savior. Good days don't happen anymore, though, so mostly he's just my master. I don't know his name; he's never asked for mine. We don't talk, we simply survive.

Bones. They catch my eye because of their stark whiteness against the gray ground. I stare at them dully, holding back as my master moves to the side of the road to check for anything useful. But the pile has already been picked over. All that's left is rags and signs of a fire with the roasting spit still stuck in the ground. I shiver. Those are human bones.

That's how it is now. Eat or be eaten. Sometimes groups of survivors even band together and keep prisoners as a living meat larder. They cut off limbs and cauterize the stumps, slowly eating their victims alive. It's a fate worse than death, and it almost happened to me.

My master returns to the road and beckons me to keep going. I try, I really do. But now that my forward momentum is gone, the weight of my backpack roots me to the spot. Instead of taking a step, I sink to the ground, limbs trembling with fatigue, head drooping. I wish I could lay down and die.

But he won't let me. I feel the weight of the canned food I carry lift as he gently slips the backpack off me and slings it across his front, now carrying both my pack and his own. His bony, white hands reach down again, grasping me and helping me up. He supports my weight until I regain my balance, then he helps me forward.

Why does he keep me going? I'm his cow. I know it, and it's frightening. He's kind, but it doesn't change what I am to him: food. He keeps me safe and fed. In return, I let him drink my blood, though 'let' implies that I could stop him if I wanted to. Our arrangement works, but it can't last forever. What he takes isn't enough for him, but it's too much for me. We're both growing weaker. Isn't it strange that in a world where everything else is dying, it turns out the stuff of our fantasies is quite alive?

I could leave. It wouldn't be hard. He treats me like his child, not his prisoner. To find me enough food and water, he often hides me somewhere safe and leaves for long forages. I could slip away any time, but I never do. He's frightening, but what frightens me more is being alone. I was traveling alone when the cannibals caught me. I knew right away what they were. Eating humans drives you crazy, and they all had that mad light in their eyes. They threw me in a pit with a man missing all four limbs. I thought I was going to die.

But he got to them before they got to me. The first time I saw him, reaching down into the pit to lift me out, his face and front were covered in their blood. He saved the limbless man too, but the poor thing didn't last long. Infection got him in the end.

Ironically, my master does the same thing those cannibals would have done, eating part of me. Except, what he takes is renewable. Doesn't that make him better? He's gentle and treats me kindly, keeping me as comfortable and well-fed as possible. But maybe he's only protecting his investment. A man and his cow might be symbiotic for a while, until the man decides he wants steak for dinner. He's killed others and drank their blood. Why not me?

Yet, he's the only reason I'm still alive. The hope of survival with him is far better than the certainty of death, or worse, without him. So I stay.

I don't know how much longer we walk before he stops me again. Looking up, I half expect to see more bones. But he points to the side and I follow his hand, peering through the gloom of day that's now darkening to night. The road we've been following south has come to an intersection with a small hill beside it. On the hill sits a house with a few outbuildings. It looks thoroughly deserted, and so potentially safe. My spirits rise a little. At least we'll have shelter tonight.

We climb the hill cautiously, layers of ash muffling the crunch of gravel and dead grass under our feet. I wait in the yard, nervous and shivering, as my master checks the buildings. When he returns, he beckons me inside the house.

Though an omnipresent layer of dust covers everything, the house is in relatively good condition. Rearranging furniture, we make a small camp in the living room. The old couch is soft and comfortable, so I lower myself onto it with a grateful sigh, resting tired and weak limbs. Being in a house again is comforting.

Besides the couch, there's also a small wood-stove. Open fires are dangerous; they easily catch the attention of any scavenger for miles around. But a stove would hide the light, and the darkness would hide the smoke. My master gathers wood from a woodpile outside and starts a tiny fire.

The flames' warmth feels like luxury beyond belief. Sitting on the coach in front of the stove, I carefully peel away layers of cloth around my hands and feet to reveal bare skin, airing them for the first time in days. I drape the tatty gloves and socks on the hot metal of the stove, hoping they'll warm without getting singed.

My master stays away from the fire. He doesn't seem to need warmth to survive. He wears only one layer of clothing, and whenever he touches me, his body is always cool. In a way, it's unfortunate. With no body heat, he can't help keep me warm on nights when a fire is too risky. But then, considering what sharing body heat would involve, I'm glad his physiology makes it useless anyway.

While I warm myself, he takes supplies from our backpacks and makes a meal for me. I always find this ritual amusing, wondering if he fixes my food because I 'fix' him his. He certainly doesn't eat it himself. So far, he's survived on just my blood and that of the roaming bands of thugs who sometimes attack us. He always dispatches them with cold efficiency and then gorges himself. When that happens he doesn't need to feed from me for a while, which makes me grateful, scared, and reassured all at the same time: grateful to be spared a few weeks more, scared at what he's capable of, and reassured to know I'm worth protecting.

Those brief encounters are the only flashes of color in our otherwise gray and lifeless journey from north to south, seeking a warmer climate and the possibility that somewhere civilization has survived. So far it seems a foolish hope, but we keep going. With the sun, moon, and stars hidden behind thick layers of cloud we use a compass I found in an abandoned house to guide us.

My master finishes his preparations and hands me the bowl, along with a precious cup of water. I take both carefully from his hands and hunch closer to the warm stove. Tonight's fare is baked beans mixed with pork squares. I close my eyes, trying to forget all else and lose myself in the taste of food and the cool kiss of water in my throat. When I open them, my master has disappeared. I'm not worried, I know he'll be close by checking for danger.

As I mournfully scrape the last bite from my bowl, he reappears to clean and stow our things. Watching him, I have a sudden thought which threatens to quirk my stiff face into a tiny smile: my master waits on me hand and foot, as if *I'm* the master and not the other way around. But the smile dies when I remember that, no matter how kind he is, he still drinks my blood. He could snap me like a twig if he wanted to.

This dichotomy of safety and danger, kindness and cruelty, hope and despair stretches my nerves to the limit. But it's better than just danger, cruelty, and despair, isn't it?

I hope, and I assume he hopes, that somewhere on earth there's a place better than here, that someplace escaped the destruction. Maybe somewhere there's still green. That's why we walk day after day, through the dead fields and broken cities. That's why he cares for me and why I let him drink. It's for the tiny glimmer of hope that somewhere it's better, that we might be saved.

Having finished his meager chores, my master approaches the couch, making me tense. I know it's time. Every third night he drinks. Resigned, I hold out my wrist and look away. I stopped shaking like a leaf after the first few times; the horror fades with repetition.

But instead of taking my wrist, he presses something hard and square into my hand. I look back at him, surprised, then glance down to see a plain wooden box, scuffed with age and gray with dust. There's a tarnished turn knob on the side and I realize with disbelief that it's a music box. He must have found it while searching the house.

He gestures toward the box, watching me intently. Trembling a little, I draw it to my chest and carefully lift the lid. It opens with a creak of rusty hinges, and a high, tinny tune begins to play. I don't recognize the song, but it doesn't matter. In that moment it's the most beautiful thing left in the world. I begin to weep silently, sitting curled up in front of a warm fire and listening to the first music I've heard since the war.

Closing my eyes, I sway to the rhythm as it repeats, the tiny cylinder inside the box turning again and again. Its sweet but haunting tune reminds me of a Russian music box my father gave me when I was a girl, brought back from a business trip to New York. That intricately painted box had played a similar tune. A wash of memories bursts forth as I remember, making my long-numb heart ache with bittersweet longing for all I've lost. I remember that once my family was alive and well. Once, I wore new clothes, ate fresh food, lived in a house, and went to school. Once, I had a life.

Abruptly, the music stops and I open my eyes to stare dumbly at the box, dazed by the rush of emotions. My master reaches out and turns the knob, starting the music again. I blush, embarrassed, but the music soon swallows me up once more and I forget everything else. When it reaches the end of its cycle again, I turn the knob myself, never even opening my eyes.

After the third turn he takes my left wrist, gently pulling my hand away from the box. I keep my eyes closed and concentrate on the music, so I barely notice the bite. Maybe that's why he gave me the box, to make things…easier. I find I don't care. I'm just grateful for his gift and the happiness it brings me.

The feeding seems to be over more quickly than usual. Whether because he took less blood or because the music made time fly by, I don't know. As I consider this, he carefully cleans and bandages my wrist, though the bite wound is always gone by next morning.

After that there's nothing left to do but sleep. I curl up on the couch, cranking the music box over and over until I drift off. I sleep more deeply than I have in a long time. Absent are my usual nightmares of explosions, everything falling, dying, and burning. Absent too is the horrible vision of an insane man, teeth red, blood dripping from his lips as he holds a severed human arm in one hand and reaches for me with the other. I dream only of sunny, green fields where a soft breeze carries the far off notes of half-formed music.

I wake with a start, a cold hand clamped over my mouth. Everything comes into sharp focus and I realize it's my master, crouched on the floor next to the couch. Once he sees I'm awake he holds a finger to his lips, shushing me. I lie still and listen, fear building in my gut. After a few tense moments, my ears pick up what he's already heard: car engines.

Struggling, I try to sit up so we can grab our things and run, but he holds me down and shakes his head, pointing to the window. I realize day has come, though the dim, gray illumination penetrating the ash cover can barely be called day. The house is surrounded by miles of flat, open ground, so they'll see us if we run. It would be safer to wait for them to pass by. If they don't, my master can ambush them when they search the house, unawares.

I try to relax, but worry seeps past my defenses. What if there's a lot of them? What if they have guns? Nervous tremors seize my limbs while my master seeks out the best place for me to hide. The sound of engines grows closer. I try to swallow my fear as it threatens to turn to panic, but a nightmarish image of the cannibal from my dreams fills my mind and I can't block it out.

He settles on the hall closet for a hiding place. Huddled on the floor among the boots with coats brushing my head, I clutch my knees to my chest and watch the door close on the only friendly face I know, possibly the only one left in the world. Muscles tense, I try not to shiver as I listen hard, hoping to hear the engines pass by and continue on their way.

Instead, I hear the crunch of gravel as the vehicles turn off the road and drive up the hill. The rumble of engines approaches the house and I wonder who they are. A brief but burning desire shoots through me to run outside and throw myself into their arms, hoping for rescue. But that would be foolish. Eat or be eaten. Only those who have fought and killed for it have access to working vehicles. To them I'd be nothing but fresh meat.

The click and bang of car doors opening and shutting mixes with the sound of voices calling out to each other. With bated breath, I wait for the screams that mean my master has attacked. But there is no din of panic or slaughter. Perhaps he's considering the best way to strike without getting shot? I know one or two bullets won't kill him – I've seen him shot before – but what would a hail of bullets do?

The sound of voices grows closer, and I hear footsteps on the front porch. The front door creaks and someone enters the house, moving right past my hiding place. My body starts shaking violently and I have to resist the primal instinct to flee. Barely daring to breath, I bite down hard on my lip and the pain helps me focus. I have to trust. I have to wait. My master will get rid of them, I know he will. He's just biding his time and letting them separate.

Sure enough, a scream and a burst of automatic gunfire sound outside. Instead of feeling happy, my heart sinks. The thought of machine guns has the fear in my gut now clawing at my throat. If my protector, my sole chance of survival, is killed, my fate will be horrible. At best, I'll slowly starve alone in the wilderness. More likely, though, these men will find me. If I'm very lucky, they'll kill me quickly.

Even as these desperate thoughts swirl in my head, the screams outside grow louder and bullets begin to hit the house. I hear sickening crunches and tearing sounds. To my horror, the man who entered the house doesn't run outside to help his friends. He backs up slowly, further down the hall. But he doesn't get far.

I hear the front door burst open with a tremendous bang and the sound of splintering wood. The terrified thug in the hall screams and gets off one burst of bullets that sprays wildly around the hall before his scream is abruptly cut off.

The piercing echo of fully-automatic fire rings loudly in my ears. Dazed, I wonder why I'm slumped against the back of the closet. Then I remember: something punched me in the shoulder. I suddenly feel ice cold except for the bloom of fire in my shoulder, and finally realize I've been shot. That's when the pain hits, forcing a feeble whimper from my lips.

My master must have heard it, because he's suddenly there, kneeling beside me. His worried face swims in my vision as he scoops me up and takes me to the couch. My head lolls back over his arm, and I catch a glimpse of a decapitated body bleeding out on the floor.

I feel him lay me gently on the couch and start removing layers, bundling cloth, trying to staunch the bleeding. I wonder vaguely, in that detached sort of way of someone in shock, if he will lap up the blood seeping from my shoulder. Then I realize he won't need to, not with all the men he just killed. My last thought before I pass out is that I'm glad he won't have to bite me for another few weeks.

For a while, I swim in and out of consciousness. Dimly, I sense my master lift me and I hear a car door open and close. Then vibrations and a slow swaying lull me into oblivion. When I wake, the vibrations have stopped. My whole body aches and my shoulder is on fire. I can't move without pain shooting through every nerve attached to that side of my body. It's hard to breathe and I feel too weak to sit up, so I lie still and listen.

Someone moves nearby and a hand slips under my neck to gently lift my head. I taste the tang of metal as a cup is pressed to my lips, and I try to drink. The cool water is a sweet relief, but some of it goes down wrong and I cough reflexively, opening my eyes and seeing a startled look on my master's face. He hurries to prop me up, but the coughing hurts so much I almost black out. When the fit finally subsides, I taste blood in my mouth.

He tries to feed me something hot and liquid, but more often than not I start coughing again. Finally, I give up and go limp, hoping I'll pass out again so the pain will stop.

I do pass out, eventually. Time blurs as life becomes a cycle of vague waking and fitful sleeping. The pain which greets me upon waking is so bad I start to wish I won't wake up again. My master tries to make me eat and drink, but I can't keep much down.

Time passes. I'm moved sometimes, but I rarely bother opening my eyes. My body has started to burn with fever, and the constant coughing takes every ounce of strength I have. It leaves my throat raw and swollen, and I stop trying to drink what's given to me.

At one point I feel cool skin pressed to my lips instead of cold metal, and I taste salty blood. I wonder dazedly why he's trying to feed me blood, but I'm too tired, in too much pain, and too delirious with fever to care. I cough it up like I do everything else I try to drink.

Between fevered nightmares, I wonder why my master is working so hard to save me. Surely it would easier to drain me, move on, and find someone else who's not on their deathbed. The question comes to me easily enough, but the answer is out of my reach.

A while later, I don't know how long, I wake to the sound of tinny music. I manage a half turn of my head, and crack my eyes open enough to see a blurry image of my master, sitting cross-legged beside me. He holds the music box in his hands and is staring down at it. At my movement he looks up. His face has pale streaks carved through the gray smudge of ash covering his cheeks. I try to remember what makes streaks on a dirty face, but my mind won't focus, so I just relax and listen to the music. It soothes the burning in my body as I lie there, my breathing shallow and labored. There's so much I wish I could tell him, things I want to say before it's too late. But my thoughts are scattered and my body weak. I barely have the will to keep breathing, much less talk. Is this what it feels like to lose hope?

Yet despite the pain, I'm at peace. This is a better way to go than starvation or being eaten alive, and I'm so tired of the constant fear, the constant struggle.

I wake again, this time to the feel of cool, soft skin on my lips. At first I think my master is trying to give me blood again, but its coppery taste is absent. The sensation leaves, and I hear something I've rarely ever heard before: my master's voice. It startles me so much I open my eyes. Throughout all our time together he has uttered barely a handful of words.

'Please, live,' he says, voice broken and hoarse from disuse.

I want to, then, because he's asking, because he's speaking. His eyes are so sad, yet so beautiful as he stares down at me, and I finally realize he just kissed me. His lips are incredibly soft, and his eyes speak all the words in the world.

But, it's too late. I struggle to keep my eyes open, to keep looking at him while my breathing grows more and more shallow. I don't have the strength to keep going. Everything has left me, drained out slowly over the months. The blood and nutrients still left in my body aren't enough to heal my wound now beset with infection.

Yet there is one final thing I need to do. Why, I'm not sure, but it seems important. I just need him to know. I try to speak, even as darkness nibbles at the edge of my vision. It comes out a dry whisper, the words leaving me along with my last ounce of strength.

'My… name… is… Hope.'

A sad smile touches his lips as he sits there, leaning over me, and I feel something wet splash onto my cheek. The last thing I hear before the darkness swallows me up is his voice, whispering in my ear.

'I know.'

The Drone Room

Nicolas Watson

The fate of humanity will be debated by two old, bald, white men sitting comfortably in a boardroom. They are Mr. Lowry and Mr. Poloni. For the most part, they are indistinguishable from one another in appearance: with one exception. Mr. Lowry's remaining tuft of white hair, u-shaped and clinging to the base of his skull; is cut much shorter than Mr. Poloni's. When they speak however, you will note that Mr. Poloni still has a hint of a New York accent (lower East side) where as Mr. Lowry is from Berkshire. Both share in rounded cheeks, and paunches. Charcoal-coloured, well-tailored suits help shape their less than impressive physiques into proud Doric columns of stability in a world crumbling around them.

The boardroom is situated on New Zealand's South Island, nestled near Lake Manapouri. It is in the top floor of a squat and sturdy 6 floor office building. Within the building is all that remains of humanity's economy. The ones and zeros stored in its powerful and quadruple backed-up servers, represent 4.7 trillion Euros. Of course it should look far more resplendent, but it had to be built quickly, and strongly. Some luxuries will be afforded to the auspicious site, like our fellows' boardroom.

It did not receive marble floors, so it makes due with polished concrete. It has oak panelled walls and a fine and large table made from reclaimed fir, with seating for a dozen. The windows can be tinted to the senior executive's liking, to Mr. Poloni's liking. They are set to their 'dusk' configuration. This allows the dying embers of sunlight to wash the room in magic hour's warm glow. Mr. Poloni pours two substantial glasses of Isle of Cranachan 22 year old Single malt. Notes of toasted oats and raspberries warm the men's palates as they sit, and drink.

Mr. Poloni is proud of his boardroom, and the supremely important work that is being done there. He feels that though times are tough (and indeed they are), this place should represent the aspiration to which humanity would return. Of course the soft Corinthian leather lounge chairs next to the fireplace (some thought this addition comically anachronistic) belongs in the world's last corporate headquarters.

Once settled and meaningful pleasantries have been exchanged, Mr. Lowry comes to the matter at hand. 'I wanted to meet here because there's a concern over the… sensitive nature of what I've learned,' the Englishman says.

Mr. Poloni is able to boast that, 'There are few places left more secure than this room.'

Mr. Lowry takes a moment before continuing. This is not for dramatic effect but to allow him to enjoy the taste of the whisky, as it breathes on his palate.

'No doubt. I have, through some effort, gained access to the drone room.'

Mr. Poloni sits up attentively, he loses his cordial demeanor.

'Would you like me to continue?'

The drone room is located 30km to the northwest and is buried an undisclosed number of meters beneath one of the mountains of a former national park. It has one bunker-like entry point, which is accessed by a funicular railway carrying a unit of the world's remaining armed forces. Along this railway a mobile ski division patrols the mountain side. Scanner drones hover high out of view monitoring heat and movement signatures. Everyone is heavily armed and stimulated to maximal tolerances. It is not advisable to even think fleetingly about this location. Mr. Poloni knows this, because he had to finance the project to build it.

'There is no way you could have accessed the drone room,' says a grim faced Mr. Poloni, with the additional thought to himself: 'without me knowing it.'

'Well, it cost me a tidy sum of money, and I had to forget some key information about a senior civil servant, but there I was.' Mr. Lowry calmly retorts.

'I got in their little train and met some jittery friends along the way. They are rather attention starved. There were enough layers of security to make me feel quite confident my money was well spent. But I really did need to know the things that only they could tell me. And show me. I didn't expect that to be honest.' He takes a drink; Mr. Poloni does as well and relaxes, eager to hear more.

'Regardless, eventually I was escorted to an air lock and was left to wait. Some time passed, automated doors opened and there it was, the control room for their global operations.'

'No civilian should have access that room.'

'I agree with you on that point Mr. Poloni. Nor should a civilian be able to speak to the pilots that are in there either. But I did. And do you know what they told me?'

Mr. Poloni has no idea. This whole scenario is beyond him, it is a violation of pivotal security protocols. In his mind, he whirls through his contact list to find who possibly allowed this egregious breach.

'What?'

A wry smile appears on Mr. Lowry's face, briefly.

'The pilots are reporting complete systemic failure for food, water and air purification.'

Mr. Poloni thinks about this for a moment, and then says:

'It has been reported. The last I saw they were still hopeful...'

Without a word, Mr. Lowry lowers his head, and shakes it, slowly back and forth.

'They showed it to me.'

At this point Mr. Poloni puts his whisky down on a small table in front of the fireplace. The noise of glass on glass echoes in the practically vacant boardroom. His eyes dart back and forth; trying to read Mr. Lowry for any tells that he had made this all up. There are none.

'What did you see?'

'One of the commanders acted as my tour guide. He correctly assumed I was to have full disclosure and let me have it. Our little jaunt started in California, and we moved from sensor drone to sensor drone scanning for signs of life. It was a quick search as there were no such signs to be found. It was a desert, as far inland and to the north as Illinois. Granted, there was a tremendous amount of dust in the air, so I held to the belief that there could be pockets of life, an oasis perhaps.'

He takes a drink, and continues...

'My pilot said nothing. The visuals and data spoke for him. I knew things had gotten out of hand in the outside world but that level of devastation did not make sense to me. I asked him to show me the Great Lakes, the North, there would still be water and life there. Water yes, but frozen and glacial. Life, however could not be found. The weather patterns had stagnated to the point that an unsustainable draught and heat settled in the South and the creation of new Ice Age in the North.'

Mr. Poloni shook his head and stated that: 'This doesn't make sense.' Mr. Lowry had once shared that view, but had seen visuals proving it; the jet stream held permanently in place, thus amplifying the ecosystems on either side of it. The hope that life could exist on the borders of permanent winter and the dessert lands proved false. Crops in these 'sweet spots' had been blighted.

Mr. Lowry explains: 'I had gone to the room to check on our 'Robustus' brand wheat crops, something I wanted to use here this summer. What I saw was sludgy fields of rotten vegetation, with no signs of growth.' His drink comes right back to his hand and Mr. Poloni takes a large gulp, wiping his chin with his arm sleeve.

'What about greenhouses – they must have set some of them up in the 'sweet spots'?' With his hands rubbing his temples, then his eyes, Mr. Lowry explains the theory that the armed forces worked out. The grid had failed along the East coast. They could see collapsed power towers and lines lying under the snow. The thinking was that the weather in the north made access to maintenance impossible. The lack of maintenance seemed to have shut down the highway infrastructure as well. In the North, roads were only discernible by the streetlights that had yet to fall. In the South thousands of cars were abandoned in bottle necks on either side of collapsed bridges or flooded out tunnels.

'Heating, air conditioning, food preservation, and fuel for flights ran out. Each system ground to a halt. It looks like it could have been years ago' said Mr. Lowry. He looks out the window, it is no longer tinted; and he sees the sun disappear behind the fiord.

'Any pockets, villages still…' stammers Mr. Poloni.

Mr. Lowry shakes his head.

Mr. Poloni takes pride in his ability to stay calm in any situation no matter of the challenging headwinds he would have to navigate through as a captain of industry. But the outright annihilation of life in his country manages to crack the façade. 'Those idiots!' He throws his glass against the fireplace. Mr. Lowry flinches at the display. 'How could they let it get to this? Could they really not cope without us? All those protests, all that anti-capitalist crap. Look what they did with it.' Mr. Lowry thinks to himself, 'Well we didn't really leave them much to work with to be honest.'

Mr. Poloni steadies himself, he looks at his fireplace, littered with chards of soaked crystal. He thinks for a moment. 'What about Mexico, the Caribbean? Further south – Brazil?' In contrast to the stagnation to its north, the Gulf of Mexico and below are ravaged by near constant and brutal tropical storms. The service had lost 17 drones this month alone.

'Unfortunately force 6 hurricanes have pretty much wiped the slate clean there. There had been a carrier unit sent, but they were lost at sea trying to save anyone remaining. Any further chance of rescue was deemed too costly and potentially futile.'

Mr. Lowry learned this from a team from his company that had been dispatched to Haiti, tasked to try and grow modified grains. They had shown promise until most of the Island was washed away.'

'The rainforests?' blurts Mr. Poloni. 'There might be tribes and people in there right?'

'Not really mate, that was mostly deforested before the relocation.

What was left burnt down.'

'I should have been advised, I should have known.' Mr. Poloni says, looking down at a small pool of whisky.

'The whole continent was lost. Same as the North, but reverse the weather patterns and extremes.' As Mr. Lowry follows Mr. Poloni's gaze, he continues. 'They had a huge fleet of drones scanning for remnants of drug cartels. I think they would have recruited them, but it seems they all took care of each other. There was evidence of violence. Sorry, saying that, I saw that in every abandoned city. People turned on themselves sadly, when their governments faltered.'

'They should have survived. There was the means. We just needed to re-establish a foothold here. We would have reached out.' Mr. Poloni says. 'They brought this on themselves. They deserve what they got.' Neither of the men dwell on the idea of merit and what was or wasn't deserved; they were focused on their own problems. Mr. Lowry's crops had been refusing to grow despite science. The consolidation of the world financial system had to be completed. All financial institutions merged into one bank, under the stewardship of Mr. Poloni. Both men were kept alive and, well, flown and preserved away from the rest of the ravaged planet. 'We can still fix it. There's got to be something we can do, with the drones. We can have the drones fly relief missions.'

Mr. Lowry places his empty glass on the table in front of him, holding it from the base and muting it with the fleshy side of his index finger. There is a crackle from the fireplace as a log splits in two, red flames lap glowing orange cinders. He entwines his fingers and takes a deep breath. Then, looking up at Mr. Poloni, he speaks slowly, deliberately. 'There is no one left to help.'

There is only the noise of the fire. There is the smell of whisky, and the smoke of the fire. There is Mr. Poloni's jaw dropping open, wordlessly. He computes, he plans and scans every possibility in his mind, reaching around corners, thinking outside boxes, but finding nothing. Almost nothing. There is the pleading question. A last ditch at hope. One more moment before there is no other way around the truth. The redundant question. He asks it. 'What do you mean, 'no one left'? There must be someone. Somewhere…' And again, silence. Mr. Lowry shakes his head which rubs his collar; a friction noise of neck on cotton is the answer.

The two men sit for a moment in comfortable chairs, by a fire, in a climate controlled office building. Mr. Poloni bleeds cold sweat down his spine. It beads in his armpits, though concealed by his light woolen suit.

Mr. Lowry's facts are far more chilling. 'The drone surveillance program has not had a single detection of human life for two months, and six days,' reports Mr. Lowry. 'You know the scope of their reach. Two months, and not one blip of life out there.'

Slowly, Mr. Poloni raises himself out of his chair. He takes a few steps around it, turns and leans over the back. 'Europe, had fortified cities, catacombs, monasteries and castles. There could be people held up there.' He holds out a hand to Mr. Lowry, pleading for any chance. Mr. Lowry looks him in the eyes and says, 'Gone. No signs of life, anywhere.' His body collapses onto the back of the chair. His weight forces the legs to screech loudly as they dig into the floor's polish.

From his chair Mr. Lowry delicately explains that 'There were signs of fighting pretty much all over Europe.' He gets up from his chair and continues to speak. 'Not large battles or anything, just people driven to the brink. Like you say the castles and walled cities did pose a reasonable chance of harbouring survivors, but when the drones arrived all they found were corpses.'

Mr. Lowry comes to Mr. Poloni's side; he stands there next to a crumpled man.

'But, they… there had to be people helping them, armies or… We need to keep checking' says Mr. Poloni, his eyes and cheeks red.

'The cities showed signs of disease as well, hospitals were surrounded by the dead. They – the soldiers, – think that all across the world, the infrastructure of life fell apart and simultaneously nature worsened. Health and security services were stretched too thin. People couldn't cope.' Mr. Lowry says, calmly.

Shiny leather shoes click their way from the fireside and head for the panoramic windows facing the west. Mr. Poloni rubs his eyes and looks out to mountains, a silhouetted mauve. He folds his arms over his chest. After a moment the sound of well-heeled shoes is heard again as Mr. Lowry joins his host. He too looks out to the nearly empty world.

'I guess Africa, Asia, Australia too, they're all gone' murmurs Mr. Poloni, 'I don't know what to say. What are we doing here? What was the point of, all this, if there's no one else out there.' Placing his hands in his trouser pockets Mr. Lowry elaborates. 'I couldn't believe it either. I guess it's different for me because I saw the devastation on the monitors. They showed me the time lapse observations too, the geosync shots showing zero disturbances to the dead.' He pauses, and turns to try and make eye contact.

Mr. Poloni continues to stare out the window, so Mr. Lowry continues. 'I asked about isolated tribes, or people hiding in the jungles. What they saw confirmed the desolation. All large mammals are struggling and dying as well. The extinction event is crossing over multiple species. Complex life is dying off on Earth. It's down to the weather patterns. Their food sources have stopped growing, or breeding.'

This shakes Mr. Poloni; he turns and asks 'What's happening to wildlife?'

'They don't know.' Mr. Lowry turns away and walks back to the fireside. The boardroom is silent, and the men stand apart.

'What about your crops?'

There is no answer.

'I said, what about your crops? They were meant to be able to survive extremes. I saw your data during the procurement, it looked promising.' Mr. Poloni stands firm, walking steadily back to the fire so he doesn't have to shout. He keeps his voice a shade under booming, almost accusatory.

Mr. Lowry sits in his large comfortable chair and admits that 'There were massive shortfalls in the third and fourth generations. I think, and we haven't been able to fully confirm this, that there were issues with pollination. The relief crops failed about 2 years ago. It all went downhill from there. The GM crops couldn't produce enough, ours were dying, people weren't replanting. Seeds were stolen, sold, and horded and eventually eaten.' He holds his hands in his head. 'That's why I went to the room. I was summoned. They wanted to show me my failure.'

'My God! Who, I mean, it's one thing the world ending, out there. But why bring you in to see it?' Mr. Poloni stoops over his slouched companion.

'The military. Look, we thought the crops were going to thrive! We had no concept of them even struggling. We thought we had this all solved. That's why – that's why we planted here too, for us.'

It takes Mr. Poloni two seconds to process the information. He is a man who has had to deal with failure. He is good at assessing it, learning from it, learning how his people would cope with it. Knowing what was at stake should the failure be allowed to happen again.

Mr. Poloni nods his head, and with a calm and sympathetic voice asks 'Do you have the capability of saving our crops before the 3rd generation?' Mr. Lowry looks up, shaken. 'Yes, but we thought we had all the bugs out of the last batch – and that's killed billions!' Sitting down, Mr. Poloni holds his hands up and tries to calm the broken man across from him. 'What about local crops? Or, fishing? Did the drones see life at sea? Basically, what are our contingencies here?'

The questions serve to refocus Mr. Lowry; he sits up and remembers himself. 'Yes, there are local crops. We'll be working closely with the military to cultivate them, and we're looking for any signs of trouble with our product. But the sea, yes there is still life out there. Without the fisheries industry, stocks will rise. But like I said, there's the massive shift in global weather. We have no idea about long term effect on sea life, or if it will be feasible to fish. Storms out there are massive. We've been very lucky here so far to be honest.'

The optimistic tone quickly disappears however, and Mr. Lowry's eyes drop to the floor. He is silent. Mr. Poloni makes a move to place a hand on his shoulder but Mr. Lowry sits up and says.

'I'm sorry; I just remembered the coastal scans. They held on for the longest. Ships were being tracked out at sea about 3 months ago. Some must have been successful for a time. The bodies on the shore were horrible. Gulls and other scavengers got to them I suppose. It was all so terrible. The pilot had been flying a squad of drones back here for maintenance, so what I had seen was from the North Island.'

It was very close to home, all the death of the world. It was one island away. It sent a shudder through Mr. Poloni, knowing that they were the final isolated pocket of human life, on a dead world. This wasn't the Mars mission, where men arrived to explore a barren red wasteland. This was death, and decay. It was whatever vegetation could survive, piercing concrete, trying desperately to erase humanity's stain. Then, in a panic he thinks of a last devastating horror humanity could inflict on what was left on Earth.

'What about the power stations? The nuclear plants, would they have been decommissioned?' Mr. Poloni eyes bulge; he grabs Mr. Lowry by the lapels. Mr. Lowry is taken aback by the terror of his companion and responds that 'Yes of course they were all shut down. It was done by the military so the survivors couldn't be killed by melt-downs, or dirty bombs by the fatalists.' Mr. Poloni shakes the seated man. 'I know that, but what if they got them working again while we were here?'

That is enough for Mr. Lowry. He pushes back his scruffier doppelganger and stood up next to him. 'Calm yourself man. The drones aren't just flying around for humanitarian reasons. Their primary mission is looking for threats. Reactivations, detonation of armaments, radiation leaks, have all been scanned for and there is no sign of any of it.' Mr. Poloni calms down. 'I'm sorry. This is all just too much.'

'It really is.' Agrees Mr. Lowry and adds 'the fatalists were right. It is the end.' The New Yorker looks puzzled. 'But, you said the problem was neutralized, and that the crops should be fine and are backed up. How is this the end?'

Mr. Lowry chuckles quietly to himself. He picks up his whisky glass and pours a full glass. He attempts to down the drink in one draught but coughs hoarsely and spurts whisky and spit into the dead fire. The liquid barely hisses on the burned out logs. 'The crops ain't gonna work mate.' He coughs again. 'The drone fellas know it. The military know it too. They're keeping quiet about it though. They know who they have tucked away here in our little corporate nest. Our wee pillow Fort.'

Mr. Poloni is looking at the man's face with an air of desperate curiosity and betrayal. Mr. Lowry's face is hardening into a rictus grin. Mr. Poloni slowly, almost imperceptibly starts to back away from him. 'Gregory, what are you talking about? They are here to help.' Greg Lowry snorts, then chuckles. 'Come off it. Are they hell! As soon as my teams started falling over dead and the crops turned to brown mush, that was it for me, mate. I'm done here. You are too by the way.' Lowry takes another huge gulp of whisky.

Mr. Poloni turns and casually heads for the exit, but Greg calls to him, 'Don't be like that Randal. Come on, be a big fella. Let's talk this out.'

'We are done here' says Randal Poloni, pushing over the 7 foot glass sliding door.

'Not yet Randy!' Mr. Lowry shouts as Mr. Poloni is about to close the door.

He pauses to listen. 'Not yet man. Listen mate, I've had a bit of time to think it through. I know what we have to do to solve the army problem, okay?'

Mr. Poloni takes a step back in the room. 'Greg, I don't believe you. I think you're having a breakdown. It's perfectly understandable considering the amount of stress you've been…' Lowry waves the comments off, but in doing so loses his grip on the whisky glass and it goes flying. It crashes into the fireplaces grey brick work, exploding on contact.

'Sorry, it slipped.'

Mr. Lowry looks at the mess he just created. 'They are in babysitter mode now Randy. Think about it. The world's most powerful people gathered here in one place. The last place on Earth. Randal. What is power though, when we don't have the guns?' Mr. Poloni comes back into the room; he stops at the table.

Lowry continues. 'We caused this all; your banks, my crops, and chemicals and products. Together, we did not give a toss about anyone outside of rooms like this.' He holds his arms out, the Chairman Christ. 'We are the most dangerous men and women on the planet. We are statistically more psychopathic, calculating, dare I say evil than any other sample group alive, or dead. The guys with the guns, they know this and they are prepared for us. Once the food starts running low, we'll be shifted around the Island, divided. When all the food disappears we'll weakly lash out. But to no avail.'

Mr. Poloni sits at the table and pours himself a glass of water. He drinks and asks 'Yeah, then what? They draw at noon, winner keeps the planet?' A smile comes over Mr. Lowry's face. 'You're not so far off.' Mr. Lowry has calmed and is intoxicated; he swerves as he walks, but joins the conference. 'Look, I get it. It's my fault okay. I've destroyed the planet.' Mr. Poloni scoffs. 'Well, fine. The rest of the world helped, but my crap plants were pretty the much the last nail in the coffin. Which was a shame really, I actually tried to make them for the benefit of all mankind! No good deed I suppose. Well whatever, I'm not letting a bunch of tough guy civil servants take the world. No, I'm going to end it.'

'Oh great, what are you talking about now?' Mr. Poloni leans over to Mr. Lowry, but he does so in a manner that obscures his left arm. Said arm reaches for the conference phone, and with his index finger he presses the call button and his middle finger mutes the device.

'I switched the orders.' says Mr. Lowry.

'Huh?'

'I switched the orders. The army requisitioned unmodified crops from the eastern farms. I don't own those farms, but I do run the logistics for agricultural transportation. Their food gets hauled around by MY trucks.'

'You gave them your crappy seeds, but why?'

'Why? Well, look if we're going out, we're damn well taking every-one with us. We're not going to let the army win. They'll have their own clever system of the fittest people in their ranks breeding away under the mountains. Once all the rich folk die out and the planet reboots, they'll pop out of their caves and start it all over.'

'Uh huh. And that's a bad thing is it, the survival of the species?'

'They don't deserve it. They didn't work for it like I did!'

Lowry stands up and heads for the door. Mr. Poloni sits up and talks to the conference hub. 'Christine, did you get all that?' The voice of Christine is crisp and clear, with a hint of Southern California. 'Yes sir, I've forwarded it to General Sheppard.' Poloni leans over to end the call but thanks Christine first. He stands up. Lowry is frozen in his tracks.

'Well you were right about one psychopath I guess, you pathetic failure.' Lowry is silent. 'They might have your trucks already on-site. They may well have started planting, but it is certainly not too late for them to switch the crops. I have faith in our men and women in uniform. Together, with the businesses that didn't lead to the collapse of the global food supply, we'll find a solution to this, and we'll go on. We've got this. You certainly don't.'

Mr. Lowry stares at Mr. Poloni. All is quiet. Poloni has a hint of smile in the corner of his mouth. Lowry suddenly turns and bolts for the door. 'Hey, get back here you crazy….' Mr. Poloni chases after Lowry and the two slam into the doors, jowls smearing the pristine glass and rattles the panel, its metal struts clang as the two portly men fall to the floor. There they wrestle. Titans of industry, ties being pulled, fine cotton shirts pulled out from their overpriced, well-tailored trousers. They grunt and snarl at each other, their shoes skidding on the floor, shrilling, squeaking as one white floppy walrus tries to gain ascendency over the other. Panting and sweating, Randal Poloni traps Greg Lowry under his bulk. He has his hands around the man's neck.

Security arrives at the door, and with a bit of effort they get the sliding door back on the mount and push it open. From underneath Mr. Poloni, Mr. Lowry pleads for his life. 'Please, please don't I just, I just want to…'

'I don't care what you want! You're a sick man, you don't deserve to be here.'

'I know.'

Mr. Poloni hears this, and notices the man's face turning purple, eyes bulging, with Poloni's hands around his neck. He releases his grip. Mr. Lowry coughs and spits, the security guards help their CEO to his feet. Mr. Lowry sits up eventually. Catching his breath, the security detail allows him that.

'I didn't switch the crops. I just thought about it.'

'Yeah sure. Alright, Murray could you escort...'

'No honestly, I didn't. The army can check anyway to confirm. No I thought about switching it, but I knew that would never work.'

Mr. Poloni's glare softens towards the defeated man, he furrows his brow.

'So instead I just hid a nuclear bomb that I bought off the Russians, well I think they were... '

Deep within the Mountains of New Zealand's South Island a rumble is heard, and light erupts violently upon the last dregs of humanity.

Before the Crack

Christopher Adams

They predicted it would start sometime after nine thirty on Thursday, or before midday on Friday - Saturday lunchtime at the very latest.

The microwave buzzer broke Peter's innocuous stare out of the corner window. The lazy haze in which he had settled gained fresh vigour and purpose through the heated beans.

Peter's sniffling never ceased; it was natural compensation for the leaking. The sniffling came involuntarily, and was to be expected with the circumstances. But as Peter shuffled from the windowsill, cocooning himself with the bedsheets as he went, a sudden attack came upon him. He was caught ill-prepared, and was too slow in reaching for the handkerchief. The aftermath was devastating. A monstrous load of nasal mucus and syrupy fluid ejaculated from each nostril, coating the hastily drawn bedsheets with a thick pocket of human slime. There was silence in the wake of it. Then the familiar *bing* of the microwave began repeating itself from the kitchen. The gaps between each note narrowing, like an insurance salesman at a doorbell, paying no care to the obvious predicament of the occupant.

Peter couldn't worry about the microwave or the beans. Aside from his escaping fluids, he knew that time and its inconveniences weren't comprehendible - for salesmen or kitchen appliances. He altered his course to the bathroom, scarcely acknowledging the cat as he shuffled by.

He blew into a ball of toilet paper and proceeded to clean his face of the leakage. The shelf above the toilet was littered with small bottles and tablet sleeves: aspirin, paracetamol, a half-full bottle of whisky, ibuprofen, lemsip powder, a tiny bag with the remaining dashes of cocaine, and nicotine patches were balanced around the shallow edge.

He tore open the Lemsip pouch, scattering it into the base of a cracked mug that lived on the side of the sink. Conscious of the spillage hazard, Peter filled the mug to just over half way, well before the forked crack began its ascent to the ridge. He agitated the cure with the bottom of a toothbrush and what was left in the whisky bottle before raising it to his lips. Peter knocked back the mixture with a single gulp and an accompanying cringe. The sharpness of the dash provoked seven deep and increasingly violent coughs, before the fit settled into short and mild splutters. He swilled the mug and returned it to its place before taking down his underpants. Peter gathered his dressing gown on one side of his body before he sat down; the way girls tie their hair on a particular side to show the better half of their face.

The low hum of the building's boiler network moaned from behind the toilet. The vibration found its way through the loose fittings and untightened nuts and bolts of naked pipework. It crooned varyingly. Pitch and volume rose and fell as if in an argument. Paint had fallen away from the walls through years of reverberations, and pockets of rot revealed the crude fixtures of the building's arteries beneath a flimsy chipboard surface. To a guest it would have been intrusive or uncomfortable, it may have even put them off urinating, but to the occupant it was warm and enveloping. The faint murmur created a familiarity of setting and a sense of motion for Peter. He often thought it must be what a long-haul flight through the late hours felt like, with nothing but the powerful swirls of jet engines and thirty five thousand feet separating you from the earth. It swallowed him into a little universe of safety, as if a sleeping octopus held the room securely within its warm grasp. The microwave's *bings* persisted in the adjoining room. Peter flushed.

By the time he had reached the kitchen and lit a cigarette, the beans had cooled. Peter silenced the microwave and began stirring the contents of the bowl, startling the lingering cat with sporadic coughs and splutters from a thickening smoky haze. Sensing an imminent dismissal, coupled with the diminishing prospect of more nip, the cat retreated to the kitchen table and took immediately to licking himself. He understood when time wasn't convenient and, as a result, moved from flat to flat in accordance with his fancies, making the most of each occupant's good nature and hospitality. Percy did have a home, but for now here was as good as anywhere, and he had found that nobody else was in.

Peter shuffled into his slippers. The sensation was always comforting to him; it reminded him of shaking hands with an old friend, or stepping on a washed up jellyfish as a child. However, in recent months, it had become a necessary reprieve from the tiles on the kitchen floor. It was here that the flat was coldest. Even the cat would skip with urgency and speed across its surface for the warmer clime of the carpet, as though he were late for a meeting.

The apartment block was always cold now. The draught in the corridors came about you harsher than ever, and even taking a shower was a serious risk. Even under regular circumstances, the heating system was more of an aesthetic concept than a working utility. The pipes clattered and flexed but to little effect; the block was old, cheap, and uncared for. The landlord of the building was a short southern man in his forties. He wore a flat cap indoors and spoke every sentence as though it were a favour. Ever since the announcement that the heating allowances for each flat had been reduced, it had only been working for two-hour periods in the evening. Peter exhaled a cloud of Benson and simultaneously raised a spoonful of beans to his face, as a mechanised clock ornament performs two motions in perfect synchronicity.

The kitchen and lounge area of the flat were shared, and there was a short corridor that led to Peter's bedroom and bathroom. The space was small and cluttered; human occupation evidenced itself on most surfaces around the lounge area and the room wore an intrusive suggestion of body odour, though friends occasionally commented that the space suited Peter.

The flat was particularly quiet today. Despite the pipework and the microwave and the sniffling and the octopus and the cat and the slippers, the flat was quiet. Thoughts of a half-eaten tuna pasta salad, or something else that may have satisfied, floated listlessly above Peter's head. He might have made spaghetti or lasagne if he had the ingredients, but he knew there was little gain in filling the shelves now and going out in the cold air would only aggravate his condition.

Peter switched on the television; a nondescript copy of a superior brand. It was nineteen inches across and *supposedly* HD, ready for films or computer games. Peter didn't care much for movies, and hadn't played a computer game for at least fifteen years. He wasn't entirely sure why he had acquired it in the first place. His sister, Sarah, had upgraded to a wall-sized home cinema system and Peter's flat needed furnishing at the time. Anything that filled space and came without charge was happily received at the time.

Peter's thumb repeatedly inputted commands, making strangers come and go from the screen. The action of the thumb increased as the world appeared and disappeared through avenues of sight and sound. It was somewhere in-between sitting down, taking the last life of the cigarette, eating the baked beans, and listening to the strangers in his room that it happened as it always did. Peter wasn't particularly fond of television, but was complacent running through channels. It had a peculiar effect on him. It reminded him of sitting in a lukewarm bath, drawing no pleasure from the situation but equally having no dispensation to get out. Peter always drew positives from any situation, however, and the content of the programme could have been an hour-long broadcast of the colour beige as far as Peter was concerned. But it passed time, so he sat and watched the same old news be told to the same old world. Noises and colours stealing away time before anybody realised that it is missing, like a trick coin fool-ing a passive viewer, seemingly spinning through a static axis. He sat alone; the cat wasn't interested in the news and had evidently grown bored of licking himself. Neither Peter nor the cat could be sure of the other's current location.

The same scene had occupied every screen for the past seven months. News broadcasts, documentaries, debate programmes, lifestyle shows and reality television had become a kaleidoscopic barrage of believers, deniers, truth proclaimers, screamers, weepers, fatalists and crazies, all filling the last pockets of time with theory, opinion, jargon and noise. Peter was still behind its pace, he hadn't caught up with the momentum but, since his predicament had bedridden him for the last week, he was a little more up to date on current issues.

Without conscious decision, Peter settled the television on one of the main terrestrial channels and gathered the remaining beans on his spoon. A brunette news reporter was interviewing a family on the screen. Their house was offensively large, and unreasonably clean. Peter responded immediately with a contemptible groan and thought of changing channels, but the trick coin gained momentum somehow. It put any dispensation to look at something else away, and Peter knew the other channels would only be showing something similar.

The family appeared happy to be together. The children wore clothes that looked the sort from designer catalogues and the kitchen seemed to be chiselled from a single block of marble, all the things that people hoped for. They spoke about 'togetherness' and 'what was really important' for a number of minutes. The whole spectacle was ridiculous to Peter. A violent outburst of coughing and facial leaking nudged any of its intended effect from his mind, and several beans escaped his mouth and back into the bowl. The final scene of the feature was outside the house, using all the most impressive angles. The parents placed their hands on the children's shoulders and spoke about how they would spend the day: 'cycling as a family' and 'preparing a home cooked meal'. Peter switched the television off at this and reached for his cigarettes. The sound of the cat gnawing at the drywall could be heard from the spare room. Small stirs of something beyond words made itself known in the pit of Peter's stomach. He hadn't visited his mother for weeks and had cancelled his last golf game with his father to see Eve. *I couldn't risk giving them this.* Peter proceeded in the direction of the kitchen. He was sure it was for the best; his mother suffered from terrible asthma in the winter and giving her a virus would not have been fair considering the timing.

Peter returned to the kitchen and opened the fridge door, making a beer can topple from its place. It rolled across the kitchen floor, finally settling against the table leg. As Peter let the foam of angry fluid gush into his mouth, he became aware of a faint but steady noise coming from the world downstairs. It sounded like the beginning of a football match a few miles off and, moving to his corner window, Peter could confirm that the city's structure was leaking with people. If the light were not fading so quickly, he would have been able to distinguish faces. Hundreds were gathering in the square; the side streets and alleyways burst like swollen tributaries as people flooded into the square like water joining a lake.

And, for what might have been the two hundred and thirty fourth time that week, thoughts of speaking to Eve were chiselling into his head.

After the news credits had rolled, a message announcing an alteration to regular viewing filled the screen, and a female voice spoke with a conscientious and apologetic manner. Peter thought it was the perfect tone of voice owned by somebody you would love your parents to meet, but couldn't particularly imagine yourself fucking. He would have shared this thought if anybody was present but, since he couldn't be sure if the cat took offence easily, he kept it to himself. She announced: 'due to unforeseen technical difficulties, tonight's regular schedule of the Celebrities On Ice final has been cancelled. Up next is the usual eight thirty showing of Question Time. We apol-ogise for the cancellation.'

Peter reciprocated, 'At least that is something,' to the woman on the screen, but she had gone.

Peter switched off the television and resumed his lazy stare into the universe. He wouldn't have been able to say when he started alternating his gaze between the sky above and the people below. Peter thought how many of them were looking up at the sky like him, or looking at each other look up at the sky. Peter couldn't have been sure how long he pondered this for.

The sky outside hadn't changed. It had been this way for the last week, though the faint line above the world had grown more dis-tinct in the last few hours. Clouds occasionally drifted past, hiding the imperfection with their closeness before passing. The faint glimmers of light that managed to break through wore a colourless haze, like paint watered down at the end of a tin.

Peter wasn't a lazy man by nature; he had studied the line diligently over the last week but repetition had enabled a natural ambivalence. To him, it may as well have been the stray visiting cat that is fed and bedded through common decency before moving on.

He placed a cigarette between his lips and opened the window, lifting a match to his face then letting it fall to the streets below. The only thing noticeably different tonight was the air which had gradu-ally thickened throughout the day. Normally the fourth floor window would draw in a rush of evening air and erase any stagnancy in the room, but opening it tonight felt like getting into a long standing car on a hot day, as if the world outside had been parked for hours in the baking sun.

The slow night emptied the room of air and filled it with an opaque closeness. Coupled with Peter's sinuses it gave the impression of being at the bottom of the ocean, as though a thousand tonnes of water had filled the little flat and the pressure was physically working to smother and crush him within. He exhaled deeply and took a large gulp from the beer, one motion anticipating the other. The discerni-ble gaps between one person and another were thinning in the crowd below. If it were a little clearer Peter would have been able to make out features, but the last light of the sun was fading behind the clouds and it looked as if it would rain.

The thoughts of Eve had gained momentum. They were running about the air in the room, gasping from the pressure and pushing against the ceiling. Eve wasn't particularly Peter's type. She listened to Buddy Holly records and spoke with unwarranted enthusiasm at staff meetings. Nevertheless, she made Peter laugh and sketched funny drawings of Mr. Gardner sometimes. She was another mid-thirties divorcee, with two kids from a teenage romance gone sour. She and Peter had gotten together after a night drinking with work col-leagues. They had enjoyed themselves, and held each other on the Saturday morning but nothing became of it. Monday was another Monday and they were both insistently complacent about the episode, so much so no real conversation ever happened about a 'we' or an 'us' or even an 'it'. Peter scanned through his phone contacts; he didn't know what he would gain by speaking to her. Potentially a break from only having the cat to talk to, potentially somebody to share the tuna pasta salad with. The dial tone started.

All too quickly the tone was cut, 'Oh – Eve. It's Peter.'

There was enough of a pause for him to regret his decision.

'... Peter... Peter, how are you?' she opened, that same enthusiasm reserved for staff meetings was there. 'How're you feeling?' followed.

Peter returned, 'Oh pretty awful still, I can't seem to shake it.'

'I'm sorry to hear that; have you tried those Lemsip powders? And are you eating fruit and taking vitamin tablets? They will help strengthen your ...' she spoke with textbook false sincerity.

Peter didn't answer either of her questions. 'Do you have plans for tonight?' he started, quietly surprised at the directness of his question though she seemed unfazed.

'I'm taking Samantha and Charlotte over to my parents, we're cooking dinner and watching this dancing show that mum loves.'

Peter spoke, 'The final is cancelled tonight. Technical difficulties, they said.'

'Oh that's a shame, we'll just enjoy our meal then.'

'That sounds nice,' Peter replied. There was an exhausting pause, the kind Peter could tell his grandchildren about. 'How has the office been this week?' Peter wasn't a good talker, but gave the appearance of listening well.

Eve inhaled as though about to retrieve something from the bottom of a swimming pool, 'Stressful in the run up to last Friday,' she started, 'orders and statements aren't getting to the right people on time.'

'Typical mess,' Peter returned confidently. 'Almost glad I've been dead to the world.'

'It was dull without you. I was hounded by Gardner for most of the week,' Eve stated.

Peter laughed, 'Any questions come up on 1980s cricket players and you'll be well prepared.' This wasn't a funny joke, but Eve laughed anyway. 'Sounds silly considering the circumstances, but I've actually missed work this week. The people, anyway. Some of the people.' Peter didn't mean to go this far, or leave this long of a gap between speaking. Aware of the space not being filled, Peter spoke suddenly, 'Were your yoga classes running this week?' The seconds folded and stretched around themselves.

The same inhale came again, as though preparing for a deeper dive in the pool, '… Listen Peter, why don't you come and be with us?' Eve said. The false sincerity had vanished now. Something else replaced it. Peter could hear the cat pawing at the tassels of the sofa cushion.

'That's really kind, Eve, but I wouldn't want you or your family catching this, especially … - I mean - considering the timing.' Just enough moments went by for an IT technician to think of a lie, 'I've got some jobs to do around the flat too. Tidying up and feeding the cat… thank you for the offer though'.

Eve didn't reply and Peter couldn't be sure if she had actually heard him.

'Anytime, Peter.' She said eventually.

'I hope you have a nice evening Eve. Take care.' Not waiting for a response, Peter closed the line. There are particular situations, with particular people, who have experienced a particular breed of pain, that an understanding is reached of not saying too much, or if possible, anything at all.

After the phone call, Peter collected a handful of potatoes from the fridge and placed them in the microwave. He wanted something tangible and warm to go with the tuna pasta salad. The red timer wound down into smaller and smaller digits as the potatoes rotated.

Peter decided it was best to take a bath, but due to the negation of heating allowances, he had found that three full kettles of boiling water were required to make it worthwhile. Peter returned from his first journey to the bathroom with a small bag of cocaine, and emptied the contents into a even line. He took a five pound note from his wallet and rolled it into a tight, thin straw and inserted it expertly into his right nostril. He made a short, quick motion along the table and the white dust disappeared. He then returned the dampened note to his wallet.

Boiling kettles, filling the bath, repeating the process: this was a welcome model of structure and order for Peter. The electric burble of the boiling was a pleasing steady tempo and rhythm. It wasn't intrusive or frustrating like the microwave, and far more natural. It was like jazz in upmarket restaurants, the kind that is played at a volume where you can barely discern the beginning or end of a song.

The faint line hovering above the world had lengthened and thick-ened in the sky. It was as if paint had been too swiftly applied to an under-coat, and quiet cracks were beginning to branch out from each heavy brush stroke. The surrounding sky was also different. Shadows fell peculiarly on the buildings below and seemed unsteady in their depth of cast. They appeared to be peeling away from their natural posts, drawing towards the line in the sky like dust being sucked from a carpet. Peter thought there must have been a sunset somewhere, he had seen them before and was sure they happened. The dyed sky shifted, almost in response, and faint glimmers of light could be seen splitting the inky clouds, but an overwhelming refraction swallowed them into the emerging vacuum. The crack widened and expanded. The starless sky was finishing its last day.

Peter studied the line and finished the tuna pasta salad. He had emptied the kettle into the tub twice already and was waiting for the last boil. Once ready, Peter added the steaming fluid to the bath. He lowered his body, coughing as his testicles met the steamy surface. Before long, he had acclimatized to the temperature and let himself drift once again in to the little universe in his bathroom.

The air in the flat was perceptively heavier by the time Peter had dried himself. The thickness and humidity of the room was dense and close, as though the octopus had awoken from a nightmare and suddenly tightened its grip too far, bursting the seams of the flat and letting the night flood in through the gaps.

Flus and men worsen at night and Peter began to feel the accompanying light-headedness of his condition. He noticed that the edges of shapes were blurring. The bookcase, sofa and kitchen table were etching away, as if the contrast on a television screen was decreasing, or he was wearing goggles underwater. Peter suddenly felt his nostrils tickle and was immediate with his next move. He masterfully wrapped the handkerchief around his nose and trapped the escaping mucus in the vacuum of tissue. He waited several moments to ensure the situation was under control before cleaning his face of the residue and placing the material in his dressing gown.

The crack ate away at the horizon.

Gaseous clouds and forks of electricity shivered and warped around the main line before an increase in pace tugged them to an aperture of blackness. Road signs and bicycles could be seen hovering in the sky outside Peter's flat like balloons. They hung slowly and listlessly before a sudden change of angle pulled them towards the splitting skyline. It reminded Peter of a game he played as a child when his parents took him to the country. The four of them would throw sticks over one side of a bridge and race to see which one would emerge on the other side first. He remembered that it was important to start your stick where the current was strongest; he learned that his stick would suddenly gain momentum as the shape of the riverbed changed and if he did this, he would win. Peter consulted his watch. It read ten forty five.

They said Saturday afternoon at the latest. That's what they said.

Outside, cars, people and buildings were floating weightlessly upwards and gaining terrible momentum at a set distance from the crack, hanging effortlessly until a sudden jerk gave way to a steadily increasing pull into nothingness.

The off-shooting cracks were racing across the horizon now. The night sky was a memory, creaking apart in front of the world as a boot presses too heavily on weak ice. The night sky and the million year old light from the stars, as precious as time, was now a thin veneer - and a clumsy foot pushed through to the cold dark beneath.

Peter shut off the lights around his flat and drew the curtains closed. He popped out two paracetamol tablets on the kitchen table and poured his last beer into a short glass. He finally switched off the kitchen light and whispered, 'Percy, here puss.'

Nothing stirred in the flat.

He waited a few moments for movement but nothing came. Peter knew that he might have slipped out while he was in the bath. Before long, the tablets took their effect and he slipped into a deep, nasally snore.

At twenty four minutes past eleven, the cat grew uncomfortable with his position behind the sofa and casually sauntered into Peter's bedroom. Percy found his usual place in the crook of the man's thigh, and fell immediately to sleep.

Last Night

Sheila Adamson

I remember when I first heard about the Asteroid. We'd been talking about death earlier that day, one of those intellectual conversations that Aaron liked to start. We were meant to be students, after all.

Dan refused to get into the philosophical spirit. 'I'd like to die crashing my Ferrari after a high speed chase with the cops.' He was such a rebel.

Hayley had to go one better. When I first met her I instantly liked that about her; the wild things she'd say, the way no one ever really knew what she was thinking. Four months of sharing a bathroom was taking the shine off.

'I would like to give my life to save others,' she declared. 'To close the Gates of Hell.'

'Why would your death close the Gates of Hell?' I asked. The others gave me a pleading look. Hayley and I were arguing a lot and it was getting on the guys' nerves.

'It's the symbolism of the sacrifice, Jen,' Hayley explained patiently. 'The triumph of the human spirit.'

'I think I'd prefer not to die at all,' I said.

'Everybody dies,' said Aaron.

'Not Jen,' Dan laughed. 'She's too stubborn.'

That was what they thought of me. I was the practical one, the never-get-the-joke one, keeping the kitchen almost clean and handing my assignments in on time. Thanks to my mum I'd learnt early-on how to be the grown up.

It was later that day that I saw the news item. An asteroid had been discovered on course for Earth. The article was jokey, talking about a 'potential collision' in the headline and then backtracking in the small print. Of course it wouldn't actually hit. Just a near miss. A bit of excitement in geek circles. I mentioned it to Aaron, to show I really was on his wavelength. We talked about humanity's death wish and the appeal of disaster movies. I held my own. Threw in a few references. He threw in more. But I think he was a little bit impressed.

And that was that. For about a week.

It was Hayley who announced casually one night, 'So this asteroid is going to kill us all.'

'I thought it was going to miss,' said Dan.

Aaron pulled a face. 'They don't seem so sure anymore.'

Obviously, Hayley had decided to go with melodramatic rumour as opposed to actual facts. 'We're all going to die,' she said, with some relish. 'In, erm, three weeks and two days time.'

'Of course we're not,' I said sharply.

'Asteroids hardly ever hit planets,' said Dan. 'I read that.'

'Something killed the dinosaurs,' said Hayley.

I lost patience. 'Oh come on, Hayley. An asteroid is not really going to hit the Earth. Even you can't think that.'

She pointed her fork at me and gave me her utterly serious wide eyes. I was growing to hate her utterly serious wide eyes. 'Three weeks, two days,' she said. 'We'd better get ready.'

Ready? What did that even mean?

I refused to give it any thought.

Other people did. And that was strange, because officially there was nothing to worry about. The BBC news had a graphic to prove it. Yet queues of shoppers were clearing tinned food and toilet rolls off the supermarket shelves. At first we laughed, because where was this panic coming from? The same distrust of science that made idiots refuse to get their children vaccinated? Pudgy-faced politicians appeared on every TV and media outlet to assure us that everything would be fine. The Asteroid – which had acquired a capital 'A' by now – would 'come close', that was all. The worst case scenario was that it would explode in the upper atmosphere, causing a shock wave. We might experience 'some disruption and damage to property.'

The Internet begged to differ.

Everyone had a prediction. Even if it did explode above ground, the Asteroid would burn off oxygen from the air and we'd all suffocate. Or, no, it would hit, instantly destroying everything beneath it and in a wide radius around ground zero. Those who weren't killed straight away would be caught by the rain of ash and fire. Or, we'd starve to death as clouds of soot blocked out the sun. The collision would set off earthquakes and tsunamis all round the world. Or volcanoes. Or all of the above.

Some of the people saying this sounded like they knew what they were talking about. The scientists who were wheeled out on the news sounded... not as convincing as I would like.

'Whatever way you look at it, it's serious,' said Aaron. He was the most obsessed of us, devouring every scrap of information and trying to sift fact from fiction. I couldn't work out whether he was trying to prove that the government was wrong or that they were right. Whenever I saw him there was a frown on his face. It was almost as bad as when he broke up with his ex.

'It's not going to happen,' said Hayley. I sensed a pronouncement coming. 'Don't you see? This is a CIA plot.'

'What?' I couldn't get enough scorn into that single word.

'Well, you said it yourself, Jen,' she said reasonably. 'This whole situation is crazy. We don't really believe an asteroid is going to wipe us out. Do we?'

Aaron, for once, was the one to take up the gauntlet. 'Every amateur astronomer on the planet has seen this thing in the sky. It's heading towards us.'

'Oh, yes, of course, that part is true. But it's just like all the other asteroids that come by the Earth. They explode way up in the sky and it's no big deal.'

'It was a big deal in Tunguska,' said Aaron. 'Even that one in Russia a few years back caused a massive shock wave and it was only a few metres across. This one might be two kilometres.'

That was another thing that nobody seemed able to agree on – the exact size of the object hurtling towards us. Every national government spokesman estimated low, whether it was the UK, the US or China. Everybody else assumed they were lying.

Hayley sat back in her chair with her wise face on. 'Just you wait. Come the big day, everyone will be cowering in fear. And then there's a mysterious explosion up in space. Boom! Asteroid gone. Thank you US government, you're our heroes. And suddenly we find they've got a ginormous space missile platform in orbit. But nobody objects because they just saved our lives. Win-win.'

'You are certifiably insane.' I couldn't listen to this any longer. 'The CIA. For god's sake. And is Princess Diana involved too? Elvis?'

'Maybe they killed Diana because she knew about the plan,' Hayley said thoughtfully. Dan made the mistake of laughing. She warmed to her theme. I had to escape.

So I shut myself in my room and worked on my essay. Other students had started to murmur and suggest all classes and deadlines should be cancelled. Quite a few had stopped coming altogether. Not me. This would all blow over in time, wouldn't it? In years to come we'd have a good chuckle about it. And in those years, I'd want my degree.

I had plans for my life. Or, at least, I planned to have plans. The future was this glorious, bright haze of uncertainty. A blank sheet on which anything could be drawn. I'd worked so hard and things were finally coming together. I had friends. I was learning how to talk to guys. How to take my time and be patient and see what developed. Like with Aaron. I wasn't going to leap in and make a fool of myself over a passing crush. I was keeping my cool.

And I needed time.

Suddenly it was hard to get food. People left for the country as if somehow that would help. Shops closed. The police prowled the streets to keep order. Then, to make sure everyone was really calm, they broke out the army.

Mum kept phoning me. Usually drunk. 'I wish you were home, Jenny,' she'd say. 'Why don't you come home?'

'I have classes,' I told her. 'I can't come home.'

The week before the impact the university closed. Neither the staff nor the students wanted to be there. But where should we be instead?

The government told us to go to work and keep the country operating normally. Food still needed to be delivered, water and electricity supplied. Hospitals and doctors had to stay open. The army guarded supermarkets and enforced arbitrary rules on the maximum amount of anything that you could buy at one time.

It was madness. It couldn't be happening. It couldn't be happening to us.

Most people turned to drink. The drug dealers were raking it in. The police didn't even try to stop them. They had enough to do with the random outbursts of violence and attempted looting.

Some people killed themselves. Aaron said that maybe they were trying to wake themselves up. 'You know, if you're dreaming. When you die in a dream you wake up.' His voice had a strange, empty quality. I couldn't tell if he thought this theory actually made sense.

We were in the street, heading for a shop that we'd heard was still serving. The ambulance that cruised past us had no siren. What was the point in claiming to be an emergency? The whole world was an emergency now.

Aaron looked up at the sky. There was nothing to see in daylight. Nothing but the clouds of a standard Scottish winter. They said you could see it with ordinary binoculars now, if you were in a dark enough place. In the city it was never dark enough. We wouldn't see it until it was right on top of us.

I wanted to tell him it would be all right. I wanted to tell myself it would be all right. I wanted to punch something.

I wanted to kiss him.

None of us were getting what we wanted. Not anymore.

The government announcements sounded stranger and stranger, like a hypnotist trying to convince you that you were a chicken. 'There is no need to panic. We ask everyone to stay indoors and only travel if it is absolutely necessary. If you have elderly neighbours please take a moment to check that they are all right.'

And some people believed them. But all the time there was the doubt and the not knowing and the people screaming all over the Internet about doomsday. Religious nuts handing out leaflets on street corners. It was all the fault of gays or reality TV shows or whatever you didn't like.

It was a world that nobody wanted to live in anymore. Except that we wanted even less to die.

We couldn't talk about anything normal. We found ourselves playing raft debates to decide who should be allowed into the government's secret bunkers and who should be left out. (There had to be secret bunkers, right?) Dan, high as usual, worked himself into a state. He said if any bastard let Elton John in he would kill them with his bare hands. 'A few good songs in the Seventies and he dines out on it for life? Give me a fucking break.'

But we had to thank Dan. He supplied the dope and none of us were too proud to join in. It helped a little. It made sense of the fact that nothing made sense.

I wanted it to be over. More and more I just wanted it over.

So that we could go back to normal.

Slowly, tortuously, the days ticked by. Nothing felt real. I drank a lot. I shouted at Hayley, at poor gormless Dan, at stupid miserable Aaron. I shouted at Mum and told her to stop calling every day, since when was she Mother of the Year? I drank more.

Dan made it his mission to have as much sex as possible before the end. It was surprising how often he pulled. Girls were lowering their standards. Hayley was certainly lowering hers. I wouldn't have touched some of her efforts with a barge pole.

One night Aaron hooked up with his ex. I don't think it did either of them much good.

I wasn't ready to give up all my common sense. This couldn't really be the end. It couldn't be. I blamed the useless politicians who couldn't explain things in a way that people would believe. The scientists who should have been on TV, demonstrating how the Asteroid would break up in the atmosphere. Where the hell were they? Why had they allowed everyone to believe the worst?

I gathered up our large collection of empty bottles and lugged them down to the recycling point. One by one I threw the bottles into the bins, trying to make them shatter as hard and loud as I could.

But now we're here. Today is the last day. Tonight is the last night. At about four am we should know, one way or the other.

I sleep late, hoping to work through my hangover. In the end I have to get up. The flat is a mess. More bottles, empty glasses, overflowing ash trays. My stomach turns.

There is nothing on TV except old movies. Against my will I turn to the news. There's the prime minister telling us to stay indoors and keep calm. Pictures of the Asteroid taken by orbiting telescopes. For the millionth time, I hear about the explosion in the air, the shock wave, stay away from windows, etcetera.

And I don't believe it. I just don't.

This Asteroid is big, ridiculously big. Everybody knows. The government desperately wants us to keep calm, not because it will do any good, but because they don't have anything else to offer. That's the truth, isn't it? Who am I kidding?

I can't talk myself out of it anymore. I'm too tired. Too scared. There's a hollow in my stomach. I sit frozen in front of the TV, unable to think of anything to do.

Aaron drifts in and sits beside me, nursing a coffee. For a few minutes he watches the news silently. None of it seems to surprise him.

'Why aren't they doing anything?' I demand.

'They probably are,' he says listlessly. 'Behind the scenes. They'll have tried to blow it up. Maybe they're still trying.'

'They're cutting it pretty fine.'

'Yeah.'

We wait for our last minute dramatic rescue. The hours tick by. Nothing changes.

Hayley doesn't come home until late afternoon. She looks terrible. She doesn't talk about it.

And now it's evening. The number of hours left is in single figures. The four of us sit in our shabby living room, watching TV because we can't help ourselves. Hayley is quiet. It unsettles me. I ask if she's all right.

'Yes,' she snaps.

I don't pry.

Dan shakes us up. 'Come on,' he says. 'If this is the end no way we should be wasting our last hours like this. We should be making the most of them.' It seems a friend of a friend has the run of a big house, not far from us. 'Go out with a bang,' he says. 'Party until four and then keep on partying.'

I shrug. It all sounds irrelevant. Like a moth drawn to a flame, I turn back to the news. Again. The others yell at me to switch it off. There's no change. No announcement of a sudden, brilliantly successful missile launch. Just footage of people rioting in India.

Dan perks up. 'We should go out and steal something.'

'Steal what?' I say.

'I dunno. What would you like?'

I can't make sense of the question. 'What use is a new TV if the world is ending?'

'It doesn't matter!' he says. 'Don't you want to do *something*? Don't you want to break the rules for once in your life?'

Maybe I do. I'm not sure what I want anymore. Dan is determined. Somehow the four of us find ourselves walking into town, looking for action. For some kind of adventure. It's cold. Rain spits from the sky. You can't see any stars or oncoming asteroids, only the orange glow reflected from the street lamps.

There's very little traffic. But it's not quiet. From some windows we hear loud music, parties starting early. A mass of voices singing hymns in a church. Not *Abide with me*, thank God. I don't think I could bear *Abide with me*.

We also hear the rumble of an armoured car approaching. The army are still here. I wonder what they're thinking, what orders they were given. Do they know what's really going to happen? Or have they just been left behind as cannon fodder, to patrol the streets and stop riots? Doing their duty right up to the last minute. Just, you know, not saving us.

'This isn't a good idea, Dan,' Aaron says quietly. 'Let's go back.'

Dan doesn't move. 'We can wait till they're gone.'

'Why?' I say. 'What's the point?'

He swears. 'Don't you want to…? Just to…?' With an inarticulate noise he kicks a nearby signpost.

'We'll go to the party,' says Aaron. Not words that usually come out of his mouth. 'Come on, man. Let's just… get wasted.'

The last hours. The party is in a detached house with its own grounds, a three storey monster of a place with pillars at the door and cornices on the ceilings. Somebody's parents are away. If the world doesn't end tonight they are going to be so pissed off.

The rooms are jammed with young people, many of whom I know or recognise. Dance beats thump. Alcohol flows. Pills and powders change hands. Partying like it's 1999.

I can't do it. I can't get in the mood. I feel queasy and I don't want to talk to anyone. Maybe it's a remnant of the hangover. I fill up on vodka to see if it helps. It doesn't.

Before long we get split up. I catch sight of Dan doing his best with puppy dog eyes on a cute Goth girl. In another room Hayley is dancing wildly with her eyes closed. Aaron I can't see. There's a smash of glass behind me. Oops. There goes a crystal vase.

'Hey, Jen.' A guy from my class sidles up. 'How're you doing?'

There is no sensible answer to that question.

He nods. He swears. Then he nods again, as if to say he's covered it. Which I suppose he has.

I drain my glass and look up to see his eyes fixed on me. Startled, I stare back. He lifts his hand and strokes my face gently.

Jesus! I jump back, banging into a table and knocking over a glass. Red wine drips onto the carpet.

'Come on,' he says. There's a mixture of pleading and impatience in his voice. 'Last night. Don't you want to be with someone?'

'No!' In the nick of time I stop myself from saying *Not you*. I elbow my way through the crowd and up the staircase, hoping to get some space.

It's not much better on the first floor. Heavy metal and lots of bong action in one room. Couples and threesomes twining themselves in the bedrooms. Queues for the bathrooms.

This is it. This is how we use up our last few minutes of life. Our idea of a blaze of glory is getting out of our faces and snogging someone we don't even like. Dear god, is this the best we can do?

In a little room that's kitted out as a study I slump in a chair. Below me muffled music vibrates. Shrill laughter and occasional squeals tell me that everyone else is having fun, oh so much fun.

I'm not.

I don't want to die.

Idiot, idiot. Should have thought about this sooner. Shouldn't have spent all that time shouting at everybody who told me what was coming. Should have done something worthwhile, made sure that there was some joy in these last few weeks. I think I spent most of them worrying and being angry.

For the first time it strikes me what a waste it was.

I don't know what to do.

Oh god, Jen. You've got three hours left. How can you make these three hours count?

Well, I could go back downstairs, grab the first guy who seems willing, and have sex. It would be nice to feel alive in that way. Been a while, let's be honest. Maybe if I shut my eyes it would feel okay.

Or maybe I should... should what? What does make me happy? When have I enjoyed life the most?

I think of times with friends, those rare days when everything came together. Not usually something planned as an 'occasion'; times when you just had the right people and everyone was in a good mood and we all made each other laugh and felt at ease. When the unexpected happened in good ways. Or when I got into university and Mum was so proud.

It always seems to need other people. On my own I can be peaceful. Content. But for real happiness you need someone else. You need someone you love.

I don't think I've loved enough in my life. And now it's too late. Far too late.

I think about what I want in these last hours. I think about Aaron.

I work my way back through the house, in and out of various rooms. I can't find him. What was I waiting for? Good grief, it hardly matters now about acting cool. There's no time left to be embarrassed.

Dan and the Goth girl are going at it with gusto. Good for Dan. But Aaron isn't here. I squeeze back into the main hall. It's almost impossible to move. With brute force I make it to the kitchen.

Where I find Hayley sitting on the floor, her back to the oven, holding a bag of ice against her cheek.

'What happened?' I ask.

'Fell over,' she says.

'Oh. Thought for a moment somebody punched you.'

'Maybe they did. But it wasn't you, so tough shit.'

I can't leave a remark like that dangling. 'What do you mean?'

She waves her free hand. 'You don't like me. It's no secret.'

I start to deny it but I don't know why. Maybe this is the time to get a few things off my chest. 'You irritate me sometimes, okay. And you keep on doing it, even when you know I don't like it.'

'Doing what exactly?' she demands.

Around us party goers jostle back and forwards, filling up on drinks. But it feels as if we are alone.

'It's all the shit you say, Hayley. Always trying to get a reaction. You just make stuff up.'

Hayley stares at me as if I'm mad. 'So I make the odd fucking joke?'

'It's not the odd joke. It's all the time. Hayley, the world is ending. I don't want a joke. I don't want a reaction. I want friends. I want something in my life that is real.'

'And I'm not real?'

'I don't know. Are you? It's hard to tell.'

Hayley swallows and places the ice against her cheek again. Her eyes have gone a funny bright colour.

'Sorry,' I say gruffly. 'You wanted to know.'

'I'll tell you something real,' she says in a choked voice. 'The world isn't ending. That's what I think. This thing is going to hit us and god knows how much damage it will do, but it's not going to kill us all. Not straight away. If we're not in the immediate impact zone we'll survive.'

'You've changed your tune.'

'No. I'm like you. I didn't believe it. But now I have to. Now I have to face up to it.'

I know what she means. I snag two beers from the fridge and hand her one.

'Have you thought about it, Jen?' she says quietly. 'Thought about what it will really be like? After this?'

'Nobody knows. Everybody opens their mouths and spouts opinions but nobody knows.'

'I think it will be bad.' She looks at me. 'Everything will break down. We'll be fighting to survive. And I don't know anything about fighting. Dan doesn't even know how to steal a TV from an empty shop. We're not cut out for this. None of us are.'

I would like her to be wrong. But she could well be right. And it's not a world that I'm cut out for either.

Hoarsely I say, 'I suppose we'll need to rely on each other, then.'

'Great,' she says. 'So I'm screwed.'

'Hayley, I don't hate you! I just wish you'd say what you really feel.

All the time I've lived with you I've never got to know you. It drives me crazy.'

'Tell you what I feel?' She scoffs faintly. 'You'd just laugh at me, Jen. That's all you do.'

Not sure that's fair. Guiltily, I mutter, 'It stopped being funny ages ago.'

Hayley takes a swig of her beer. 'Well, I'm sure it'll be hilarious as hell tomorrow.'

'Look,' I say uncomfortably, 'I think you're right. It's going to be grim. So let's not fight. Okay?'

She shrugs one shoulder and concentrates on her beer.

'I want to find Aaron,' I say. 'I'm worried about him.'

'Of course you are.'

'Help me look? Please?'

She hesitates. But then she drags herself to her feet. 'I think he went upstairs.'

'On his own? Or…'

'Oh, calm your hormones. On his own.' She starts to push through the crowd. I follow.

We find him in a room in the attic floor, probably a former servant's bedroom. Like me, he'd gone in search of solitude. Unlike me he's standing at an open window looking out. The room is icy cold and I wonder how long he's been here.

'What are you doing?' I ask.

He doesn't turn round. 'Don't you think that maybe… maybe it would be best just to…? You must have thought about it.'

'Thought about what?' says Hayley, always a bit slow to catch on. He looks at her. He looks at the window. We're fairly high up.

'Aaron,' I say firmly. 'We talked about this. It's not a dream. You can't wake yourself up by jumping.'

'I know. But you can take control.'

'Control?'

'You can die straight away,' he says. 'Or you can die slowly. Which would you prefer?'

He looks at me, a genuine question. He must have some doubts. He hasn't jumped yet.

'Well, this window won't do,' says Hayley briskly. 'You'd probably break your leg. That's all. Pretty shit way to spend the last... let's see... two hours of existence.'

'Have you never wanted to fly?' Aaron says, in an odd, not-quite-Aaron voice that spooks me.

'Falling isn't flying.'

'It is – for a second. For one second you could be exactly what you wanted to be. Isn't that as good a way of dying as any?'

'It doesn't matter how you die. Your life isn't a poem that somebody reads in a book. Nobody reads it. Nobody cares about the punch line.'

'It should matter,' Aaron says quietly. 'That's what so wrong about this. It's so pointless.'

'You want symbolism?' I can't believe he'd be so stupid.

'The triumph of the human spirit,' Hayley says softly. 'I wonder what that would actually be?'

'Not this,' I say firmly. 'Definitely not this.'

Aaron doesn't speak. He stands at the window sill, staring out. The wind is getting stronger. The huge old trees in the garden are whipping around like they're trying to uproot themselves and evacuate. In the dim light I see tears shining on his cheek.

'Aaron. Oh god, Aaron, please.' I put my hand on his shoulder, bad idea or not. He doesn't move.

'We're scared, Aaron,' says Hayley. 'We're shitting ourselves terrified. We would appreciate it if you would help out with that.'

'How can I help?' he asks. 'How can anyone help?'

'By being our friend,' I say. I edge closer and let my arm curl round him. I can feel his breath shuddering in his ribs.

A gust of wind rattles the glass and we rock back automatically. Hayley swears and grabs the window, forcing it closed. With some effort she twists the handle and secures it. Suddenly it's a lot easier to stand upright.

In that moment of quiet it hits me how good it is to breathe without effort. That here we are, indoors, warm enough, perfectly comfortable and well fed. Safe. And that this might be the last time I ever feel this way.

I can't help it. I can't stop the tears.

'Please don't leave me,' I say to Aaron. 'Please.'

He sighs. 'Jen…' I can hear it in his voice. Damn it. The answer I didn't want. But he holds me anyway and for a moment I can pretend.

For a second, falling is flying.

'Let's go,' says Hayley plaintively. 'Let's find Dan and go. I want to be–'

'Home,' I finish for her. 'Safe. Together.'

Not many of those words mean much now.

We find Dan in the garden, throwing up. He can barely walk. Luckily it's not far. And the night is surprisingly bright.

We look up. Above the clouds, where the moon isn't, there is a glow in the sky.

The future is coming.

The future is here.

The War

Jade Dovey

Humanity had survived its First World War, and then its second, and yet now it looked as if we had barely make it out of the third alive.

The years since our victory for the second time had past with reasonable joy, and sorrow equally. Then came the threats, the terror of not knowing who the enemy was, or if there even was a real enemy; especially after the internet was used to spread fear and panic among us, like a virus infecting blood. People became infected with fear, sick with it. They pointed fingers at anyone who was different, anyone who they deemed a 'threat', acting like children who didn't want to take the blame for something they knew they had done wrong.

After 9/11, everyone wanted to have a face, an image of someone to blame for the devastation caused. It came in the form of the Al-Qaeda, and its founder, Osama bin Laden. I still remember where I was when they announced his death, sat in college watching the President break the news to the world. Everyone had cheered once we had been told, but I had remained seated. I wasn't quite sure why, but I had been filled with the uneasy feeling that it wasn't the end. It all seemed too easy, too simple. We had wanted someone to blame, and so when someone had been presented to us as simple as handing soup to a starving man, he was killed and the world had rejoiced. Without trial or anything. Just shot. Everyone had boasted about how killing him had been justice.

Justice?

I'm not too sure I know what the meaning of justice is anymore. Or if anyone really knows.

After that came a brief wave of relief. But then suddenly there were others, the 7/7 bombings in London, the bombs scares and hijacking of countless airplanes, the wars in Syria, Afghanistan, Pakistan, and Iraq. Everyday people lost their lives to war and yet it was a war everyone was too scared to face. To really stand up and say, this is it. This is how humanity ends. Because every time I watched the news, I found it harder and harder to see the humanity we were supposed to have.

Humans without their humanity. That was a new one.

Then it really started. Whispers that North Korea had nuclear missiles trained on America, rumours that Mexico had bombs targeted for Britain, and doubts about what the Chinese had up their sleeves. Panic began to fuel fights in the streets, in parliaments all over the world, and even at peace summits. The world was at a tipping point and everyone was jumpy; no one wanted to set off the first bomb.

To this day we still don't know who it was to strike first.

But then everyone was second.

My world exploded one day in a fog of ash and smoke so bitter I couldn't breathe. Terror had been painted on everyone's faces, and we had all ran in panic trying to find shelter. Most didn't make it. I had been out shopping with my mum when a bomb was dropped in the car park, the shudder that rippled through the ground was enough to throw food to the floor, break lights, and take our feet from under us. After the initial shock I'd helped my mum up, looking around in panic and seeing everyone else doing the same. It was when the ringing in my ears dulled that I heard the screams.

Myself and my mum were already inside, luckily, and I thought more had run in, but once the manager had gotten a hold of the door controls and locked them, I knew there were still people outside. I ran to the doors, watching through the glass as luminous green gas clouded from the crater on the far side of the car park and came towards the shop, engulfing around fifty people in an initial wave. The gas couldn't reach us; it began to fade into the air after twenty seconds, but we had to watch as about a hundred people choked on their own breath outside. They spat bile and blood while their eyes rolled and their skin crawled as if live insects were underneath it.

My mum had tried to turn me away but I had wanted to watch, as sick as that might sound. I wanted to see what we were doing to each other. I wanted to see the pain people were causing because of fear, because of mindless, blind panic.

And oh, did I get my wish and more. As I stood there, their skin bubbled, and their throats worked to clear their airways of spittle the colour of mustard. If it had been because of radiation then we would have all been effected. But this was the gas; someone nearby had whispered about how it reminded them of the effect chlorine has on the human body and I couldn't help but remember Wilfred Owen's poem.

Gas! Gas! Quick Boys!

Quick indeed, but no one was quick enough to escape it. I watched as, like starving animals in a mindless haste to reach a rotting corpse, those left outside climbed on top of each other, ripping our hair, punching, screaming, and biting each other to get to the doors. Only to slam against the glass in limp forms onto the ground, unmoving.

An elderly man beside me began crying thick tears that fogged his glasses but he didn't reach up to wipe them away, the basket in his hands trembling.

'It's happening again.' He had said, his voice cracking as he watched the people with an unwavering sorrowful gaze. 'Again and again and again, why won't it stop? Why can't we stop?'

Later that week I had been watching the news, dotted with countless reports of more gas bombs, and of radiation leaking into the drinking water in Australia, killing millions. Then came the bigger bombs, nuclear attacks were made on South America, during which Brazil was almost literally taken off the map; the number of dead was too large to comprehend. I could only imagine the state of the rainforest now, or the fate of the tribes living in their branches in complete peace and harmony.

We couldn't even find out if any of them had survived, but the lingering hope remained.

Then, there were rumours whispered on the streets that people from Alaska and Canada were crossing the Bearing Strait land bridge into Russia to get to Europe; they were that desperate to escape the gas bombs that were dropped every day into their untamed environment. Those who did manage to cross into Russia didn't make it very far, bombs were dropped onto the frozen land a few days later. The images of the devastation came through on the news from a helicopter as the radiation in the ground was so thick, it latched onto whatever touched it. Animal and human alike.

In all of this, I wondered about the animals. Which ones were surviving, which ones were dying. No one else seemed to really worry about the wildlife of the earth and what impact the bombings were having on them. The radiation alone would have devastated their numbers. I often wonder how many species are now extinct. People in my home town had tried to save their pets, dogs, cats, birds and hamsters but all in vain. Some ran away, others died when there was no more food. People prioritised their own families before the family dog, and for that there were piles of animal corpses in a mass grave outside nearly every town or village.

When another round of bombings happened, there were a couple dropped on our main road and the surrounding fields, only one hit a house killing the family inside when the roof collapsed. Once people heard the roar of overhead planes there was a flurry of panic when they started to realise that they carried nuclear bombs.

Nuclear bombs in England.

The snobs must have had a field day.

The bombs didn't detonate right away, they were all put on a timer. I still can't fathom why someone would bother with a *timer* on a *nuclear bomb*. But who can reason with or understand madness? A couple of friends had told me how they gone past with their families on their way to the bunkers, and had seen the timers on the bombs; stereotypical big red numbers counting down. I wasn't sure how that was meant to be comforting, but I suppose the little irony in the situation was humorous. So while these bombs counted down, the remaining population, including myself and the remaining half of my family, clambered into hastily made underground bunkers by the military.

Bunkers no one had known about until the attacks had started.

It seemed the military had been preparing for this kind of thing for years. I can't say I resented them for not telling us, I was just glad to have somewhere to hide. Not only had the bunkers been waiting for us, but different families were assigned to different bunkers, keeping the masses from crowding into one. After the chaos we had witnessed in the last months, the startling order that was presented to us was a shocking change. Many argued with the soldiers about the proceedings and demanded to be told what was happening, names were thrown about as if they were money used to bribe, but I doubted even the soldiers knew or even cared who any of us were. Once people began to figure out where they were putting us, panic once again erupted. Children screamed about not wanting to be buried alive, parents worried about their child's claustrophobia or their aunt's asthma. The sad truth of it was that no one had any real answers or solutions, but no one wanted to admit it. So we'd all scrambled into the hole in the ground and huddled like the pathetic, scared creatures we were, relying on each other for warmth and comfort.

Once the doors had shut and deafening darkness had enveloped us, I remember how the whole world shook when the bombs finally detonated. I thought the ground would collapse around us and suffocate us all. Two hundred people were crushed into the same bunker for weeks on end, all the while, bombs rained down on the ground above our heads. I thought I'd never see the light of day again. I thought I'd never breathe fresh air again. All we knew while in there was the artificial light from wind-up torches and battery-powered lamps, and the stale tang of sweaty bodies and musty blankets. Tinned food had been stock piled so we didn't starve, but that didn't stop sickness from spreading throughout everyone in the bunker. Several people had come down with the flu and with limited antibiotics I had given my share up. The medical officer assigned to our bunker had looked at me like I was insane. My only response was to shrug and say,

'I'm allergic to it anyway.'

She'd given me a sympathetic glance before rushing off to treat her patients. Days afterwards two people had died from a high fever that the doctor didn't recognize. She said it might have been a reaction to the small amounts of radiation we were all exposed to while topside. It made sense. Especially when twelve others found that their skin had reddened and rid itself of all hair in places. Both signs of contact with radiation.

They all died within the week before we got out.

The medical officer suspected cancer.

I suspected she was right and dreaded to think about how many more of us had cancer and didn't know it. Probably all of us. I'd stopped being optimistic while in the bunker watching children die whimpering about wanting to see the sun one last time. I stopped being a lot of things whilst I was in there.

At the end of a month and three weeks, we were suddenly being hauled out of the bunker by other soldiers and onto the soil like they were pulling weeds. No forewarning meant that people struggled against the rushing hands and loud voices suddenly penetrating into the bunker, telling us we had to leave. It was hard to believe that the land above was safe. I thought maybe that we might die in the bunker and it looked like everyone else had too. On the ground again, I'd struggled with the sunlight piercing through my eyes and skull, blinking away the bright pain until I saw what was left of my home.

In short, nothing.

The ground was pimpled with craters as wide as houses, the land scorched in places and in others fumes left the soil in sickly gas bubbles. Trees dotted the land like bare quills, their greenery stripped. In many places there were piles of rubble that resembled what once have been buildings, and dented husks of metal, half melted and barren that must have been cars and buses. There had been lumps lay down the road of what I had first thought to be the tarmac of the road buckled and broken, but then saw the twisted lump of meat that resembled an arm and realised they were the unfortunates who hadn't gotten underground. I should have known by the smell of cooking flesh that lingered in the air, but my rational brain had shoved the knowledge aside in favour of ignorance.

Ignorance had been bliss.

As the remaining people had climbed out the hole in the ground behind me, gasping in lungfuls of air, I had remained stock still, scared stiff of what would happen to us now. The world around me had crumbled into chaos like a kicked sandcastle; what good could possibly come of all this torment? How could our lives ever again be peaceful?

After only a brief moment to stare at what had happened while we were underground, as one we were ordered into a bus and driven away. Bags of our hastily packed belongings were shoved into our hands, and packets of dried food were thrown at us among orders to save it for the journey. Suddenly I felt like we were in disaster a film, not for the first time, but now we felt a little bit like cattle being herded for slaughter.

We were being evacuated.

Evacuees, like during the war. We looked like children, what with the way the remaining members of the army, special forces, RAF and countless other militias shepherded us along. Mindless, terrified children, praying this was all a nightmare.

One terrible, terrible nightmare.

After the evacuations I found myself on the very edge of north Wales, staring out to sea as if I could fly over its depths and find somewhere safe to hide my family. How I wished to be far away from what was happening to me. Reports afterwards were few and far between, with only brief messages about the total dead or dying from radiation or cancer caused by radiation. In short, the world was falling apart, still, and it looked like it couldn't be saved.

I often found myself crying when I thought about how easily this all could have been avoided. If only people communicated and talked out their problems instead of just being children and spying on one another. If peace had been practiced like we lied to ourselves, consistently and without fault, and with belief in what was being spoken. If only we could have spoken the truth as easy as speaking a lie, what might the world have become?

An eye for an eye makes the whole world blind.

How could they not see that? Why did murder condone murder? Why did anyone think that this war was doing any good?

War is never the answer. We just struggled to realise that there was a better way. Violence was a base instinct of ours, and it seemed no one could let go of it.

I remembered those charity adverts about getting water to third world countries, or helping those after the Nepal earthquake or the Syrian refugees; one line they kept repeating was, 'No one is born to die'. I always found that redundant. Everyone is born to die, death is inevitable. What they really should have said was that everyone was born to live. Everyone deserved life.

Now it looked like no one would have that privilege without knowing how many had died to ensure they survived all of this. That was not the type of guilt that should be placed on a child's shoulders. But I believe it will be inevitable.

Now my world is walled off, completely. The habitable land is now cordoned off into three territories, mine is what is left of Europe, there is also most of North America and Canada, and nearly all of Africa. Everywhere else has been lost to the radiation. What's left of the government say that those lands will probably never again be inhabitable, and that we are safer behind the walls they so honourably built for us. Leaving the walls to journey into the wastelands would mean suicide, and the government didn't condone suicide anymore.

They don't allow a lot of things anymore.

Once communications were fixed so that we could speak to the rest of the world, and the higher ups had conferred with each other, a few new laws were passed and a couple of hard truths explained to the remaining public.

The killing of anyone or anything was punishable by a life of servitude to the government.

Jobs were no longer optional or chosen, but given and could not be contested.

Reproduction was mandatory because humanity was now an endangered species.

So many had died in the genocide that humanity itself had started, and now humanity was near extinction. Ironic, huh? There's not many who would agree.

My name is Keri Blake and this was how the world ended, and a new, smaller and much darker one began.

It's Always the End of the World for Someone

Pete Sutton

She left Simon another message.

'It's me. He was worse yesterday. I'm going to the hospital now. He'd love to hear from you. I'd love to hear from you. I know, I know, you only switch your phone on once a week when you come down off the mountain top. But... Christ Simon, it's coming. The end is coming I... we... Fuck just come home. It's close.'

She stabbed the end call button and wiped a tear away. Took several deep breaths, buttoned up her coat and opened the front door. The weather was suitably apocalyptic. The forecast was for winds of fifty mph, with gusts up to eighty. She'd heard someone say on the bus that unusual solar activity was to blame for the weather. She had bigger things to worry about, and no time to read the news or watch TV.

She grabbed her scarf close and scuttled down the road to the bus stop. She glanced ruefully at the car but had foregone its comforts for her nightly trips. Fucking government, paying hospital parking was a sickness tax.

The bus, when it finally arrived, was steamed up and smelt of wet dog. She sat by the window, wiped a clear area and watched the streets amble past. She remembered when their car had been steamed up, at Bridgend, eating fish and chips. Dad laughing, Mum happy, Simon reading a book about space, and her? She had always tried to hold the family together. Telling jokes, keeping everyone talking to each other. Her eyes misted up yet again. She remembered Dad wiping the steam away and pointing out the stars to them. Simon had got his love of space from him.

Now Mum was gone, Dad was sick and Simon was on the other side of the world staring at the stars through a massive telescope. Actually, that bit wasn't even true. The telescope measured radio waves, or X-rays or something and he just studied the computer. Why he couldn't do that online she didn't know. Today was what? Saturday, Simon would be checking his phone tomorrow. Although his tomorrow was several hours behind hers. He hadn't been there when Mum… when it happened. Just blew in for the funeral. She tried to make him stay for a while but no luck. Since Dad had been ill she'd had no time for herself. She was too busy to find someone to support her, the way she supported everyone else.

Simon's last message – he hadn't called when she was at home, hadn't answered when she phoned back, was about esoterics, the 'cosmic wind' and a breakthrough that'd make him famous. She was glad and angry.

The bus farted to a stop and she glanced out the window to see that it had arrived. Last stop. Final destination. Another tear leaked out of her eye despite her best efforts, she ground her teeth. She swished off the bus to the monumental stone monstrosity that was the hospital; as black as a cancerous lung. Anyone watching would have seen her square her shoulders, like trying to shift a heavy burden, before entering the waiting entrance under sheets and plasterboard still.

They were still working on it, seemed to have been for the longest time, she had no idea what they were doing. The foyer changed weekly, all temporary walls and taped off areas, a constantly changing maze she had to negotiate to the throbbing heart of the hospital. Everyone seemed to take the two massive lifts; the stairs were directly opposite but too much effort for the sick and the well alike.

She climbed aboard a lift alongside a bed; being wheeled from God knows where to places best not thought about. The silent cadaverous old woman in it looking like an injured bird swaddled in clean white sheets and vomit coloured blankets. She averted her gaze from the old dear only to catch one of the porters perving at her. She shuddered and was grateful when they remained in the lift as she got out. The large hall was shaped like a H with narrow corridors like veins heading north and south. She walked down one that went south. To the ward her father was on.

She conscientiously used the alcohol gel and went straight for the third bed on the left. To her father. He was asleep, although nowadays it was hard to tell because he slept with his eyes open. The oxygen mask had slipped and she absent-mindedly straightened it as she kissed his waxy forehead. The tears that had been threatening ganged up and came all together. He had been such a strong man, a tall man, her father; a solid, albeit almost silent, presence throughout her life. Now he was reduced to a few flesh covered sticks and a beak-like face. Where had all his weight gone? It had seemed to boil off him over the last few weeks.

She took her seat, grabbed the book off the bedside table, a Stephen King, his favourite author, and, wiping her eyes, started to read.

She hadn't got far when the nurse came and spoke to her. They had increased his pain meds. They were treating him for an infection. They thought he had pneumonia again.

'Have you managed to get in touch with your brother?' The nurse, whose name she was ashamed to have forgotten, asked.

She shook her head.

'He'll get in touch, on Sunday right?' The nurse said.

She swallowed and blinked away even more tears and nodded. The nurse placed a hand on her arm. 'He needs to come soon.' She said and there the tears were again. Seriously? She wondered how one person could cry so much. She must have been responsible for dehydrating a lake's worth of water, one plastic cup at a time. The nurse placed one in her hands now and passed her a tissue.

'It won't be long now. He may not even wake.' The nurse said sadly, patting her awkwardly on the shoulder. She wandered on to the next bed which held a fat old man, who shat himself very day when the nurses turned him to prevent bed sores.She had not yet become used to the smell.

She smoothed her father's yellow-grey hair from his sweaty brow, and used a sponge to wet his lips as the nurses had shown her. She replaced the mask, sat back down, and started reading again.

Once visiting time was over and she was buttoning up her coat the nurse, who was going off duty, came to see her again.

'Come in early tomorrow love and stay as long as you like. You won't be in the way.'

She nodded gratefully. 'Thank you.'

'Just get that brother of yours to come home, before it's too late.'

At home she sank into an exhausted slumber. She seemed to have no time to herself. She had been visiting him daily for months. Get up, eat breakfast, go to work, nip to the hospital lunchtime, go back to work, go home grab something quick to eat, visiting hours, go home, sleep, repeat.

Today, being Sunday, she slept through till ten AM and cursed herself for being so lazy. She got ready and walked out into the wind. It was blowing a gale; a struggle to make headway. At the bus stop she watched as an old woman with a hip problem was blown over. She stood up, ready to go and help when the bus turned up. As it came to a stop she dithered until she saw that two shop assistants from the shop opposite the bus stop had come out to help the old woman. She got on the bus which sailed down the road serene amongst the flying debris, leaves, small branches, litter, all thrown like a giant child was kicking through the streets with glee.

The hospital was unusually empty when she arrived. The bus had been empty too, now she thought about it. She made the usual trip up to the ward. Made sure nothing had changed. She took out the birthday card she'd picked out during a more hopeful time. A picture of Tommy Cooper on the front. A recording of a few of his catchphrases played when it was opened. She put it on the bedside cabinet.

'I know it's not your birthday for a few weeks but I thought you'd like to open your card now. It'll cheer you up.' Her throat felt swollen, as if she was the one who'd had the surgery. She tucked him in and then glanced at the clock.

She made the long trip outside and tried Simon's number again. It was about 8 AM in Chile but she didn't care. She needed to get through to him.

'Hello?' A sleepy voice answered.

'Simon? Thank fuck. Why haven't you answered any of my calls?' She was equally angry and relieved. He answered!

'Sis? Wait a second.' There was muffled rustling and she thought she heard a woman's voice say 'who is it?' and she definitely heard him say 'It's my sister, I'll be five minutes.'

'Sis?' He said, loud and clear.

'Five minutes?' She said coldly.

'Shit. Listen, that was just to mollify Sandra.' He said, sounding sheepish.

'Who's Sandra?' She asked.

'No-one special. Listen I have to tell you something important.'

'No. You listen Simon. Dad's… He's… Fuck, he's… you need to come home as soon as possible. Shit, it may already be too late. You have to come home. He… it's the end Simon, the end isn't far.'

There was silence on the other end.

'Simon?'

She heard him take a deep breath.

'I'm really sorry about Dad but that's just it, Sis. It *is* the end.'

'What?' She said, not catching on.

'This is about more than Dad. I don't think I'll be able to come. Like I said I think it's the end.' Simon said.

'What do you mean? Why can't you come? Can't you make an effort? For Dad? For me?'

'Look I'm sorry Sis. I really am, I'd love to come but it's just not possible. Remember that thing I said would make me famous? It's coming. There's a massive wind coming and it is going to blow us all away. Everyone.' He sounded tired, resigned, wrung out. Pretty much like she felt herself.

'A wind? What? Simon you aren't making sense.' She couldn't work out why he couldn't make the trip. 'Why can't you just leave it for a few days? Come home.'

'I can't. I can't explain the science behind it quickly but it's coming, today, tomorrow at the latest. It's going to blast away our magneto-sphere, it's going to blow on the sun like it's a candle in a draft, there's going to be a solar flare like never before. We're fucked Sis. The planet is fucked. I won't be coming home. Come tomorrow there won't be a home to come to. I'm sorry. I love you. I love Dad too. Let him… let him know for me?'

She could hear him sniff, imagined the tears running down his face.

'So that's it? For everything? I thought… I don't know what I thought, you said it was big, that it'd make you famous?' She didn't know what to think.

'It's much bigger than we thought, we've run the numbers again, sharing it with the world, but the government, ours and others are burying their heads in the sand. Can't blame them really, what'd it achieve if they told anyone? We think it's going to blast us. At the very least it'll blast the satellites out of orbit, keep the airplanes grounded, fry communications, anything with electricity. Some people may sur-vive it. As long as the cosmic radiation doesn't cook them. I… I'm sorry about everything. Live for yourself tonight. It's our only choice.' She heard a woman's voice calling his name in the background.

'Shit…' she said, bewildered.

'Quite. Listen, Sis this is probably the last time we'll speak. Even if the wind doesn't wipe out all life on the planet I'm thousands of miles away and it'll be back to the age of sail, if we're lucky, if we survive this. I'm sorry I've been a shitty brother-'

'Simon-' She tried to interrupt him, he needed to let her speak.

'No let me finish. I should have been there to help you and Dad look after Mum. I'm sorry. I should be there now. I thought I had time. That we had time. I… I'm sorry. I love you Sis. Tell Dad… you know. Goodbye Sis-'

'Simon wait!'

The line went dead and she frantically redialled. It went straight to answerphone. 'Shit!' She shouted, she redialled and his phone was obviously switched off. 'You selfish bastard!' She yelled, then, after a short pause, 'I love you too little brother,' in a much quieter voice, then texted him and with tears running down her face she walked back to the ward. Could he be right? He seemed pretty sure and the conversation seemed final.

When she arrived she was surprised that there were people around. Nurses bustled about looking after the patients who sat shell-shocked in their beds in various states of consciousness. Should people know? She thought about shouting it out. People should be with their loved ones. But, she thought sadly, they'd just think she was mad, maybe ask her to leave. Best to leave them alone. Ignorance was bliss. She sat next to her father's bed, picked up the King novel and started reading.

When her father started to breathe slower, missing breaths, she held his hands and spoke about how Mum loved him, how she loved him, how Simon loved him and, that, as long as there were people alive who knew his name, he would live on and be loved. His eyes stared into the vast unknown. His breath caught, rattled, caught and stopped. A tear fell from her eye onto his cheek, it looked like he was crying. As she kissed his forehead, his muscles were already relaxing, making him look at peace for the first time in months. Then the lights went out. The sky was filled with an eerie green glow. The Northern Lights?

At first she thought the silence was just that she could no longer hear her father's breath, but soon realised that all the machines had stopped. All she could hear was the wind, which clawed at the building like a raging demon. She looked at her phone. It was dead. The world held its breath, then people were shouting for the generators to start, rushing around, trying to bring order to chaos. She stood slowly, put the book down, on her father's chest, spine up like a landed moth, then walked to the main hallway, onto the stairs and up. Behind her she heard the shattering of glass, the howling of the wind and many voices raised in a chorus of fear.

On the roof she marvelled at the sight of a dark city which seemed to undulate in the lambent emerald of the light in the sky. Up here the demon wind was ripping the flimsier structures apart and debris flew all about. She fought her way to the edge of the building and hung on to the railing as the wind tried to snatch her away. She wished Simon could have come home, that her mother hadn't had been taken away from her, that her father could hold her and tell her everything was going to be okay. She looked out across the blinded city, hearing the screams carried upon the demon wind. She wished she could see the stars.

Everything Old

Andrew Wilmot

'What do you remember?'

Alice opens her notebook to a fresh page. Stares at the clock. 'Tell me everything,' she says. 'Don't worry about whether or not you think it's important – just say what you see.'

She writes *Scene One* at the top of the page, underlines it twice.

Jackson nestles his upper body into the gym mat-thin mattress. The cot's hinges squeak; it wouldn't be long – days, a week, maybe – before the bolts would have to be replaced to keep it from crashing to the floor. Alice immediately starts to calculate how much rice she would need in order to make the deal.

'It's the day before my twelfth birthday,' Jackson says. 'I remember me, Jamie, and Nick – they were my friends – we were riding our bikes around the green out in front of my house.'

'The green was a field?'

'No, not really. It was just this circle of grass and trees, like in one of those whatchamacallits – a cul-de-sac. I tried to cut through the middle and hit a rock, or a root sticking out of the ground and went over the handlebars, face first into the dirt.' He frowns. 'I cut my palms up pretty good, landing like that. Felt like fire the next morning.'

'And the trees?'

'Oak, mostly. Real swell for climbing. And there was this large flat stone we used to play around at the centre of it all. In the summer, the whole place smelled like sap and fresh-cut grass. You'd stand out there and inhale and you'd know which of your neighbours were having a barbeque that night.'

'What happened after you fell?'

'Jamie went and got my mom. She took me inside to get cleaned

189

up. Wasn't till we were in the bathroom that I started to cry. I fought hard when she tried to put disinfectant on my wounds, but she kept me from squirming free. She just watched me, waited until I looked her right in her enormous blue eyes. In that moment it felt like she was trying to steal the pain for herself. She said, 'It's okay, Jackie baby. You're okay. These things happen. But you know what? When you heal up, your skin will be tougher than ever.' And wouldn't you know it, while I was busy staring into those giant blue eyes of hers, she'd gone ahead and cleaned my palms without me even noticing.' He sighs. 'She was a real good lady. Best there ever was.'

Alice stops writing. 'That's great, Jackson. That'll work. Now, did you bring what I asked?'

Jackson rolls to one side and reaches into his back pocket. He produces a faded colour photo with boxed edges. The woman in the photo looks in her mid-forties, about the same age as Jackson is now. She has a head of thick brown curls down past her shoulders, and she's wearing a red and white polka-dotted sundress straight out of the 1950s.

'And the rest?'

Jackson produces from another pocket a small, crumpled paper bag, the top rolled shut. Alice takes the bag, unfurls it and peers inside.

Rice. Enough for a week, she thinks, even after Nessa's cut.

'It's okay?' Jackson asks.

'It's perfect.' Alice rolls up the bag and places it atop the wooden nightstand with the cracked left leg in the corner of the room. She opens a drawer and removes a translucent capsule the size of a baby toe, which she passes to Jackson. He swallows it without hesitation, leans back again and shuts his eyes.

Alice places the photograph of Jackson's mother in her lap. 'I want you to clear your mind. Focus only on my voice.'

A woman in a white nurse's uniform helps Jackson to his feet an hour later. He leaves Alice's room an ashen mess, face streaked with tears, and makes his way to his suite on the lower levels.

Nessa enters the suite, which is no wider than a shipping container and only half as deep, as Alice is busy changing the sweat-dampened sheets. She is tall and lithe, like a brittle stalk alone in a winter field.

'He looked satisfied.' Her words prickle with authority.

'Catharsis is rarely pretty,' says Alice.

'Days out fishing with Dad?'

'Mother, actually. Dressing wounds, being all protective.'

Nessa scoffs. 'Typical.' She notices Alice's notepad on the chair with the picture of Jackson's mother still attached. 'Could she *be* any more of a housewife?'

'What can I do for you, Nessa?'

Nessa crosses the narrow room in two strides, fingers the brown paper bag atop the nightstand.

'How much?' she asks.

'Two cups. Should last us a week each.'

Nessa sighs dispassionately. 'You might as well hear this now. I'm upping quotas. Starting next week, sessions cost four cups each.'

Alices tenses. 'That's too much. People won't pay.'

'They will,' Nessa assures her. 'They'll complain at first, but they'll bite. They won't have a choice in the matter. After all, the sting of inflation is nothing compared to what we can offer them.'

Alice is about to protest when Nessa cuts her off.

'I've a new client for you,' she says. 'Name's Meags. She's mid-tier – her parents are scientists, work down in Processing.'

'How old is she?'

'Twenty-two.'

'Twenty-two? That means-'

Nessa nods. 'Are You up to it?'

'Do I have a choice?'

'None whatsoever.'

'Three o'clock,' Alice says. 'I'll be ready.'

Nessa produces a plastic bag and proceeds to dump in half – more, likely – of the rice, seals it, and leaves.

Nessa calls it 'staging'; Alice prefers 'mise-en-scene.' Its clinical designation from the time before was RT-7800.

Now everyone just calls it Retro.

The capsules were developed at a university research lab seventeen years prior, mere months before the Scorch hit. Those who survived holed up wherever they could find shelter.

Nessa had been a part of Retro's development. Its intended use, according to her, was to better facilitate hypnotic psychotherapy by inducing a meditative state free of thought, thus leaving the user open to suggestion.

These days, it offers the Bunker's denizens a window into the past. *Their* pasts.

Nessa set up shop soon after she arrived at their safe haven – a decommissioned military research facility burrowing several hundred feet into the earth – lugging behind her a pair of rolling suitcases filled with everything she was able to smuggle out of the university lab. She promised those willing to pay (in cash at first, later in supplies and food) the opportunity to step back in time and experience all that they had lost.

She wasted little time training a small group of 'Therapists' to aide their clients in the reconstruction of their pasts. Retro freed them from their present, she said, opened their minds to narration. It was a public service.

Alice believed Nessa in the beginning – they all did. Over time, however, she began to question Retro's worth. Were they truly offering catharsis? Or was it nothing more than bamboo shoots beneath their clients' fingernails – a torturous reminder of what couldn't be reclaimed?

And what, if anything, could a girl practically raised beneath the surface have to remember of the world from before?

Meags arrives promptly at three the following afternoon. Alice opens the door, ushers her inside. She notices right away that Meags is out of breath and offers her a cup of water.

'I'm good,' says Meags. 'Was working down in sewage treatment, lost track of time and had to sprint.'

Alice imagines the poor girl running up the long spiral staircase snaking the heart of the facility and wonders how often she makes the journey. For someone like her, raised in the facility, it was the only commute she'd ever known.

Meags is short for her age, Alice thinks. Barely five feet, with thinning brown hair cut short above her ears and sun-starved skin – like jaundiced leather stretched over a squat department store mannequin.

'Make yourself comfortable,' says Alice.

Meags sits on the edge of the mattress, bounces lightly. 'Shit, and I thought my cot sucked.'

'Do you know how this works?'

'Yeah. I think.' She passes Alice a paper bag. 'Will this cover it?'

Alice takes the bag, peeks inside. She has to keep herself from audibly gasping.

Strawberries. Honest to fucking goodness, strawberries. The smell hits her before she even notices the intense red colour, so sharp it wants to cut straight through the bag. How in the…? Meags's parents. Of fucking course. Alice was beginning to understand Nessa's insistence.

Meags lies back on the cot. 'To tell you the truth, I don't know why I'm here. It was my parents' idea. They think I'm depressed or something.'

Alice places the bag of strawberries on the nightstand and picks up her notepad. She sits in her chair. 'Are you?'

'You're actually going to try and analyse me? I mean, no disrespect or nothing, but this is all bullshit. Isn't it?'

Alice blushes. 'I'm just making conversation, Meags. That's all this is: you talk, I listen. And if I've done my job, you'll leave a little lighter than when you arrived.'

Meags sighs, unconvinced. 'So what do you want to know?'

'That depends. What do you remember?'

'Just in general, or– '

'From before.' Alice writes *Scene One* on her notepad.

Meags shuts her eyes. 'Not much. Moments. Images. Nothing linear.'

'Just start with what you do remember. We'll build from there.'

'… Dirt. I remember what dirt felt like. I remember how it smelled, especially after it rained – that kind of old chalk smell. And I remember going out and playing in the mud when I was supposed to be inside, taking a bath.'

Alice jots the information down, point form. 'What else?'

Meags proceeds to describe the home she had lived in with her parents. 'It was a beach-front bungalow, with this rickety wooden balcony on stilts. Mum always warned me against going out on it. She said it wasn't safe, that I had to wait for Dad to replace the rotting wood. A lot of things needed repairs. But Dad was always too busy with work; he spent most days in the greenhouse with his fruits and vegetables. He was learning how to clone them.'

'Can you recall a specific day or event? One that jumps out as being especially significant?'

Meags ponders. 'Not really. I just remember… it was bright.' She holds out her hand, observes her greyish skin beneath the dim industrial lamps. 'I used to glow.'

Alice swallows the spark of an idea she feels emanating from the pit of her stomach. Meags's memories are spotty at best, which makes things difficult – unless – 'All right, Meags. That's a great start.' Alice retrieves a Retro from the nightstand, hands it to Meags. She swallows readily, as if it were candy.

Alice thinks to herself, *she's in, full stop.* 'Now, I want you to clear your mind as much as possible. Focus only on my voice. Can you do that?'

'Do you have enough to go on?' Meags asks drowsily, already slurring her words. 'Am I… will I wake up back above?'

'In a matter of speaking.' Alice clears her throat, leans forward. She says to herself, *this is going to be different.*

And for one hour, the shortest, greatest of her life, Meags is a being of pure energy. Hers is a world of her own creation. She opens her five-year-old fist, her palms smooth as glass, and releases her hold on the sun. She curls her toes into the dirt, squeezes them, makes fists with them.

Briefly, the universe encircles her, cocoons her. Her nervous system is alight like crystalline fire. She stares at the planets and stars orbiting her and believes. *This is how it should be.*

When the hour crashes to an end and the last of Retro's effects wax clear from her vision, Meags feels as if she's run a lap around the world without ever stopping for a glass of water.

She lurches upright, leans over the cot's edge and gasps. 'What did you do to me?'

Alice places her notepad on the nightstand. She, too, is panting. 'What was it like? What did you experience?'

Meags takes several heaping breaths. 'I… I was infinite. I don't know how else to describe it. What did you—'

'I made you glow,' Alice says.

For the following week Alice is unable to sleep. She continues with her usual slate, assisting her clients in recreating scenes from their pasts. She feels like how she imagines a film director must have felt, before the Scorch; she manufactures memories, pulls entire lives from the ether. She is music, art direction, and editorial all at once.

Normally she was satisfied by her work; however, in the days since her session with Meags, Alice had been feeling as if there was something missing. She tried to explain it when Nessa came and took her share of the strawberries, salivating over them like a dog to a raw, bloodied cut of steak, but she could not have cared less.

'She was happy?' Nessa asked.

Alice nodded. 'I think … yes. She said she'd be back.'

'Then do whatever you need to do.'

But Alice was still trying to figure that part out. Meags hadn't given her much to go on – basic abstractions and little else. She hadn't known what the result would be when she strung together the obfuscated shards of Meags's time before the Scorch, but what had happened… Meags had remained on Alice's cot for several minutes following the end of her session. 'You made me glow?' she said. 'What does that even mean?'

'I gave it back to you,' Alice said. 'That feeling of being infinite. You might only have fragments to pull from, but those bits and pieces have none of the context of trauma or reality to burden them. Your memories are scattered and surreal, but they are also free.'

And I can make you freer than any person here, she added silently.

She waited eagerly for her chance to do it all over again. As expected, Meags arrives on the specified day a week after her first visit with another paper sack full of strawberries and, this time, a few blueberries as well.

Alice inhales the almost forgotten sugars before placing the sack on the nightstand. She regards Meags, who appears less sure than she'd seemed the previous week.

'What's the matter?' Alice asks.

'I feel weird about this.'

'Weird how?'

Meags shrugs. 'It doesn't feel right. Like, it's not my world up there. Never was, not really. I wasn't alive up there long enough for anything to really be mine.'

'Meags, even if you'd been born down here, you'd still be as entitled as any of us to the world we had. Actually, I think you're luckier than most of us.'

'Seriously?'

Alice nods. 'We remember what was lost. Your memories offer a glimpse of paradise; ours are a prison – we're stuck staring through bars at what we'll never have again.'

Meags nods solemnly and Alice motions to the cot. She feels her heart start to race as Meags assumes her position. Reaches for her notepad, her pen.

'Now, let's begin.'

Alice had always liked her job – that's what she says, anyway, when Nessa asks at her twice-annual assessment. The fact of the matter is she learned to love what she did. It wasn't easy in the beginning, accepting that her previous life's work had no place in their 'ark,' as Nessa had taken to calling it. A screenwriter's worth was moot when faced with the sudden near-elimination of one's entire species. But Nessa had seen her potential and enlisted her to help craft a new, functioning society with the work they did as its foundation. The Bunker had a small, working government and had established a set of laws and regulations adapted from life before the Scorch. Items giving special care to overpopulation and long-term sustainability were incorporated as a means of prolonging their stay beneath the surface, until such time as they were forced back above ground. The hope, unlikely as it seemed, was that by then the surface world might once more be habitable.

It was a fool's hope, Nessa confessed to Alice and the other Therapists at the start of their training. Which was why they were needed. By offering glimpses of what was, Alice and the other Therapists afforded those in need a rush of endorphins, of bliss, to remind them that not all was lost, regardless of how dire things seemed.

For Nessa, who used whatever resources she could spare to barter for the items necessary to engineer more Retro, their clients were the blood that pumped through the heart of the ark, and they would keep it beating strong for as long as they could.

For Alice, it was a chance to create again. Only now she found herself uninterested by the rank and file of her usual day-to-day: men and women regurgitating days of yore, recalling first jobs, first loves – last loves – and all points between. Some wanted to return to their days at school, while others sought to recreate times with their parents, their siblings, their childhood best friends.

Meags asks on her third visit if Alice has ever taken Retro herself. Alice shakes her head. 'Why not?'

'We're not allowed,' Alice says. 'We've got to stay present. We can't ever lose sight of what we're here to do. The responsibility of being tasked – trusted – with other people's memories.'

'That doesn't seem right.'

'Maybe not, but it's the life I chose for myself.'

'What did you do before?'

Alice thinks. 'I wrote movies,' she says. Realizing Meags had probably never seen a film, she adds, 'I told stories.'

'How did you come up with them?'

'From my life. From the lives of those around me.'

'You're still doing that,' Meags says. 'You're still making movies.'

Alice smiles sadly. 'In a manner of speaking. Yes, I suppose I am.'

Meags hands a photograph to Alice on her fourth visit. It shows a man, a woman, and a small child.

'This was taken when I was just three or four,' she says.

Alice pushes the picture away. 'No, don't show me that,' she says, seemingly repulsed by the image.

'Why not?'

'I don't want to be limited by anything.'

'Limited?'

She cradles Meags's head between her hands as if it were a delicate vase. 'Your memories are untethered. There's nothing holding you back – I can take you anywhere.'

Meags looks at the photo. 'This... is holding me back?'

Alice takes the photo and, to Meags's horror, tears it in two. 'Forget everything about this,' she says. 'Your mind is a more powerful tool without instruction.'

Meags stares down at the two halves of the photo on the ground. Alice takes her seat, folds her notepad over to a new page.

'Let's see what more we can discover.'

An hour following the end of Meags's session, during which she had danced her way across the surface of a lake and swan dived off the world's edge, Nessa opens the door and enters Alice's suite. She finds Alice sitting on the edge of her cot, eyes closed, kneading the bed sheets with her hands. Alice doesn't realize that Nessa is even there; she blanches upon opening her eyes and seeing her superior standing obstinate like a skyscraper.

'Catch you at a bad time?' Nessa says.

Alice clears her throat, stands. 'I was just thinking,' she says quickly.

'You always think like you're having an orgasm?'

Alice's face reddens. 'I wasn't– ' But Nessa isn't paying attention. She heads to the nightstand, opens the paper sack sitting there.

'Less than half what she paid last time,' Nessa says. 'Are we offering sessions on layaway now?'

'She said she'd bring the rest on her next visit. It won't happen again.'

'It doesn't happen *ever*.' Nessa pauses. 'Tell me, rabbit, do we have a problem?'

'A problem? I don't know– '

'Yes you do, so don't give me that. I asked you to take that girl on as a favour to her parents, and now I hear you're rescheduling clients to fit her in whenever possible. And at a discount.' Nessa tsks. 'Dear rabbit, you've gone too far down this hole. It's time to come up for air.'

Alice bristles at the storybook metaphor. Her own mother used to do that to her when she was growing up, years before the Scorch. Rabbit, she called her, always late, never ready for anything. Rabbit, *he* called her after mother had gone away; little rabbit, he'd scream when she did something wrong, when she wasn't there when he wanted her, when she went and hid in the basement.

Nessa knew this – a part of it, anyway. Heard it back when she first interviewed Alice for the job; she fit the profile of people who could manage beneath the surface. Who could hold it together; who didn't want what the others wanted.

Little rabbit. White rabbit, always late.

'Time to come up for air,' Nessa says again. 'You're slipping. You've gotten too invested in this girl.'

'I'm not,' Alice began. 'It isn't what you think. I'm fascinated by her. She's helping me hone my skills.'

Nessa crosses her arms.

'Honestly.' Alice draws an X over her chest.

'I hired you because you were supposedly strong enough. There wasn't anything up there for you.'

'There isn't. I swear it.'

Nessa considers Alice's claim. She holds steady for a full minute before taking the paper sack, departing with its entire contents.

She doesn't say it, but Alice understands the warning she has just received.

Meags's entire universe is a system of dark tunnels and recycled air. It's all she's ever known. Inside her head, though, were worlds of colour, shape, and experience pieced together in dreams. They were memories, and though abstracted to the point of nonsense, she still clung to them.

Alice starts asking several of her clients what they remembered – really remembered, from their infancy. Not just something that happened during your childhood, she instructs, but what you *wished* you'd seen, past the unadorned curtains of reality. Most look to her as if she's grown a second head.

'I don't get it,' Jackson says one afternoon. He checks his watch. His session is nearly over and Alice is still asking him the same question, over and over again. 'You want to hear my dreams from when I was a child?'

'Not your dreams. What you dreamed during the day – the things your mind put into the world to make it seem... less real.'

But Jackson just shrugs – they all shrug – and says, 'I don't know what you expect me to say. That was a long time ago.'

What he's really saying, though, is that he doesn't remember. Like nearly everyone Alice asks, the fragments left from the world before are already dream enough. For Meags, though, it is all she has – like someone who stared too long at just a corner of a painting, noting swatches of colour instead of the image as a whole.

Jackson leaves Alice in her chair, looking disappointed. He takes the bag of rice he'd given her at the start of his session and exits, says he'll come back the following week – they could try again then.

Alice wakes in the middle of the night to a belt being looped around her at the waist, going all the way around her cot. Through the dark she sees the soft gleam of a white nurse's smock, like a ghost in a darkened hallway. She tries to move her hands but finds her wrists have already been bound, plastic zip ties fed between the wire mesh of her cot below the thin, flat mattress. Alice struggles, briefly, and then capitulates. Nessa leans forward, materializing from the dark. She's seated in Alice's chair.

'I asked if we had a problem,' Nessa says. 'You lied to me, rabbit.'

'I didn't.' Alice fights her restraints, but to no avail.

'It's all right.' Nessa reveals a notepad, places it on her lap. 'We'll get you right for work again in no time.' She writes *Scene One* at the top of a fresh page. 'Tell me what you remember.'

Alice shakes her head. 'Don't do this. Please. I'll stop seeing Meags.'

'Were it so simple.' Nessa taps her pencil against the page.

'I don't have to tell you anything,' says Alice.

Nessa sighs. 'Sooner or later you're going to get hungry or need the restroom. You'll tell me then what I want to know.' She pauses. 'So I'll ask you again: What do you remember?'

Alice shuts her eyes. 'You already know about my past.'

'I didn't ask about your past. I want to know the first thing you remember. Don't think, just say it.'

'…A door.'

'And?'

'It's in a dark room. It's made of wood and… there's no knob on one side.'

'What does the knob look like on the other side?'

'I don't remember the other side. I just know it was there. That's how it opened.'

Nessa writes *Scene Two* at the top of the next page. 'What was on the other side?'

But Alice does not respond.

'The sooner you talk…'

Alice shakes her head. Nessa sighs and reaches into the nightstand. She takes a Retro from Alice's supply and passes it to the nurse crouched bedside. The nurse forces the capsule past Alice's lips and clamps her hand over her nose and mouth until she swallows.

Nessa grins. 'There now, that's a good rabbit.'

Alice breathes heavily, watches as the dark room inflates. 'My mother used… used to callmethat.' She slurs the end of the sentence, three words melding into one.

Nessa waits until she's positive the drug has taken full effect. 'Tell me about her. Your mother. Was she on the other side of the door?'

'The door?' Alice says drunkenly.

'It was made of wood,' Nessa says. 'And it had a knob on just one side. Can you see it?'

And Alice is suddenly standing in front of it, the door she'd told Nessa about. She glances down and sees knee-high socks and a short dress she'd been given for her sixth birthday. It's dirty and torn, and she wants to pull it down off her shoulders. She can't, though, because she's worn it every day for a week and the straps at the shoulders feel as though they've fused with her flesh.

There's a voice in her head she feels she should know but can't quite place. It asks what's out there, on the other side of the door. She places her hand against the wood, feels every notch, every crack, every splinter exactly as they had been. She tastes the concrete of the cellar like a damp dishcloth scraping the back of her tongue, listens for the exact sound of footsteps approaching the door from the other side – the alternating thumps and creaks of the stairs she knew were there but had never descended of her own accord.

Then: a hand on the doorknob, fussing with the lock but not opening it. Alice makes fists with her hands, shuts her eyes and holds her breath until the rustling on the other side ceases.

She stands still, faces away from the door.

And waits.

She wakes and looks over to Nessa, who appears unimpressed. Nessa motions to the nurse, who starts removing Alice's restraints.

'I can't help if you won't let me,' Nessa says. She goes back into the nightstand and cleans out Alice's remaining store of Retro. 'And that means I can't trust you to do your job.'

Alice swings her free legs off the side of the cot, lowers her head as Nessa and the nurse pass by on their way out of the suite.

Nessa pauses at the door, looks back. 'What was it about that girl?'

'Meags?' Nessa nods. Alice thinks. She could try and explain how she'd envied what Meags remembered of the world – or didn't, as the case may be. She could reveal how Meags had allowed her to create in ways she hadn't in years.

'She was a puzzle,' Alice says at last. 'She remembered so little… I wanted to help piece it all together. It was – I enjoyed it.'

'There's more. Something you're not telling me.'

Yes, there is, Alice thinks. But what could she say? That she'd found a dying light in the middle of a howling void?

'Go back inside,' Nessa says. 'I'll give you another chance. Let that door open and you can have your job back.'

Alice shakes her head. She remembers well enough, without the aid of Retro, the apocalypse that preceded the Scorch. There was more hope in exploring the world beneath than in returning to that basement.

Nessa closes the door behind her, leaving Alice alone in her suite. In the course of a day she'd lost all privilege; she would be forced to find her way as the others had. But what she'd lost in terms of a sense of purpose, of honour, she'd gained in the memories Meags had revealed to her.

They were fleeting, fragments of a world with no through-line, no sense of linearity or destiny. But they were vibrant, and full of life all the same. She could return to them in her mind whenever necessary.

They were fluid, malleable. Like dreams made real.

They glowed.

What Remains

Joanne Marjoribanks

It was remarkable how people fought to preserve their lives even as their ends were inevitable.

From her vantage point halfway up the base of the Eildon Hills, Hannah gazed down at the frenzy of activity in the town below. Were she closer to the ground, she would have heard the sounds of car doors slamming, people yelling, maybe even sirens if any of the emergency services vehicles were still in operation.

Her parents had left yesterday to join what remained of Hannah's family, where they had gathered in one of the few still populated towns in the South of Scotland. Even as she had hugged them and promised to see them soon, she knew in her heart that she would not be following them.

There was no point in running from the destruction that would soon consume the world, and Hannah refused to be driven from her birthplace. She would meet death where she had met life, allowing its conclusion to complete a circle rather than an abrupt end to a line she couldn't help but wish was longer.

Death was a solitary experience, and Hannah had chosen the manner of hers. She was certain that her parents, for the little time they had left, would feel anger and sorrow when she didn't join them. The thought made her feel guilty, but she forced the feeling aside. If the afterlife really existed, then she would apologise to them when she saw them there. If it didn't, then it hardly mattered what she did now.

Besides, the petrol stations had been drained weeks ago, and she would much rather be up the Eildons than in her car hoping that what little fuel remained in her tank would last until she got to where the rest of her family were. Spending her final moments stranded by the side of a road was not the ending she wanted.

She had returned to her parents' house in Melrose a week earlier when it had become obvious that remaining in Edinburgh, or any city for that matter, was certain death. The Soldiers had attacked the city not long after she had left, and the once beautiful capital now lay in ruins, its residents either dead or recruited to the Soldiers' cause.

That was all that remained now, death or the Soldiers, and even they would die soon anyway.

The Soldiers of what, no one really knew anymore. What had begun with the rise of anti-Western terrorist groups and sporadic attacks had eventually coalesced into an irrepressible force which spread across the world and swept up recruits from everywhere it touched. Families and communities were ripped apart as the Soldiers' ranks swelled to the point that there was no longer a need for suicide bombers, or lone gunmen picking off random targets.

They had become a unified army. Relentless. Unstoppable. Even as the world's military tried to fight back, they succeeded only in turning the dead into martyrs, whose spirits conjured up yet more Soldiers to continue the fight against the non-believers. Being unafraid to die made them feel invincible, and they walked the streets with impunity armoured with an unshakable faith in the righteousness of their cause.

The last broadcast Hannah had heard from the only operational radio station within range claimed that the Soldiers were close to seizing control of Her Majesty's Naval Base, where Britain's Trident nuclear missiles were located. They had already taken those held in Georgia's Kings Bay, and were awaiting their UK counterparts' take-over before detonating the warheads in catastrophic synchronicity.

It wouldn't be long now. Mere hours, most likely.

The Soldiers would die too, of course, but that was their intention. After death they would be re-born into a new world and live for eternity as the chosen ones who had purged the earth of heathens and sinners. Paradise by way of global genocide, so they believed.

Hannah had never been particularly religious and harboured more agnostic inclinations, much to the chagrin of her Protestant grandmother, but now, as she looked down on her once peaceful hometown that would soon be lifeless and deserted, Hannah wondered how anyone could believe in a merciful God anymore.

Averting her eyes from the scene and breathing deeply of the chilled autumn air, Hannah gathered her resolve and turned to continue her climb.

She had spent countless hours of her childhood and adolescence exploring these mysterious hills. She recalled with fondness days of rolling down the heather laden slopes with her friends, feeling the rush of both fear and excitement that they might stumble upon the lair of an Adder snake, or fall into a hidden crack in the earth. There had been dozens of picnics enjoyed while nursing grazed knees and elbows and spinning outlandish tales of the danger and adventure to be found around every tree and boulder.

Hannah missed the innocence and joy of those days desperately, and the echo of those memories had drawn her back there to spend her final hours in their company. It pained her to think that many of the friends who formed part of those experiences were already gone, alive now only in her fond recollections of them. It was little comfort that she would soon be joining them.

She had not made it more than five minutes farther in her journey before she came across what at any other time would have been an unremarkable sight. A man with long, unkempt brown hair was sat propped up against a large rock, one arm draped around the back of his black Labrador who remained stalwartly by his side. Hannah vaguely recognised him but couldn't recall his name, and felt her pace drift to a stop as she gazed at who she realised might be the last human being she would ever see.

The man languidly turned his head in her direction and held out the half empty bottle of Famous Grouse whisky that Hannah hadn't noticed he was holding. She hesitated for a moment before finally shaking her head in response. As tempting as it was to take a seat next to the stranger and allow the alcohol to calm the tumultuous emotions churning inside her, it felt wrong somehow.

For the next few hours at least, she would be alive and feeling, and she wanted to experience every facet of what remained of her life no matter how painful it was.

The man shrugged before turning his gaze back towards the horizon, legs stretched out comfortably before him as if he were witnessing a glorious sunset and not the end of the world. Hannah continued to stare at the man and his companion for a few moments more before she moved on.

She would soon come to a crossroads in her climb and would be faced with the choice of scaling either the medium sized Eildon with its gentler ascent and firmer footing, or the largest with its scree covered slopes and steep incline.

There was, of course, a third option of continuing straight across the grassy plateau which connected the two larger Eildons and through the verdant meadows towards the third Eildon.

Hannah had always felt bad for this much maligned Eildon, so often dismissed as a meagre hump on the landscape not worthy of climbing. There were those who even doubted its existence and claimed that there were only two Eildons, simply because they were the largest and most visible. The Romans had known the truth when they had named their nearby fort Trimontium – The Three Hills – and climbing all three within one day had been a rite of passage in Hannah's youth that she had proudly undertaken.

Hannah paused in her ascent and weighed her options as though the decision were the most important one she had ever made. Finally, she decided on the larger Eildon. It had always been her favourite and it felt right to scale its scree strewn slopes one final time.

Reaching the plateau Hannah turned right and walked up to the base of her chosen Eildon. She gazed up at its towering height and allowed herself to imagine that it was somehow tall enough to enable her to escape the destruction soon to be unleashed upon the world. That if only she could reach the top she would be spared her fate and be allowed to live out her days among the rolling hills of her home.

The moment of indulgence was brief, and Hannah pushed it aside as she began to climb.

It didn't take long for the difficult terrain to become hazardous. The loose rock fragments shifted beneath her feet and she was forced to lean forwards to keep her balance, her breath coming in short, sharp bursts of exertion. As she climbed higher, the wind which had been merely a light breeze at the base of the hill now whipped about her face with increasing velocity, and she felt a flash of vertigo as she scrambled to keep her footing.

On her left she passed a large boulder which she had used many times in the past as a spot to stop and rest. She placed her hand against its grainy surface and closed her eyes, taking comfort in the solidity and seeming permanence of a part of the earth that had been there for longer than Hannah had been alive. In that moment it was hard to believe that it would all be gone in a matter of hours.

She briefly contemplated taking a seat, before the fear of meeting her end having only made it part of the way to her destination spurred her onwards and she continued to climb. Nearing the summit, the terrain eventually became firmer and she felt the relief of grass and dirt beneath her feet again.

Pausing to catch her breath and pull her wind-whipped hair from her eyes, Hannah looked out across the landscape. The well-worn paths of centuries of footsteps snaked across all three Eildons, like grassy rivers carving their way through the earth and the ever present patches of purple heather.

It was easy to understand how so many legends had been born here. Hannah had grown up hearing them, and they continued to enchant her even as an adult supposedly beyond such childlike wonders.

The most well-known of those legends came to the forefront of her mind and she smiled slightly at the memory of hearing it for the first time as a child.

Centuries ago, a man named Thomas of Ercildoune was seated beneath the Eildon Tree which had once stood atop a hill just outside of Melrose. He was greeted by the Queen of Elfland who sat astride a white horse. She bewitched him and took him deep into the hidden caverns beneath the Eildons, where the fairies lived. Once there she gave him the gift of foresight, and upon returning to the surface he found that he could prophesise the future and was incapable of telling a lie. His prophesies were spun into rhyme and he became known as Thomas the Rhymer.

What happened next was often merged with other legends. Some said that when he died he became immortal and went to live beneath the Eildons with the fairy folk. Others claimed that legions of sleeping knights loyal to King Arthur lay in wait in those vast caverns, while Thomas spent his immortal days gathering horses in preparation for the day when they would reawaken.

The mind conjures up strange notions when it is faced with extinction, and Hannah found herself wondering if Thomas the Rhymer had foretold the end of the world, and in preparation had spent centuries readying King Arthur's knights to come forth and reclaim it once all the mortals were gone.

A cold gust of wind caught Hannah off guard and pulled her from her fantastical imaginings back into harsh reality. Shivering, she turned and made her way along the path until she reached the spot she had chosen for the end of her life.

Two stone structures stood steadfastly before her. Less than two metres in height, they had been erected in memory of Sir Walter Scott, one of Scotland's greatest writers who had loved and been inspired by the Eildons. One was a cairn with a plaque set in its side commemorating the life of the poet, while the other was a pillar with a rounded top in which was set a silver circle. Etched into this circle were the names of towns and cities in Scotland and beyond, each one with a line pointing in a different direction with a number in kilometres indicating the distance to that location from the spot where Hannah stood.

She traced her fingers over the engraved names of places that were now in ruins. London. Edinburgh. Even some of the larger towns named there did not exist anymore, at least not in a recognisable form. The Soldiers had made sure of that.

Unwilling to dwell on the pain and injustice of it, Hannah moved away from the monuments and took up a position where she could see her hometown. It was likely deserted by now, its streets silent and empty. The thought filled her with a profound sense of loneliness that made her suddenly wish that she had gone to be with her family. The familiar landscape began to feel less like home knowing that the houses below were empty of anyone who loved her.

She was pulled from her sombre musings by the sudden sense that she was no longer alone. She snapped her head around to her right and caught sight of a figure coming up the same path which she had walked up earlier. Head down against the wind with hands jammed into the pockets of his washed out jeans, the young man had apparently not yet noticed his audience.

Hannah almost laughed at the cruel irony of a universe that would bring her to the end of her life only to have her met there by the last person she would have wanted to see.

His name was Tom Harden, and he was an ass. His cocky arrogance and flippant disregard for learning, or for those outside his privileged social circle, had irritated Hannah from the moment he had joined her high school in their fifth year.

Her studious attitude and serious demeanour had frequently made her the target of his lewd jokes and disparaging comments, and she was glad that in the ten years since graduation she had not laid eyes on him even once.

Yet, here he was. Her last chance for human interaction before the Soldiers snuffed out her life.

He had almost reached the spot where Hannah was standing when he finally looked up and saw her. He stopped short, clearly surprised to find anyone there, and for a moment appeared to consider turning around again.

The sudden urge to call out to him came as a complete shock to Hannah. She realised that she didn't want to be alone, even if that meant spending her last moments with Tom Harden. Only her pride and intense feelings of dislike kept her from opening her mouth, and she settled instead on making her face appear relaxed and non-confrontational.

It was the best invitation she could offer him, and he took it. Closing the distance between them, Tom came up to stand beside her, briefly meeting her eyes before turning his gaze out towards the same landscape that had previously captivated Hannah's attention.

She was suddenly conscious of how she must look. She had given up trying to tame her chestnut brown hair when the supply trucks had stopped coming and hair products had become a long forgotten luxury. Her once buoyant tresses now hung limply about her face, coming to rest just below her shoulders where she could feel them rising and falling against her neck with the wind.

Her clothes were not much better. Her jeans were stained with grass and patterned with dried droplets of muddy water, while her old, woolly cardigan did little to hide the creased faded t-shirt underneath. It had been a while since anything in her wardrobe had seen a washing machine, not that there was any electricity to power a wash cycle anyway. Or an iron.

Tom looked much the same way Hannah did. His jeans were dusted with grit and soil, and his formerly white t-shirt was smeared with muddy fingerprints where he had obviously repeatedly wiped his hands. Flicking her eyes to his hair, Hannah found it absent of the gel he had so religiously applied as a teenager, and found herself feeling better about her own tangled locks.

Judging by her and Tom's appearances, unkempt and scruffy was the dress code for the apocalypse.

She wanted to say something to him, but everything that came to mind felt trite and insincere. She couldn't pretend that she was happy to see him, despite the circumstances, and she didn't imagine that she was his first choice for an end of life companion either. Finally, she settled on the obvious.

'I thought I would be the only one up here.'

'Yeah,' he replied without looking at her. 'Me too.'

A few minutes of silence passed before Hannah felt compelled to speak again.

'Why aren't you with your family?'

The muscles in his face twitched slightly as a darkness seemed to settle in his eyes. His gaze remained fixed on the abandoned fields and houses below, as he replied in a voice far removed from the irreverent tones of the boy she had once known.

'They're dead.'

Of course, how had she forgotten?

Tom's parents and little sister had been in London when the Soldiers had mounted their first major assault. Hannah remembered reading their names in the local newspaper, which had quickly become little more than one long obituary as the Soldiers claimed more victims who hailed from the Borderlands.

'I'm sorry,' she uttered softly. So softly that the wind almost stole her words and made her worry that he hadn't heard them and would think her cold and unfeeling.

He shrugged, indicating that he had heard her, though he apparently thought that a reply was pointless.

Hannah sighed and turned back to face the vastness of green and brown which characterised the endless countryside of the Scottish Borders, resigning herself to spending what remained of her life in contemplative silence.

Suddenly, Tom cleared his throat and finally shifted his gaze to Hannah. He was several inches taller than she was, and she had to lift her head to properly meet his eyes.

She waited patiently, watching how the wind ruffled the loose strands of his hair while he seemed to struggle to find the words for what he wanted to say.

When the words did come, they were forced out in a rush on the back of a deep sigh.

'I know you hated me in high school. I was the idiot who didn't give a crap about lessons or homework and was only interested in getting girls and booze.'

Hannah smiled wryly. 'I would say that's a fair assessment.'

Tom looked away and sighed in frustration. 'I don't know if it matters any more, or if you even care, but everything is about to end and I don't want to go out with you thinking I'm still that guy. I'm not, and I'm sorry for the way I treated you.'

Hannah smiled slightly and turned so that her whole body was facing him.

'You're forgiven.'

His head snapped back to hers and his eyebrows rose in surprise. 'Just like that? I was at least expecting some eloquently phrased insults.'

'My life is almost over,' Hannah said simply. 'I don't want the last thing I feel to be anger.'

Tom nodded, 'I guess the past doesn't mean much when we have no future.'

Hannah frowned and replied earnestly, 'On the contrary, the past means everything. It's all we have left now.'

His voice heavy with regret, Tom replied. 'Then I wish I'd spent mine a little differently.'

Thinking of all she had sacrificed and missed out on over the years in favour of academics and ambition, Hannah whispered wistfully.

'So do I.'

They were silent after that, each lost in their own thoughts.

The sun broke through the clouds and cast the landscape below them in a tapestry of light and shadow. It would shine on even after there was no life left to be nurtured by it. Even after its light could no longer reach the ground through the choking clouds of ash and dust, it would remain as bright as ever.

Neither of them knew which one first reached for the other. It didn't matter. All that mattered was his hand in hers, and the assurance that they would not meet death alone.

Evlyn

Kevin Horsley

She scaled down between rocks and brush into the clearing, grey and
frozen lifeless with flattened grasses, and kept to one side against the
tree-line.

It had been a hard winter, but animals could still be found. She
examined every bush and turned over every log and stone. Then she
spotted the pool. She looked around and kneeled down into the mush
of brown leaves and insect husks by the water's edge. A split bone,
possibly a leg bone, stuck into the side of her kneecap out of the earth
and she shifted slightly, grimacing. She looked around again, readying
an old steel camping-cup beside her to drink from.

Up on a rise above the tree-line on the far side of the clearing
something moved in silhouette. Thin, ungainly, four-legged; a creature skulked into view, and then more followed. Creatures in a line
that stretched down beyond the rise into the next valley. Each trailing the other mechanically, differing little in the manner of the one
before it like they were a sequence of haunted images ever-revolving,
a chain begun out of only one creature and its shadow. She wondered
whether her friends had seen them also. The lead creature paused, the
others responding in kind, and she could see it sniffing the air and
pointing its protracted head in every direction, resolute, purposeful.
She remained still, watching them. The wind shifted. Yet she couldn't
be sure if the wind had shifted up on the rise also. Tree branches
swayed achingly and quieted. The creatures moved on; onwards to a
place she couldn't imagine and didn't really want to. In years past they
might once have been dogs. She leaned forward and slid two cupped
hands into the icy pool and lifted the water dripping to her face.

She smelt it first, but in the moment's indecision she had already wetted herself. She dropped her hands and the stinking water fell away into the pool and the earth around her.

How could I not've seen it? she thought. How could I not?

A ball of fur, peeled in places giving way to yellowing skin. Flies clung to it and beneath the flies something writhing and insatiate. A paw dangled down into the water and an oily film wobbled from it.

She rubbed at her nose and mouth and eyes with the ends of her heavy shawl and then thought again. She looked up at the rise to be sure the creatures had gone and then took off into the trees, breathing hard against the stench left on her skin.

After a while she found a dip between old sycamore roots that perhaps was once the depression of a dyke and growing within its base, beside a rotting log, were small sprigs of newly emerging mint, green and defiant against a backdrop of icy brown. She broke a couple and crushed the leaves in her hands, rolling them back and forth and then spat into them. She rubbed the green paste all over her face. It would do little else except hide the smell and perhaps clean her a little, though she took several more of the sprigs and tucked them into her clothing for a brew later.

Her forage had fared poorly. She skirted the clearing, and then clambered back up between the rocks to the hill crest. From this point an abundance of large boulders, tumbled together in positions only gods and geological time could have constructed, filled the upland landscape. Picking her way between them she smelled the cooking meat and her stomach grumbled.

'They've found an animal,' she said gratefully under her breath. As she approached, nearing her companions, a menacing shout broke the calm and then a wrenching scream was cut short. Thuds and shouts and howling. She dropped to a crawl and pinned herself into a nook between boulder and boulder. She edged sideways like a crab until a gap presented itself.

Murderous disaster had taken all but one of her travelling companions. Their heads disembodied. Crimson. The last of them was on his knees, chin raised into the air by the edge of some unholy cleaver which gnawed at the skin of his throat through thick black stubble. The owner of the cleaver stood to the side with both hands attached to his weapon like a blacksmith about to remove his hard-worked creation from the forge. A larger man stood looming over her friend with what looked like a sickle. Two other men and a woman, her face contorted insanely, loitered among the dead. All were bedraggled with strips of feculent cloth that hung about their scrawny bones, like they were abortions of mummification from many centuries before.

The large man with the sickle tramped about the campfire and took one end of the roasting spit in his free thick-gloved hand and inspected the animal. It was a small skinned fox, charred nicely over its entirety, smelling wonderful. He grinned and took a healthy bite of the animal's hindquarters.

'You alone little dead man?' the large man asked as he chewed.

Her friend shook visibly.

The large man looked about him at the carnage, 'I see five heads. And look. I see five bodies. Then there's you. That makes six.'

'Just kill me.'

'Good things come to those who wait, little dead man.'

The man with the cleaver giggled and her friend's chin was forced higher. Blood trickled down the blade. In her hiding place, she felt around in the dirt by her feet and took a stone. Her knuckles locked around it.

'Try and stay kneeled, little dead man. Now. I see seven sleeping positions.'

She gulped down a breath.

'A union of six sharing seven beds. The maths tells the truth. There's one missing.'

Her friend gasped and tears streamed down his cheeks leaving dirt-lined tracks.

'She died.'

'What?'

'She died. Two days ago. Fell into the river a valley over. Drowned.'

'Yet you keep her bed intact?'

'Out of respect.'

'Speak again.'

'Out of respect. Evlyn was a good friend. A good person.'

'Aye. I'm sure she was a good person,' the large man smiled and eyed each of his cohort. 'Out of respect you kept her place of rest. This is beautiful. This is truly beautiful.'

The large man walked over to the insane woman.

'Have a good bite of this,' he handed her the spit. 'It's cooler now. Go on. Take a good couple of mouthfuls. You'll need your strength.'

The large man walked back over to Evlyn's friend, still kneeling, and looked him dead in the eyes but spoke to the man with the cleaver.

'Okay. It is time.'

It was easily missed. The blade moved from the chin up over the top of the head and in one swift exile sliced the head clean from the nape through to the larynx. The rest of his body tilted forward as if on some godless pivot and blood plumed and arced with the torso as it flopped forward.

Her muscles relaxed, the energy sucked out of them, and the stone slipped from her hand back into the dirt.

She crawled away, numb. She wriggled down the hillside from where she'd come only moments earlier. She made it to the clearing and struck out through the trees and deep into the woods, stopping only to look back and pray that they weren't following. Crows called from somewhere distant and soon it was night, cold and boundless, and somewhere in the damp she curled up and tugged the now stinking shawl across her body and over her face. The shawl was the colour of the forest floor, like some deranged hermit sinking into the earth.

As she woke she found herself caught in a half-dream. It was eerily quiet, and leaves fell in ceremonial flourishes to the forest floor around her in the hazy morning light. It was a moment in her childhood. Of walking through woodland in the Lake District sometime in the very late summer, circling higher along well-trodden trails beneath a green abundance. A long lake, a mirror cerulean in the depths of the valley. She ran ahead of her parents and jumped, attempting a pirouette, to see them hand-in-hand and both smiling happily back at her. Maybe twenty years had passed, she wasn't sure. What had happened, had happened and at that moment she knew her mind had been burned with the images of the day before forever as much as the terrible days before that. This and her other memories goaded her cruelly. She was shivering. Moisture had frozen to her hair in the night.

Close by she could hear the gentle tinkling of a beck, and a moment of relief replaced her despondency. She followed it and found a dell in the trees on the curve of the beck and surveyed her surroundings for signs of movement and sound. A distant howl of some despairing creature. Nothing else. She could at least keep herself occupied for a while. She clawed a hole in the earth, several fingers deep and three hands wide, and circled it with stones.

Why keep going? she thought. She swept a hand around the outside of the stones to clear it of anything that might catch fire. She piled tinder shaved from birch bark and sticks, the driest she could gather, into a tepee. Rummaging through her thick layers of clothing she found the pocket filled with flint. They'd found thousands of flakes up in the moors in days past and she'd shrewdly stowed some. From another pocket she retrieved a rough steel bar, snapped from some old tool, and struck a good flake off it five or six times in deliberate motions until sparks scattered in a focused point at the tinder. Soon she had a fire crackling away, though she was ever vigilant and ready to bury the fire and run.

Scooping up a cupful of water she boiled it and added some of the leaves, poking and stirring them, pinching out the crumbs of unwanted forest material. She studied her shawl. It was nauseating and she wished she'd been able to change it for a cleaner one before fleeing. However, she'd freeze to death without it.

Fine rain pittered off the bare branches overhead and she cast up a hood from beneath her shawl. She drank her brew, buried the camp-fire and set off through the forest temporarily warmed.

The next day, and for ten or so days to come, parched and with glazed eyes, she roamed the woods and wild fields and valleys avoiding the desolated towns of a landscape the dead had once known. Then, starved and half-crazed she collapsed in a wooded clough overlooking a deeper ravine, into which several streams merged as a thundering fall. She rolled against the base of an oak tree, its branches sweeping low, and she shivered uncontrollably. A great fever boiled beneath her skin and she remembered the rotting animal in the pool and cursed herself, for there was no one else to curse. The sun was high in a cloudless sky and she glimpsed it beyond glittering rays through the gently shifting branches. She lifted a hand and dropped it again to her lap, and turned both palms up to the heavens and began to weep.

'Lady. Lady.'

The boy found her propped like a wilting sack of vegetation by the tree and presumed her dead until she strained her eyes open.

'Lady.'

'I've nothing,' she tried to focus.

'My name is Christopher.'

'I have nothing.'

The boy crouched beside her and looked in the direction she'd most probably wandered.

'I do not want nothing. Are you alone? Are you sick?'

'I'm alone. Go away.'

'I have tea and biscuits,' he said.

She looked at him.

'Who are you?'

'My name is Christopher. I told you. You must be sick.'

She struggled to sit up.

'My name is Evlyn,' she managed. 'Christopher. Christopher. Are you real?'

The boy didn't know how to answer.

'Do you want tea Evlyn?' he asked.

She looked at him. At his small nose and long uncombed dark hair and dark skin and nodded.

The next thing she was aware, a blue plastic beaker was urged into her hands with liquid steaming within it. She smelled the tea and her eyes widened. He placed two oat biscuits on her lap and she eyed them and then him suspiciously. She sipped the tea and took tentative bites of the biscuits, sweet and crunchy. She struggled on a shaky elbow to stand but fell to the side and vomited the biled tea and biscuits back up. The boy remained standing beside her like some stoic guard, his face impassive. He disappeared and re-emerged with a new beaker of tea, and this time with a separate cup of water.

When she drank again and felt able to walk, he led her down the ravine along a carefully plotted route, circumnavigating the falls, her knees shaking. Spray incandescent simmered across the surface of the plunge pool and he took her down and around behind the waterfall. The place was an oasis in a land only just returning from winter. About halfway, she could see that there was a fissure in the rock face. It was several feet wide and appeared to go nowhere; the back of it clearly visible as far along as she could see, albeit in shadow.

'This way,' Christopher said raising his voice in combat with the thundering water. 'It's hidden.'

They watched their footing over stone green with veridic algae.

'I don't see it.'

You could only reach it from the way they'd come. The gap was turned towards the vertical edge of the ravine wall away from them. She ducked her head and they both rounded a bulbous jut in the fissure to find it. The boy pulled away a screen made of water-warped plywood, cut and painted to the shape and colour of the stone around it. They followed the passageway, just wide enough to squeeze down, until it opened up.

Inside was a shelter constructed of wood beams and panels throughout the undercut stone. The smell of damp and the faintly stale and sour smell of human habitation hung in the still air of the cave. She wandered around examining every detail, running her hand along the lacquered horizontal beams of several beds, stared in wonder at the hundred or so books on a shelf, at niches holding candles of which there were about two dozen lighting up the cave, and finally she found a plastic backed seat such as she remembered from her brief days at school, and sat down in it by a hand-hewn wood table.

'Who made this place?'

Her voice was shaky, weak.

'My parents. Or their parents. They told me but I not remember.'

She studied the space. In the stone ceiling in the centre of the room there was a wide natural crack, filled with dark humic soil and roots protruding down like garlands into the room. Directly below a campfire smouldered. Smoke coiled upwards into it.

'No one sees the smoke above? Out there?'

'No.'

'Where does it go?'

'My Dad made tubes that go through soil. There is lots of them. Lots of pipes. They split the smoke up in soil. It is in bushes up there. There is the smell of smoke, maybe. But you cannot see. You cannot see.'

'Really?'

Christopher nodded.

'Your Dad is clever,' she said. 'Where is he? Where's your Mum?'

The boy looked away, 'They gone.'

'Are you by yourself?'

'Yes. But no more.'

Evlyn smiled and moved over to one of the beds.

'I need to sleep. I'm not well.'

'Okay.'

The boy watched her slide over to one of the beds and collapse upon it.

'I'll sleep for a bit.'

'Okay,' he said. 'When you wake I have food.'
But she was already asleep.

She suffered the waking dreams of which no soul should bear to witness. Great hulking beasts carved up the landscape around her like rampant behemoths, terrible in sight and sound, and the screaming of the dead and the maddened crushed in tumult never ceased, and many times she would wake up breathless and damp with sweat, not knowing the difference between the flickering candle-lights in the niches and the burning pyres of the villages and towns and cities on the horizon. Then she'd slip back into a world dark and without hope, for it all to begin again. Nothing made sense in this new world. But she often wondered whether it had made sense in the old, because it had ended in violence and tragedy for the few remaining people to butcher each other without mercy to survive. Her father, before his murder, had said there seemed to be a robustness; a seemingly concrete perpetuity to the human world. In fact it had proved to be built upon many thinly veiled weaknesses. Each weakness had imploded, like abnormalities in the heart of an athletic and vibrant youth.

In three days of near unbroken rest she awoke to Christopher snapping sticks and casting them into the fire. The boy brought her water and asked if she was hungry. She nodded and he went over to a cupboard. He withdrew a tin and found a seat on the bed opposite her. With a can opener he struggled until it popped open, sugary juices sloshing to the floor. She sat up on the bed and he carefully handed it to her along with a spoon. It read Mixed Fruit Cocktail on the faded label. Soon she felt right enough to walk about and leave the cave.

In time she went out and collected firewood and began to feel useful again. Animals were difficult to come by but they were there and she knew how to catch them. She fixed up some traps to catch squirrels and rabbits. Killing was something the boy struggled with, but returning with meat always brought a smile to his face.

'Christopher,' she said across the central hearth, flames stretching shadowy spectres across the cave walls behind them as they ate.

'Yes?'

'Where are you from?'

'The cave,' he'd say. 'From here.'

'But your skin. Your skin. I've never seen such a thing.'

'My Mum had this skin. My Dad had yours. From before the war.'

'It's beautiful skin.'

And Christopher would smile. Such were their conversations. Such was their quick-found bond.

'Thank you for finding me.'

Days later they were out in the woods. Buds were unfurling in the canopy. She was teaching him about plants, their various uses and where they might be found.

'I watched you for a long while.'

She looked at him.

'When? What do you mean?'

'When I first found you. You were wandering in the trees. Talking to yourself. I was scared so I watched you and then you fell to the floor. You looked weak but your face was kind. Different from others. I thought you one of them. But you were not.'

'One of them?'

'Bad men.'

'The bad men. I think I know who you mean.'

'They take my Mum and my Dad not long before I found you. I saw them taken by bad men. I hid.'

He fiddled with a loose thread in his jumper.

She shook her head.

'Why are they bad?'

'I don't know,' she said, crouching and examining a weed. 'There's no one left to stop them being bad.'

'Yes.'

'Do you know how old you are, Christopher?'

'My Dad told me once I was ten years old. But I do not know.'

'It's to do with how many times you've seen the seasons.'

'Do you have Mum and Dad, Evlyn?'

'I did. Yes. They were killed a long time ago now. Not long after the war.'

'You remember war?'

'No. Not really. I was four or five years old at the time. The war didn't last long.'

'Oh,' he looked disappointed. 'My parents talked of war at times they thought I couldn't hear.'

'The world is very different now. Very different. It would have hurt to talk about it. To tell you.'

He spoke little more after that and Evlyn wondered whether he'd meant she didn't want to talk about it either. Shortly before dusk they returned to the cave, after finding a spot by the side of a stream where the soil was raised and fairly flat; not too dry, not too wet, and surrounded by bracken, flat and brown in winter dormancy.

'Do you have vegetables?'

'What is that?'

'Vegetables. Carrots, potatoes, peas. Things like that.'

The boy moved to the back of the cave and lifted the lid of a long, thinly constructed wooden chest.

'My parents named these potatoes,' he said, presenting the discoloured tubers stacked in rows, purple shoots sprouting in places. 'There are others also. Some are planted out there. Some are planted. I show you. I show you.'

A feeling of hope filled her chest and flowed up into her head.

'That place we found. By the stream, Christopher. It could be a good place for growing vegetables,' she said. 'Fairly well hidden. You'd have to know where it was to find it.'

The following morning in the cold light they retraced their steps through the trees and pushed through the half-dead bracken.

Evlyn broke the ground with a rusted spade and pulled up a good lump of the dark loam and piled it to the side.

'This is good soil.'

Christopher slid one of the potatoes upright into the hole and then pressed the piled earth back in and around it. They repeated this process a dozen times or so until two rows were completed, contoured to the shape of the stream dribbling a few feet over. She scanned the world between the trees. So quiet. So quiet.

'It's going well into spring now,' she said. 'They'll do well I think. From what I remember.'

Christopher looked at her, 'We will eat good you think?'

She smiled, 'Yes.'

In the cave they spoke of the bad men again and where they might be living; where the boy's parents might have been taken. There were small groups that still lived in the ruined towns, she said. She told him how the towns were terrible places to pass. He went quiet and then he told her that there was such a town two valleys over near the coast, on the edge of a wide sandy river delta. Factories still smoked and the land around it, though wild, was devoid of life other than what the bad men allowed to survive amongst the horrors they committed. He was sure his parents were there somewhere but he'd never ventured anywhere close. These were the stories his parents told and his fear prevented him.

In the coming weeks great rains fell upon the woods. They would struggle out through each deluge sopping wet with cracks of thunder breaking overhead. And when the hot summer arrived and dried the ground again they toiled in their allotment in as little clothing as they'd each allow. All to survive. But for the first time that Evlyn could remember, she was enjoying life. Of course she couldn't know what this was. Only that for the first time, she wanted to wake up each morning. The sun lasted longer in the day and the nights became shorter and warmer, and soon the woods around their sanctuary were green and rich.

Evlyn couldn't pinpoint the moment she'd known something was wrong. That danger was close. Her time in the cave with Christopher stretched out behind her in memory as much as if she'd always been there, and in this she'd become thoughtlessly comfortable.

Perhaps, during one of their walks through the woods, with Christopher trailing behind her, she'd seen an unusual pattern on the forest floor. The tell-tale signs of movement, at odds with their own. The unfamiliar trample of leaves. The signs that nameless travellers had passed nearby. But she'd been blind to it.

Christopher hovered over the stream just outside of the allotment, gazing down at his reflection, playing with the surface of the water with his fingers. She'd been walking with the garden fork over her shoulder and she dropped it carefully to her side, allowing the tangs to pierce the earth. He looked up and said something about whether the potatoes were really ready or not.

'They've been flowering the last few days,' she replied. 'I'll dig some up before we check the traps. Just to see.'

'Did the flowers have to die first?'

'Not according to the pictures in the gardening book on the shelf.'

He nodded and returned to the water. Evlyn watched him for a moment and then looked out between the trees, eastwards along the sedate meander of the stream. Lines of orange sunlight bounced around between the heavily laden branches ahead. The forest was quite beautiful now. Quiet and beautiful. She swung the fork back over her shoulder.

The bracken was thick and high now, and they'd since cut through some of the large green fronds along the shore of the stream to make it easier to access the allotment. She edged her way in and set to work removing some of the potatoes. The yield was better than she'd imagined. Fist-sized and healthy-looking, with pinkish dimples in dirty white skin. She dug out the whole of one of the plants and gathered seven potatoes. She wrapped them in a cloth, picked up the fork and went out to find Christopher.

There were two men standing there, thin with tendons twitching beneath rank skin and tattered garbs. The arm of the man holding Christopher was dripping with fresh cherry-red blood. She couldn't see who the blood belonged to, but she knew by the snarling pant the man was issuing that Christopher had put up a fight. For a fleeting moment she wondered how she hadn't heard the fight. The fork dropped from her shoulder and she tossed the cloth of potatoes away from her.

'Hey, look at this,' the first man said. 'There's two of them.'

The second man's eyes bulged out of his narrow skull, 'A woman.'

'I want the woman.'

'You have the boy.'

'I want the woman.'

'Take the boy back. I'll get the woman.'

The man holding Christopher's limp body growled and lifted the boy a little of the ground and carried him off, one foot low enough to carve a path in the dirt.

'Go on. Don't worry,' the second man said. 'I'll get her. You'll have her later.'

He moved forward with one hand out to her like he was coaxing an animal out of its burrow or presenting alms to the poor.

'You must be lonely out here. All by yourself. With just your son. You'll be better with us.'

Her eyes widened, 'Get back,' she said.

'You should come…'

'Get back!' she snapped again. Her heart thumped in her chest.

The man's features tightened revealing blackened shards of teeth between thin cracked lips, the phantom of what might have been a man.

The next she knew she was on the floor, grappling against his weight. He was heavier and far stronger than he looked. She managed to force away one of his arms, and when he yanked it from her she used that same hand to scratch him hard across the face. Then she didn't stop throwing her fists up at him until he found an opportunity to counterattack. He'd been in many more fights than she. He pulled away, her fists still punching, allowing her to roll to one side and when she tried to scramble back to her feet he was on her again. One hand took her by the throat and she instinctively grabbed that hand with both of hers, desperate to slacken the pressure. With his free hand, he raised it behind him. His muscles tightened. For a split second she saw joy rupture onto his face, maniacal; a look which froze in her eyes as he drove his fist into the side of her face, darkening her world and sending his ghoulish portrait spinning.

But that wasn't the end. She wasn't out. Though everything seemed considerably further away than before. Her hands flapped about beside her. The man's breath grunted somewhere above. She shifted and found the handle of the fork and opened her eyes and looked at it. She threw her knee hard up into the man and he screamed feverishly. She kneed him again and beat him about the face. At that moment she realised only one of her eyes was working. Numbness clouded the left side of her face, but she couldn't worry about that. She rolled to one side and took hold of the fork and raised it up, just as the man was leaping upon her the third and final time. Two of the tangs went through just above his clavicle, and he dropped writhing to her side. She shuffled away from him and watched as he coughed and spluttered his final moments of life.

Christopher, she thought. Christopher. Beyond the bloodied lump of the second man she spied the trail left by the boy's foot leading a clear path through the wood. She closed her good eye slowly and then opened it again, hoping to gain a fresh view of the world.

Then she took the fork out of the man's throat and set out after Christopher and his captor.

A Veneer of Civilisation

Tim Robson

I have learned, through bitter experience, that every blissful moment in life, however intensely felt and however pivotal it seemed at the time, will one day be no more than something half remembered, a page in a novel never to be re-visited.

I have also learned that every hateful, unhappy moment in life, however brief and however inconsequential it seemed at the time, will be fated to be replayed again and again, until the end.

It is the natural order of things; hate beats love, every time. I've seen things and done things that cannot be told here. I carry them inside in that small part of my soul that forms an impenetrable core; who I was once, who I should have been. I suppose you might call it conscience or morality. Maybe I didn't start out this way but once the switch was flipped, I found I was capable of the most terrible things.

When the asteroid hit, things didn't go to pieces at once. Obviously the impacted area, covering one quarter of the planet's surface – from Russia to the Indian subcontinent - was devastated. Everything was destroyed and millions, billions, of inhabitants died instantly. Then the wave of knock-on effects hit the rest of the planet, principally massive tsunamis that flooded half of Europe and swept through the Gulf of Mexico. But the collision, and its immediate ruination, was only the beginning of mankind's woes.

Such was the size and the speed of the asteroid; it knocked the earth off course, out of its regular orbital and into a new trajectory, more than ten million miles further away from the sun. Like a celestial pinball, the Earth was now buffeted by frequent, if smaller, asteroids, which killed untold millions. A preventative and massive nuclear strike on an incoming mega asteroid ending up misfiring and laying waste to much of North America. No nukes were used again.

But the real danger came with the Earth's new orbit. It became cold – unbearably cold – as the sun became more distant. Plants, trees, animals died. Crops refused to grow. The seas frosted over, the fish died. Riots broke out across the non-devastated areas of the world; governments were powerless to stop the ceaseless fighting for food, shelter, and warmth. Millions died in the riots. Billions died in the enveloping famine.

Some governments proposed vainglorious projects to build spaceships and try and start the human race elsewhere in the galaxy. These never even got off the drawing board. Food and material shortages meant that scientists couldn't even work. Technology was going backwards, we were regressing bit by bit into savagery and the Stone Age. Science and progress were not going to help us anymore.

Demagogues and populists seized power and enacted fearsome revenge on those they blamed for the Earth's catastrophe. Women, Jews, scientists, the rich, beggars, all were killed brutally by the mobs. Cults sprang up all over the planet; afterlife crazies whose answer was to ritually commit suicide. Thousands upon thousands of people, whole families, hurled themselves from cliffs or slaughtered each other. Anarchy, confusion and violence took over.

I relive these scenes every day.

I am isolated: the remains of a top-secret research team in the Antarctic. My living pod generates its own heat, my provisions will last years, I am safe and warm but time is limited. How I got here is something that haunts me, every night, every waking hour.

My team had its office in The Falklands and a research lab on the coast of Antarctica. We worked a monthly shift rotation; two people on Antarctica, two back at the office. I was in Port Stanley with Jack, an associate professor, when the asteroid hit. As the streets around us descended into lawlessness, Jack and I planned to take the micro plane to the Antarctic base. That is when things got messy. Jack wanted to take his girlfriend, Sally. I refused as my girlfriend, Diane, had been killed in a food riot the week before. I took my festering anger out on Jack and Sally. We couldn't have five people in the hut, I declared, though up to the week before, I was happy to have six. The argument got heated. We fought. I killed Jack with my bare hands. Sally, watching in terror from the sofa in the lounge of their bungalow, hit me with a vase. I strangled her to death.

Armed with my rifle, I made my way to the airport shooting anyone who got in my way. Word got out that I knew how to fly a plane, so my departure was difficult. I started the plane and, with deliberation, ran over a group of twenty trying to block my exit. I took off with blood on the wheel and undercarriage.

The killing didn't stop there. At the pod, Sam and Miguel refused to let me join them. They were always tight. I persuaded them to open the door and shot Sam before he could raise his own pistol. Miguel tried to reason with me but I beat him to death with the butt of my rifle. Over time I disposed of their bodies.

There were others in Antarctica, I know, but not many, and they are getting fewer. I did use the radio to keep in contact with other scientists, but unwanted ears intercepted my messages and for a while I had an invasion problem. Armed with my high velocity rifle those problems ceased and, as with Sam and Miguel, I disposed of their bodies.

It was two years later when she arrived. A gale was blowing. Since the Earth had moved to its new trajectory, the storms had increased in frequency and meanness. There was an epic grandeur to their ferocity. Storms lasted months and battered my hut daily, moaning to come in and stub out this last defiant stand.

I could tell the Earth was getting colder. The outside temperature was falling consistently. The Earth was freezing to death. The human race was fated to go out, not with a bang, but with a slow, oscillating freeze. I figured I had ten years of fuel and food if I was careful. But with the temperature falling this fast, survival now looked like three years, tops.

In the middle of the storm, I heard knocking at the door. A trick of the wind, I thought. The storm-gods have developed new methods to get inside and kill the warmth. I rolled over on my cot and ignored it. But it continued. Persisted. Grew louder. I reached for my rifle.

'Who the hell is that?' I roared. 'I am armed. Now fuck off before I shoot you.'

The knocking stopped but then I heard a thud of something collapsing against the door. And a brief cry. I waited ten minutes, maybe more. I was suspicious of tricks. I would not fall for one. I opened the door, rifle cocked.

A woman lay unconscious in front of the door, snowflakes covering her inert body. I looked around – there were no other people, and so I had a choice; let her die outside or bring her in and everything that might entail inside.

Her face decided it for me. She was beautiful; full lips, lustrous hair, high cheekbones. There were signs of frostbite but this couldn't hide her beauty. She was young too, probably about twenty. Heat and food are two essentials of life. Here, on my doorstep, was a third. Mind made up, I dragged her over the threshold and into my pod.

I lay her on the bed and turned up the heating. I removed the outer layers of her clothes. Curious, I now removed her blouse and then her trousers until she lay in her underwear. I had been alone for over two years. Gazing lustfully at this semi-clad girl, I realised what I had been missing.

She lay unconscious for two days, not moving. Apart from a few cuts and bruises she appeared in perfect shape, if a little thin. How had she gotten here? By herself? On the third day her eyes opened. I was doing my exercise routine to maintain body mass, when I noticed she was watching me; half afraid, half thankful. I stopped my weight lifting and crossed to the bed. She covered herself with the sheet.

'You talk?' I asked.

She nodded and said something. It could have been Spanish.

'You speak English?' She looked confused. '*Habla ingles?*'

'*Si*,' she replied.

I suppose it was natural that if a girl turned up on my door she'd be a local. I didn't speak much Spanish.

'But I also speak English.' She said this and smiled, before shutting her eyes.

In time she could sit up and eat the warm soup I gave her. On the third day she got out of the bed and sat at the table with me.

'So, who are you?'

'I am Maria. I came from Argentina.'

'You speak good English.'

'My parents worked in England for five years. I went to school there.'

'How did you get here?'

'After the temperatures dropped, things got bad in Buenos Aires. There was rioting every night. This man, Valois, said that only by sacrificing to the old gods could the sunshine come back and the food grow again. But the only people who he wanted to sacrifice were rich people. My father was rich. One day, the mob came to our house. My father insisted that my brother and I run away through the back. My mother refused to go. The mob took my parents. I know what Valois did to people when he sacrificed. Beaten and buried alive.'

'My brother and I ran to the docks. Father kept a boat there. My brother knew how to pilot boats. We hoped to leave and find our parent's property on the island. We hoped the people were kinder there.'

'But my brother got lost. The satnav wasn't working. There was not much petrol and so we drifted southwards. But the sea iced up totally around us and we were stranded and stuck. We thought that was it.' She looked at me. 'Perhaps it was better if my story had ended there.'

'There was hardly any food on the boat; we hadn't been able to bring any. It was so sudden when the mob came. We were freezing when another boat came by on the horizon. We waved to it. It was full of bad men. They pulled alongside. My brother went to greet them and they shot him like a dog. They had different ideas for me.'

She looked at me defiantly. Was I going to be any different? I was

English, and a scientist but my desires were no different to the wild men on the boat. I had a veneer of civilisation – but once the veneer has cracked, there is no repair. She would do as I wished whether she wanted to or not.

'I was passed around the crew like a piece of meat. They were animals.' I nodded, acknowledging her, but with no sympathy. The end of the world hardens you. Too many bad things happened. One more was just, one more. We all had stories.

'One night, they were drinking and they all wanted me, so they started fighting with each other. Nasty fighting with knives and pipes and then guns. I got off the boat and ran away. I stayed near until all the noise had died down and crept back on-board. They were all dead or injured. One man, the leader, Carlos, was still walking. I killed him with a knife. Others were dead drunk so, I had to leave before they woke up. I took some food and warm clothes and left.'

'But where were you going?'

'To die,' she said simply. 'Away from the men. Just fade into nothing, here in the ice. But then I saw your light and knocked at your door.'

'How long had you been walking?'

'Two hours, two days, in the storm it is hard to tell.'

We got into a routine, Maria and I. I found she needed little persuading to pay for the heat and food in the only way she had. She acquiesced and did what I asked and sometimes appeared to enjoy herself. I knew her heart wasn't in it though. Why would it be? I was twice her age. We may have been the last two people on the planet but she couldn't hide her preferences; no doubt she would have preferred someone younger and leaner. But she was alive in my pod, so she submitted to my desires.

I stopped trying to please her and took her when and if I wanted. It was better that way. We treated it as a necessary transaction. She bore it without comment and I did what needed to be done for my own satisfaction. And then we'd fall asleep, or warm up a meal or play chess.

And so it went on, for month after month. I noticed that the food supplies were diminishing at an alarming rate. Power and heat were the same – two people can use the same amount of fuel as one. But food? That was running out fast.

Then the heating broke and the temperature dropped twenty degrees within ten minutes. I said to Maria it must have been the solar panels slipping out of alignment on the roof of the pod. We both went outside to fix the malfunction. I took a ladder and propped it against the wall of the pod. Maria held the ladder.

I hit her with a hammer as she stood outside the hut and dragged her body into the supply pod next door. The remains of Sam and Miguel hung on the rafters. All the real meat had gone and so they looked like skeletons with heads, minus their fleshy cheeks, of course. I'd stored one or two invaders there too. I'd consumed all the meat and had only the sinewy parts left. Maria would be good eating.

Maria woke up at this point and screeched in horror at what she saw. Her final scream was a plea to spare her life but she had nothing to offer me, alive. Better dead.

It is now two years later. My food has run out. My meat supply has gone. No other humans have come here. Maria was the last. I am truly alone.

It's cold, even here in the pod. My heating cannot compete with the dropping temperatures. The Earth must be slipping further away from the sun. The new orbit mustn't have taken and so we're falling deeper away into the solar system.

Before the end of the world there must be the end of mankind. And before the end of mankind there must be an end to civilisation. I had been a professor, a man of science, and I fell lower than most. In times of crisis we needed our conscience, our sense of community and yet we turned on each other as though rabid dogs. Perhaps our extinction is for the best. The flaw must have always been there beneath the veneer of civilisation we arrogantly carried as proof of our sanctity. It wasn't enough.

I'm putting my pen down now. No one will ever read this. It is last will and testament of mankind.

I'm going outside for a walk. I may be some time.

Bring-your-kid-to-work Day

David J. Wing

Looking back, I'd have to say, it wasn't all my fault.

I could have easily gone to work with Mum at the office. I could have spent the morning eating Geoff's doughnuts before he arrived and in the afternoon I could have let the water cooler run out over the carpet. It would have been a great day, but oh no, Dad had to take me to work with him.

Whoever came up with Bring-your-kid-to-work Day is a dick. Ordinarily it means unwanted distraction for the other employees and for the employer it means a slow day, profit-wise. It's not like the kid in question ever learns anything either. We just mess about, get under-foot, whine, cry and moan until we get to go home and watch *Power Rangers*.

Dad said 'I'll take him with me; it'll be good for him. Besides, there's a lot going on today and we can take this time to bond a little.'

Remember that, 'bond'.

What he really meant was - *He needs shaping up*. I'd been a touch mischievous in recent months, why? I was eight, that's surely why enough. Anyway, graffiti in the toilets and obnoxious behaviour in general doesn't make teachers happy and the letters home were get-ting all too frequent.

So off we went to work.

We drove out past the suburbs, past the new builds and the old factories and on still. After an hour I was beginning to get frustrated and started singing the most annoying songs I could think of. I even farted once or twice. Dad just kept driving. I asked 'Are we there yet?' at least thirty-three times in a row and eventually ran out of breath and flopped back into my seat. The landscape changed and before too long we were in the desert, Cactus trees and sand everywhere.

To be fair, I'd never gone to work with Dad before. Other than him being in the Military, I hadn't a clue what he did; all I knew was whenever we played soldiers, he always had to be the General.

Pulling up to the front gate I began to get an idea why.

'Colonel.'

A young private stood to attention, saluted and lifted the gate to let the car drive through. I saw this as an opportunity and stick my tongue out at the guard. He didn't flinch, no fun.

We pulled-up to a small office, surrounded by a few other small offices and went inside. Dad saluted a few more people and waved at Gladys – his secretary. I'd met Gladys plenty of times and I would later come to believe she was part of the reason for my early onset diabetes.

I palmed the candy she gave me before Dad noticed, and followed him into his office.

The walls were covered in photographs; a General here, an Admiral there and in more than one there was Dad with a President's arm on his shoulder. The family photo we took last summer on vacation in Yellowstone took pride of place on his desk.

Dad sat down a behind his desk and grabbed the phone.

'Gladys.'

'Yes, Colonel.'

'Gladys, Thomas and I are going on inspection, please call ahead.'

'Yes, Colonel.'

I was busy admiring my Dad's collection of mint WWII figurines when he slapped me on the shoulder. I jumped.

'OK, Son, time to inspect the troops.'

I beamed. This would be great.

We headed out of the office and stopped at the lift. A Lieutenant joined us and inserted a key just above the floor buttons and turned. The doors slid shut, and the lights on the buttons began to descend until they reached sub-level 3 and stopped... but the lift carried on going. I looked up at Dad and he shone a sly smile my way.

I waited and waited and after a while we came to a stop. The doors silently opened and the Lieutenant waited for us to pass.

'Colonel.'

'Thank you, Lieutenant.'

It was a corridor, a long one, but way down at the end there was a faint light, but the more we walked the more I began to feel like that light was getting further and further away. Eventually we arrived at a desk and a Private jumped to attention.

After the official greetings, Dad and the Private placed their hands on matching pads on either side of a steel panel, looked into a camera and typed in a code I couldn't see. A door seemed to appear from within the walls and then move sideways. It was thick too, almost a foot deep. The Private waited until we had walked through and then the door slid shut behind us.

We stood in total darkness. I looked up at Dad, not that I could see a thing, and waited. A noise screeched in my ears and a green laser shone up and down us then vanished. A white light glowed through the walls and a door rolled open in front of us.

We stepped forward and there it was; a big ass missile. I sort of floated over to the viewing window, unable to quite believe what I was seeing. I stared down the silo shaft, all the way to the bottom and then had to crane my head back to see how far up it went. It was white, tail to tip and around halfway up there was a painted flag and just underneath, in black pen, someone had written:

S.A.M. says Hello

SAM of course was a very witty name; Surface to Air Missile, Uncle Sam too I guess.

Gobsmacked? You could have knocked me over with a stiff breeze.

People were walking around with purpose, working hard and saluting whenever they saw Dad. I just stared at him.

'Impressed, Son?'

I think I nodded, I certainly meant to.

'Feel free to wander around. I've got a few things to work on through there.'

He indicated the silo and walked through a small maintenance door and disappeared.

I spent the next few hours wandering around and watching the men and women at their work, scarcely noticing me. I found the water cooler but I realised, even at the age of eight, that spilling water all over the place in a nuclear missile bunker was probably not the best course of action.

There were no doughnuts.

I began to lose interest. After the initial shock, you'd be surprised how quickly atomic weapons lose their appeal. I sat down on a swivel chair at the back of the control room and span a bit.

Lunchtime rolled around and the shift changed. I'd been quiet for a good while and I guess they forgot me. The doors slammed shut and before I knew it, I was alone. Dad must have been really busy because I hadn't seen him all morning and I was getting hungry. I blew my lips in a huff and slouched over to the desk.

You've never seen more buttons and knobs in your life and you'd be surprised how basic it actually was. There was a monitor above, but it looked like it hadn't been updated since the Carter administration. Budget cuts, dad would always moan about, budget cuts... I never paid much attention.

It was one long board, but split into three parts. There was a chair for each controller and a phone sat under a Perspex box. Each button had a small LED light next to it and on the screen there was a notice that read; *ERROR.*

I frowned a little and turned around, no one in sight. I looked back and a second *ERROR* message flashed up, then a third and a forth. I was becoming a little suspicious. Where had they all gone?

'Hey.'

I called out.

'HEEEY! Doesn't anyone work here?'

Nothing, no one came and the messages kept flashing and they looked angrier and angrier the longer I stood there.

When the message got specific, that's when I realised I needed to take action.

The screen read:

MISSILE LAUNCH DETECTED.

ORIGIN SOURCE: RUSSIA.

INDICATED COURSE OF ACTION: RETALIATION.

I started screaming. I'm not proud, I'll admit it, I even wet myself a little bit.

'Help! Really, HELP! Someone's got to help me!'

I ran my eyes over the console and watched the lights flickering, blinking, yelling at me to make a decision. I shot my eyes around the room again and when I saw no one and no one answered my final plea, I started pressing buttons – all the buttons.

I pressed the yellow and the blue, the green, the purple. Then my eyes rested on the big red one.

The screen was clear; it told me to do it, so I did it.

I reached out my right fist and slammed it down.

As the button depressed I heard laughing. There was an observation window high and behind me. I guess it's where the top brass watch when they do those War Games where they pretend to obliterate Russia or China or... Belgium, I guess. There was my Dad and all the people that should have been in this room, doing their jobs, but they weren't, they were laughing at me instead. Hell, one of them was even eating a jelly doughnut.

Dad stopped laughing when the silo started to steam.

The others followed suit and ran down the stairs to the control room and started scanning their hands and retinas, frantically trying to get in. But they wouldn't. I'd pressed the locking button or twisted the security knob or some such thing. They were locked out and the countdown was counting... fast.

The screen flashed Ten, Nine, Eight...

The phone on the desk rang and I smashed the perspex with more force and speed than I imagined I had in me.

'Son, press the override.'

I scoured the desk.

'It's the blue with the red around it!'

Who designed this place? That's what I wanted to know, but I didn't have time to ask the question.

'It's on the right!'

I looked.

'NO, further to your right, it's under th… '

And that's the last thing he said before *SAM* left to say *Hello* to his little red friends.

The door opened a few seconds later, but it was too late and no matter how many buttons they pressed and knobs they twisted, I'd fouled up the system too much. They'd need a week to fix it and the world would end in a little less than three hours.

The site had a bunker; convenient and stocked to the rafters with all the mod-cons and essentials and we all managed to get into it in time, even Gladys. Mum got obliterated in the retaliation of course. I blame Dad, he blames me. We don't talk much and I don't think this is the kind of 'bonding' he had in mind. Well, there's plenty of time for building bridges, mending fences, etc… I'm told around 20 years in fact until the radiation dies down.

When you look at it with fresh eyes, you might be able to accept it as a bit of a whoopsie, but at the end of the day (the end of days), who in their right mind thinks scaring a kid with the threat of nuclear devastation is a good idea? I ask you.

Crossing

Benjamin Abbott

2037, South England

You're not known to talk about the continent, why now?

Well, you've asked me, and the question is simple enough. 'What day do I remember most from our exodus?' Children always ask for our stories, but they are not stories for children to hear. Each of us have them; I choose not to tell mine. Excuses vary; a favourite is the language, how easy to pretend my tongue still struggles with English words. Truthfully, I have no desire to tread those steps again; to journey through the vividness of my darkest memories, to own my part in the actions that may have happened, things I may have done.

We don't have to talk about this now, I have others to speak with.

Maxwell agreed to tell you about the fall of London?

I think so. He's hard to read, but I have an appointment.

A fantastic story he has, darker than any you will have heard; hard to sit through but worth the journey. You are fortunate, he doesn't tell it to many. Strange the things we remember and those we forget. I've reached a point where I no longer feel I deserve to forget; perhaps there will be some absolution in the retelling.

I remember that morning. Is it daft to say I'd never seen a horse before? Perhaps from a distance, speeding past a car window, but never close enough to really tell what I was seeing. I was of an age where I was yet to leave the Swedish mountains of my birth, a landscape ill-suited to such animals.

It was near Troyes. Weary from the weeks of flight, down through Northern Europe, I was sitting high amongst the sandy grass; more alone and wretched I was yet to be, when the thing strode out in front of me. The creature moved slowly and without fear; not a trot but an elegant walk. Wild and shoeless on the soft ground, the animal's footfalls nearly as silent as my own. Sunlight ignited the sheen of its bay coat into a thousand hidden colours. I think I felt relaxed then, for a moment, blissful to watch the unexpected beauty, a comfort to know there were still such things as beauty in the world. I wondered from where the beast had come and whether it was missed. I considered the distance I had travelled and wondered if there was anyone that still missed me. The gelding turned its huge head towards me; I am not ashamed to admit I felt a gentle sweep of fear. But such majesty. The horse bent to graze upon the long and plentiful grass. As it ate it breathed through its nose, and I could hear it sigh.

Confidently, the horse moved on, down the slope of the hill, turning right into the valley; it picked up speed through the basin, cantering down a route I was afraid to follow. Tracking the horse, my eyes were drawn to the scene I was attempting to ignore.

A herd of frightened humans, pushing and stumbling to traverse that bridge. Remember there is much we know now that we did not for a long time. The falling of the age of mass communication brought unmatched confusion. Facts were ruled by hearsay and few could be trusted. We had no idea of the value of water. A colony of ants, concussed by fear and the summer sun. And the others, the one's we grew to know as 'leeches', wandering closer from their horizon. But not from mine, from atop the hill I saw so much farther, my horizon decorated by the evacuated city: grey and lonely and dead, it glared down on all of us.

He lights a hand-rolled cigarette. The scent of the smoke has a faint hint of dried poppies. After taking a long drag he offers it to his interviewer, she declines politely.

I knew I had to follow the exodus, but the horde made me nervous and I didn't trust the thick covering of trees that occupied the expanse between myself and the refugees. I looked all around me: at the slope of the hill; the wide, tapered valley; the rocks and trees that obscured the certain dangers of the climb; in the distance I saw my horse again, far downstream crossing the river. I stood, hoping the action would trigger some decisive revelation.

It was then that I was distracted by a furtive rustling sound near my feet. I bent to find a small rabbit had become entangled in the straps of my bag. As I reached down to free it, I paused. It was no coincidence that I had my knife strapped to my ankle; as I had done since I was a boy when my uncle had gifted it to me, fresh from his workshop. Carbon steel of expert quality, set in an antler grip, hand crafted and brilliant. I had often used the blade to skin rabbits whilst camping in the woods near our village; this time it was my own palm I drew the edge across. I imagine it hurt, though I do not remember the sensation. All I remember is how dark and red the blood was; so thick it did not drip from my hand. Instead running slowly in the direction of my tattered sleeve. Tenderly I placed my hand on the back of the rabbit, dragging it along the grain of the fur, slicking the poor creatures coat in my own blood. I don't think the tiny animal even struggled. I untangled its legs and set it free, bombing and leaping down into the trees.

A simple distraction. For a moment I must have been pleased with myself. As it scampered out of sight I used the last of my water to clean my wound. Be sure that I was thorough. I applied alcohol, bandage, gauze, and a leather glove entirely unsuited to the heat.

In the valley below I heard screams. I had known the effect that blood had on them, but I had carelessly not considered the incredible range of their senses. Such different species to us. Shoulder to shoulder the refugees had nowhere to run, no freedom to move or try to escape. Incensed by my decoy, the distant creatures erupted towards my hill, and between us, the line of souls bound for the bridge. People were dying before the creatures reached them. Some were trampled as the mass of frightened passengers twisted and convulsed, but some were murdered much less accidentally, over arguments at the edge of the bridge.

A cloud moves to disguise the sun and the young interviewer shivers; she watches her subject pause to pick at a scab on his hand. By accident she catches his dark eyes as they flick up; he smiles.

Those on the far side of the river looked back with a paralysing horror. You could have almost believed they were going to pass straight by, till they were upon them, till the screams became that of pain and anger. Fear came to me then; guilt would follow. In the cluttered killing field I witnessed a family make towards my hill. They were young, full of love, parents shielding the children with their own bodies as they ran. It occurred to me how very cold my stomach felt; rising up to the tips of my shoulders. Fingers numb.

With a bravery I could not explain, and I can assure you has been absent since, my legs stuttered into life, carrying me towards them. To my luck, my distraction seemed to have left the forest deserted.

A hundred sticks broke underfoot as I ran, chasing the sobs from the youngest of the family. They weren't moving fast enough. Leaves kaleidoscoped as they whipped past my eyes. And then there were no more leaves and I was momentarily static in the abandon of the valley. I spotted the family, moving as fast as they could. To my left the line disbanded in chaos. Those things totally within them now, grey skinned and empty eyed they flooded the crowd: like water filtering through sand, latching and poisoning as they drenched the caravan with their overwhelming numbers. My cheeks felt wet and cold.

A man in the crowd tripped; he fell to the ground, bag above him, pinning him down. Before he had finished gasping, there was one on top of him, mouth to his arm. A lady he had been running with stopped and turned. I imagined she was his lover, but they may have been strangers. She might have screamed as she ran back to him, I can't or won't remember. She slammed into the creature with all her weight and force of stride. I glimpsed only the pommel of the knife she drove fast into its neck. I looked away, turning back in time to see her embrace the man, who may have once been her lover, as she slipped the long blade into the back of his skull.

Beginning to gain on the family, I realised we were making progress towards the shallows the horse had crossed. Finally within earshot I tried to shout to them, but if they heard me they showed no sign. We sprinted together beside the steep bank of the river. The waters here deep and powerful. The mother was younger than I had realised, younger even than I was. She was beautiful and carried a fragile bundle of blankets close to her chest, as father ushered two young girls with increasing desperation. Soon I was able to stride with them without losing pace. Hope of us reaching the crossing with the children on foot was absent. I tried shouting again, this time they heard, staring wide-eyed at the stranger imposing himself on their escape. I called again, imploring that we carry the children. Over my shoulder I noticed several leeches pull away from the crowds, beginning to bear down on us. We stopped. The father knelt for the eldest child to climb on his shoulders. I lowered myself to speak with the remaining girl.

'What's your name?'

'Amélie,' she sniffed.

She was light on my shoulders and we moved swiftly along the riverbank. The insides of my stomach tightened as the adrenalin worked its care through my system; the possibility of our survival feeling very real, yet at the same time, untouchable.

A small dart of crimson rushing through the grass startled me, I skipped a step and nearly stumbled. As several leeches burst from the trees towards us I realised it had been the rabbit. They were many, and fast. I hadn't time to think; barely time for action. In a panic I began to lose my rhythm, feet falling against each other, I twisted reflexively to protect the child, and we fell. Rough and wet from the changing levels of the water, the steep edges of the bank bit and tore at the skin on my arm. We hit the water hard; like a looking glass it shattered, blood and sediment dirtying the waves around us. The mother was screaming. I couldn't see if they were still running but I could hear the screams above the fierce current that was fighting to consume us. We were taken. The waters, so much stronger than they appeared from the shore, lined with tracks of white, carried us in a rough flurry. I felt the pressure change as the waters shallowed, and then I felt it in my knees as we were run aground. We were exposed, free of the rapids; the shallow crossing was probably more than two feet in height but it felt like a puddle, lapping against my thighs. Surprisingly, the girl was both alive and conscious. I think I asked if she was 'all right', or something equally banal; she answered by staring down the shore to her fleeing family.

My ears popped and in the distance I heard the rapturous thunder of cannon fire. I tried to stand and wade to the far side of the shore, but Amélie would not be moved; so we stood, and we stared, and we saw it all. When the mother tripped they were so close I heard her ankle snap. And then the creatures were on her. She didn't scream after that; she just lay there. The crumpled blankets in her arms, still, silent.

'Run,' she whispered, the last sound she would ever make.

With all his bravery, her husband ran. Some of the few who've heard my recount of these events have questioned this as cowardice, they are wrong. A coward could have chosen death in that moment, but he chose to run, to try to save himself, and his daughters.

I don't think he saw the creature to his right, or perhaps he knew he could do nothing but run, but they are fast, so *fast*. Perhaps I should have shielded Amélie's eyes as the creature thundered into her father, a cheetah tackling a gazelle in a single pounce; should have picked her up and carried her quickly to safety. We watched, water to the top of my waist, halfway up her torso; we watched the struggle as father fought with fists and nails. Blood was everywhere, as it spilled it drew more of them; the shore filled with the fucking things, silently rushing to the edge of the water, then stopping, static on the bank. A macabre, grey painting, blurring our vision, swallowing Amélie's sister and father.

That was how I learned about the water, cradling a sobbing child, I suspect I was sobbing myself; everything was so wet and bloodied I don't recall what were tears and what were the dying rapids. Staring into the grey eyes of the beasts, so human, and yet, so not so. I saw it in their eyes, salivating at their unreachable prey, and I knew they could not cross the water's edge.

What happened, after that?

We walked away. What else could we do? You know the rest of the story, more or less. I don't know how we survived the coming months, or the crossing of the channel. But we did. We found this place, it was nothing like it is now but it was safe enough. Maxwell was already here, a few of the other survivors you know too, Mrs Brownless arrived shortly after we did.

Do you remember the names of the parents, or the siblings?

I was never told them. So much of that day I've wished had gone differently; a sad fact is there were more days like that to come before we would reach safety. I'm growing old, by the standards we live by now, the years of regret are starting to weigh heavy on my shoulders. You still have your name though. I'm glad you kept the one they gave you, Amélie.

Unearthed

Ben Wilmshurst

Outgoing recordings from the International Space Station, Line One.

16:04 UTC, December 3rd 2018

'Mission Control this is Commander Michael King reporting in… Yes Sir, the crew are doing just fine thank you… No Sir, nothing wrong, just hoping to confirm the identity and trajectory of the body currently… Well Sir, it's visible from here… Sir? … Sir? … …'

16:08 UTC, December 3rd 2018

'…Commander King speaking… Yes Sir, I understand… You have its location? … And this is the first Spaceguard have seen of it? … Well Sir I don't know how it could have been missed, perhaps its densi… Yes Sir, sorry Sir…We'll do our best Sir, but if there's anything we can do please call right away… Okay Sir, thank you Sir.'

17:29 UTC, December 3rd 2018

'… Commander Ki… Yes Sir, I see it Sir… We've been monitoring it and it certainly seems… Are you sure? … And that's been verified by the ESA? … I… I don't know what *to* say Sir… Is there a plan? … I don't know Sir, destruction? Escape? … There must be somethi… But… I understand Sir, sorry Sir… Yes, I'll inform the crew… Please keep us upda… Sir? … …'

17:31 UTC, December 3rd 2018

'Hi Alec, buddy, it's your father… I'm *good* thanks bud, how are *you*? … You did? That's fantastic buddy, really great… She did? … Could

you get her on the phone for me real quick please buddy? Thanks…
… … Sara? Yeh, it's me… I ugh, I don't know how to explain this but
uh… No, please just listen to me for a moment… I need you to go to
the grocery store and buy as many tinned foods and bottles of water
as you can fit in the car… Sara, please just listen… I need you to take
Alec down into the basement with the food and the bottled water
and… you need to stay down there for a while… I don't know, maybe
three days, but you might need enough food for a couple of weeks…
There's a… mass… it's big, we just picked it up and relayed the info
to… I don't know why they hadn't seen it already, that's what they're
trying to work out right now…Sara, listen, they don't know precise
details just now but they *do* know that it's on course to hit, and they
think it'll be somewhere in the North Pacific… I know Sara, but it's
big… Please, just, just stop, I don't want Alec to see you panicking…
I'm *trying* Sara, I really am trying, but there's not a lot I can do from
up here… *God*… Just please, just get the supplies and take him down
there and wait a couple days until you hear the all clear… I will, as
soon as I know… I love you… Give Alec a hug from me…'

18:02 UTC, December 3rd 2018

'… Comm… Yes Sir, I… Sorry Sir… Do you think that will work? …
And what's the predicted fallout? … *Jesus*… … I, ugh, I can't belie…
Sorry… … Yes Sir, I've informed the crew… Cliff and Volodin are
messaging their families on their personal machines, Nakagawa and
Shuysky are with me now Sir… Well Sir, I'm going to be honest, we're
feeling a little impotent here… *Hey! Stop it you two*… No Sir, nothing Sir,
just Nakagawa and Shuysky being a little loud… Well Sir do you have an
ETA? … Yes Sir, I understa… *I said stop it you two! … Let him… let him
go! Nakagawa that's an order! Let him… … … Jesus Christ… … Don't you
understand what's going on? We're all goddamned frightened but that's no excuse to
behave like fucking children! Shuysky! Shuysky! Over there, go… … Nakagawa…
That way… I don't… I don't care, go! … … Fucking unprofessional goddamn…*
… S… Sorry Sir, as I said, tensions are a little high on board but we're
under control… Please just keep us updated Sir… Yes Sir, thank you Sir.'

19:48 UTC, December 3rd 2018

'Mission Control this i... Yes Sir, I understand, but we can see...
Sir... Sir, please listen... Yes Sir... No Sir... No Sir... Isn't there still
time to try something? ... ... I know Sir, but surely you have to...
What about 1997 XF11? ... I know it's still, what, ten years from
approach? But wasn't there a precautionary strategy for... If you detonate nearby, just off the surface, surely the trajectory will... Yes Sir,
I understand, but it might be enough to... Sorry Sir... Eighteen *times*
larger? *Jesus*... No Sir, I wasn't aware it was that large... *How the hell did
we miss that?* ... No Sir, nothing, sorry, I was just talking to myself...
... *shit*... Yes Sir, I understand... I appreciate that Sir, I'm just trying
to help... I know... I know... Yes Sir... Thank you Sir.'

21:04 UTC, December 3rd 2018

'Sara? Is that you? ... How are you? Are you safe? ... No... No, not
yet... How's Alec? ... I know, but you *need* to stay down there, please...
What do you mean they haven't told you anything? ... There's nothing? ... Reuters must have *someone* in the ESA or the UN who will
have heard... Have you checked online? ... *fuckers*... Sara, just, please,
just stay down there and keep yourself safe... I don't know... I *don't*
know... All I know is that it's big, Sara, and that they're worried...
Well maybe... Just... No, nothing, it doesn't matter, just stay down
there, keep the door locked, and stay with Alec... I don't know...
I spoke to them about, uh, about an hour ago... They think maybe
within twenty-four hours but they aren't certain... Well it's moving
so fast they're having trouble... I know... I *know*... I'm sorry, I truly
am... I will, we just have to wait to see what the impact is... Yeah...
Yeah... Stay safe, I love you... ... Sara, I'm sorry... ... I know... But
I am... ...'

23:18 UTC, December 3rd 2018

'... Commander King speaking... I understand Sir... Yes Sir...
Thank you Sir...'

00:09 UTC, December 4th 2018

'Mission Control this is Commander Michael King... Sir, we have a visual on, uh, *Volodin, how many?* ...We have a visual on four, Sir... What's the range on that? ... And how long 'til detonation? ... Hmm... Well Sir, I'll be honest, it looks pretty goddam huge from here... ... ... I sure as hell hope so too...'

04:22 UTC, December 4th 2018

'... No Sir, I've not been able to sleep... I know Sir, but given the circumstances... Yes Sir... Visual on all five now Sir, yes... Three hours? ... Yes Sir... The team are, well, they're quiet for now Sir... How is everyone there? ... Yes Sir, I understand... S... Sir... I just need to ask something... Forgive me if it's out of place Sir... Well Sir, I was wondering why no one had been told yet Sir... Yes Sir, it's just that I spoke to Sara and... I understand Sir, but do you not think it will give people a chance at least to prepare? ... What about on the East Coast? ... Really? ... ... *My God*... ... No Sir, sorry Sir... Yes Sir, I understand... Okay Sir... Yes Sir, oh-seven-hundred, will do Sir...'

06:47 UTC, December 4th 2018

'Sara? ... Sorry, I didn't mean to wake you... I just wanted to hear your voice... No, nothing's wrong... No... No, honestly... How's Alec? ... Good... Has there been anything on the news? ... No... They've sent... Well, everyone... Us, the Russians, China... Well I guess they thought this was more important... They're going to try to divert it's course... No, they can't do that... I know, but that was just a film, it wasn't accura... No, I'm not *trying* to be condescending, I'm sorry, I just... ... It's just a lot safer to try to divert it... Yeah... I hope it, I *think* it will, yeah... You'll be safer down there, don't worry... Try and get some sleep now, okay? ... I love you... I will...'

06:58 UTC, December 4th 2018

'... Yes Sir, it's me... No Sir, they've passed out of view... Yes Sir... How long until detonation? ... *Jesus*... Uhm, is there anything we can

do? … Yes Sir, we will… They're with me now, yes Sir… … … Sir?
… … … Sir, are you there… …'

06:59 UTC, December 4th 2018

'Mission Control? … Yes Sir, sorry Sir, we lost contact for a moment
there… Fifteen? … *God… … come on, come on…* Sir, we have a visual
on first detonation… And a second now, Sir… Have all five, woah,
Sir we have another detonation… … Sir? … *fuck… … … … Y…* Yes
Sir… Sir, it, it seems the final blast broke it into fragments… I don't
know Sir, perhaps three larger masses and, *Jeez,* I don't know, maybe
twenty smaller fragments… *God…* Yes Sir, I understand Sir… *Hey!*
Stop it! Shuysky, stop! Both of you, stop! Cliff, Volodin, get them off each… …
… uh my God… … fuck… … … Is he? … Are you sure? … … You see
what you've done, you fucking… … my God… How deep is it? … No, we don't
have the equipment for that! … I don't fucking know… How are we supposed
to… Jesus… … … … Sir, I, ugh, we've had a, ugh, *Jeez… …* It's Shuysky
Sir, he's, *fuck…* he's dead Sir… … Nakagawa and him were… Yes Sir,
I understand… *What do you mean he's bleeding?* … Sorry Sir, I need a
moment… … … *Well how bad is it? … … Jeez… …* Sir? … Nakagawa
is losing blood Sir… He has a laceration to his face and neck… …
How deep is it, Volodin? … fuck… It looks pretty deep Sir… No Sir,
Cliff and Volodin are okay… They're with Nakagawa… I don't know
Sir… … Yes Sir, I will… *Cliff! Cliff… Try to get him stabilised, okay?* …
… Have they mapped the trajectory of the fragments, Sir? … Yes Sir,
I understand… I'll keep the line open, yes Sir… Thank you Sir… *Jesus*
fucking Chr…'

07:23 UTC, December 4th 2018

'… Commander K… Yes Sir… No Sir, I'm afraid we weren't able to
stop the bleeding in time… We just don't have the capability to deal
with an injury like that… I… I know Sir, I'm sorry Sir… They have?
What does it look like? … Shit… All of them? … What size is the
largest? … Still? … *Jesus…* The Atlantic too? … Is there anywhere
that won't be affected? … … Yes Sir, I understand… I will Sir… …

Has anyone been told yet? … Sir! … Sir you can't do that, Sir… They have a right! …… …… That's not a decision for you to make, Sir! …… …… I don't know Sir, but they might want to make their peace or… …… Don't you? … Well what if I told Sara? … You can't do that… What about Cliff? Volodin? They've got families too, they won't be able to say goodbye if you… …… It's inhuman, goddammit! …… …… Yes Sir… … No Sir… I, uh, I understand Sir… Yes Sir… …… No Sir… …… No Sir, I won't… No Sir… *Jeez*… Yes Sir, I will… How long? … *Jesus*… I'll call in thirty minutes… Yes Sir… Sir… Good luck Sir…'

07:51 UTC, December 4th 2018

'Mission Control, are you there? … …… Mission Control this is Commander Michael King of the International Space Station, is anyone there? …… …… Hello? …… …… …… *Jesus*… ……'

07:53 UTC, December 4th 2018

'Sara? …… …… Sara are you there? …… …… Sara, pick up the phone… *please*… …… …… Alec? …… …… ……'

07:54 UTC, December 4th 2018

'Mission Control do you hear me? … Hello? Is anyone there? …… …… … Oh thank God Sir, I thought… …… Okay Sir, I understand, yes… How many have hit so far? …… …… We've seen several impacts… Well Sir, there's a huge amount of dust and ash that's… …… It looks like a hell of a lot of debris entering the atmosphere Sir… *God*… There's been another impact Sir… …… Sir? …… …… Hello? … *Cliff, where did that one hit? …… …… Cliff! …… …… Where was it? …… …… shit… …… Can you see that? … There, look! …… …… What is that? … Oh my God… …… fuck… …… It must have… …… …… Jeez*…'

08:02 UTC, December 4th 2018

'Mission Control? …… …… …… …… Mission control are you there? …… ……'

08:03 UTC, December 4th 2018

'Sara... Please... ... Sara? ... I love you... ... ... Alec? ... Alec, are you there buddy? ... ... Please pick up if you can hear me... ... ...'

10:28 UTC, December 4th 2018

'Is anyone there? ... ...'

16:34 UTC, December 4th 2018

'Hello? ... ... Sir, are you there? ... ... Please, someone... ...'

22:07 UTC, December 4th 2018

'This is, uh, this is Commander Michael King of the International Space Station... ... I don't... I don't know if anyone can hear me but... *God...* Please, if anyone is there, please contact us... We've seen the craters but now the dust... we can't see *anything* anymore... ... ... Our current position is... uh... approximately uh, forty-four, seventy-seven North, one-two-eight, twenty-one East... Can anyone hear me? ... ... *Jesus...* ...'

05:12 UTC, December 5th 2018

'... ... I know no one's there but... ... Just... ... *uh, Jeez...*'

10:30 UTC, December 5th 2018

'This is Commander Michael King of the International Space Station... This message is for anyone who might be listening... or... or anyone who might hear these recordings... I don't, I don't know, I just... I... ... ... We, uh, we moved Nakagawa's and Skuysky's bodies into the Rassvet module... *Jeez...* They uh, Cliff and Volodin seem, uh, they seem quiet, a little distant... I guess they're still struggling to come to terms with exactly what's happened... It's been, uh, approximately, uh... twenty... twenty-seven hours since the first impact... We've had no contact with Mission Control since yesterday morning... Our course is as yet unaffected but, uh, I don't know what's going to happen as time goes on... ... ... As of last inspection we have enough basic supplies for the anticipated remainder of our expedition, but obviously now, I, uh, I don't know what's going to happen... We can ration ourselves a little more generously with the loss of Shuysky and... Shuysky and Nakagawa... ... ... I, uh, I... ... *Jeez*... ...'

13:01 UTC, December 5th 2018

'Commander Michael King awaiting response... ... Is there anyone there? ... *Jesus fuck*... ... Mission Control? ... Anyone? ... ...'

13:03 UTC, December 5th 2018

'Sara? ... ... Alec? ... ... Sara it's me, Michael... Are you there Sara? ... Sara? ... Sara if you get this message please call me back... Please, I just... I just need to hear your voice... ... Are you okay? ... Please... I need to know... *please*... ...'

08:00 UTC, December 6th 2018

'... ... ... Mission Control... This is, uh, this is Commander Michael King... Still haven't had any contact from Earth since the impacts... If anyone is there... Please contact us... We, uh, we are awaiting, uh... I don't know... *Jeez*... Mission Control, if you're there pl... *What the hell do you think you're doing? ... Cliff, stop! ... I said stop! ... Goddammit Cliff, are you crazy? ... ... No! ... ... No! ... I'm still the commander of this expedition, dammit! ... ... Volodin... No! ... Get away from there! ... ... It's only been, what, forty-eight hours? ... They still might be... ... You don't know that, Cliff... No you don't... ... She might still be alive... ... You can see all that dust, it must be affecting outgoing comms... ... I know that, Cliff, I know... Volodin, what about your daughters? Have you given up on them as well? ... ... No! ...Stop! ... I command you to stop! ... ... No! Stop it! ... ... Don't you dare ... You can't... ... Jeez, no! ... ...'*

09:18 UTC, December 6th 2018

'... ... ... This is, uh... ... *fuck*... ... Whoever is out there, this is Comman... This is... ... Well, I suppose I'm not the commander anymore... ... This is Michael King of the International Space Station speaking... ... My uh, my crew have... ... uh... *God*... ... I'm the only one left... ... I'm, uh... ... ... *fuck*... ...'

16:40 UTC, December 6th 2018

'This is Michael King... I, uh, I don't know what to do here... ... I guess you're not there... ... Are you? ... ... It's so quiet... ... Hello? Hello? Did someone say something? Hello? ... ... Hello, are you there? Did you say something? ... ... Please repeat... ... ... Hello? ... ... Mission Control? ... ...'

17:01 UTC, December 6th 2018

'Mission Control? ... ... I thought I heard you on the last commu-nication... Is someone there? Can you hear me? ... ... *Please God*... ... I thought I... Hello? ... ... Anyone? ... ...'

02:57 UTC, December 8th 2018

'It's me... ... I guess no one's there, but... ... I just need to talk to someone... ... ... It's been, uhhh, two days since Cliff and Volodin left... ... I... I can see their bodies through the window each time the station makes a pass... ... ... Supplies are still high here, I estimate enough food for approximately fifty-five, fifty-six days... Most of the mac and cheese packs have gone but I found some extra candy in Volodin's sleeping bag and a few packets of crackers that Cliff had hidden... ... I've had to, uh, readjust the schedule of works given the circumstances... ... But I'm continuing the research with the uh... ... The bacterium... ... Signs right now sugge... ... ... *Jeez*... ... *What's the fucking point?* ... ...'

00:10 UTC, December 14th 2018

'This is Michael, Michael King reporting to uh... ... ... My orbit has uh, has remained steady... ... The past few days I've been observing the Earth and looking for signs of the dust dissipating but thus far I haven't located any regions that look uh... I haven't been able to see anything... In fact the dust seems... To be honest I can't tell what's going on... ... Is anyone there? ... ... My plan is to continue observing and wait for, uh... I'll await contact until uh, until my food supplies run out... I think I can last until approximately, uh, sorry, yeh, I've got enough I think to last until February Second, maybe a couple days either side allowing for fluctuations in consumption... If no contact is made before that date, well, uh, I, I might last an extra few days maybe, I'm not exactly sure... And after that... I guess uh, I guess that'll be it... ... ...'

14:14 UTC, December 23rd 2018

'Sara? ... Are you there? ... ... *Alec?* ... ...'

04:55 UTC, December 25th 2018

'This is Michael King aboard the International Space Station... It's, uh, it's Christmas and uh, I'm not really sure why that's important but I thought I'd try and communicate... ... The dust is still so thick, the Earth looks like a marble that's been... It looks like someone has dropped it in the mud... ... It was so beautiful before I can't believe how different it looks now... ... ... I've been getting headaches, real strong ones... They've been stopping me from sleeping and I'm starting to notice the effects of insomnia... I, uh, I forgot to eat anything yesterday and my, uh... *Jeez...* Sorry, it's such a sharp pain... It... hngghh... ... *fuuuuckk...*'

00:04 UTC, January 1st 2019

'It's uh, it's twenty-nineteen, January First, this is Michael King aboard the International Space Station... My supplies are running a little lower than anticipated... I calculate another twenty-three days of food given current levels of consumption... The dust is... Well, if you can hear me I'm sure you know... ... I've been continuing on the T2 and the ARED to keep my strength up for when... ... uhm... if you, uh... ... ... yeh... ... ... Yesterday there was a uh, a fault notification indicating that there is some damage to one of the primary solar array panels, but so far there hasn't been any indication of

significant impacts to the, uh... ... I'll, uh... I'll keep you posted...
...'

11:51 UTC, January 14th 2019

'Someone please just fucking answer me! ... ... Please? I
can't... *Please*... ... ... I can't be the only one left... *Please God, please...
... Please make someone answer... ... I need to... ... I... ... I can't... ... ...'*

19:16 UTC, January 17th 2019

'Mission Control, or, anyone who can hear me... This is Michael King
speaking... I, uhm, I'm certain that no one is listening but... Well...
The headaches are getting stronger... It's hard to do even the simplest
tasks... I've continued my observations where possible but nothing
has changed... ... I haven't been able to exercise all week and I've
been trying to conserve food... There's not much left now, maybe
six or seven meals... I... I, uh... I don't really have much to say... I
guess there isn't much I *can* say... If it is just me I guess, I... Just...
... I don't want to die... *I can't believe... ...Please... ...*'

08:08 UTC, January 22nd 2019

'Sara, Alec, I know you aren't there, I know you can't hear me, but I
just needed to tell you that I love you both and that I'm sorry... ...
I'm sorry I wasn't there with you, for you... ... ... I've eaten the
last of the food on board now and don't know how long I'll last...
... ... I'm sorry, I really, really am so sorry... ... Wherever you are, I
hope... I hope I see you soon... ... I don't think it'll be long... My
head is, uh, it's, uh... *Jesus fuck*... ... Sorry, it's the headaches, they're...
God! ... ... I'm sorry... ...'

13:44 UTC, January 24th 2019

'... ... ... Uh... ... King... Michael King... ... I, uh... ... It's... ...I
don't, uh... ... ... Hello? ... ... Is someone... Is someone there? ...
...'

02:01 UTC, January 25th 2019

'I'm sorry Sara… … … … *I love you*… … … *Alec*… … I… … … … I'm… … …'

16:23 UTC, January 25th 2019

'… … … … … … … … … hngghh… … … … uh… … … … *God*… … *You bastard*… … … *You*… … *Bastard*… … … …'

16:27 UTC, January 25th 2019

'… … … … … … … … I … … … … … … … … … … … *uh*… … … … … … … … … … … … … … … … … …'

16:32 UTC, January 25th 2019

'… … …'

The Anatomy of Desire

Selma Carvalho

The worst of our lives had been lived and now we are free.

Outside my window, in the commune I share with 200 others, the rain is a mere drizzle of pure, ice-cold water. Fifty years ago, it would have been dirty as dishwater; a putrid flow of contaminants raining down incessantly until all hope of surviving it had vanished. The prophecies about climate change had all come true. Before the rains, were endless days of sun. The trees stood singed as if a volley of thunderbolts had burnt them, and a carpet of arid land unfurled itself over the plains.

All that is a thing of the past. I live in an old disused aircraft hangar converted into a large dormitory. There are hundreds of these abandoned airfields littered across the country, rigid in structure and Spartan in furnishing, except for the complex gadgetry left behind in the control rooms. We can't find a purpose for the gadgetry. We're told to use them as aids for the simulation games we play all day, which they say will eventually coax our nerve centres to feel empathy.

I stretch my legs on the bed I'm sitting on. They ache occasionally from the shrapnel embedded in them and on rainy days from the cold. I see Jenny turning in her sleep two beds down from mine. She is what, in the old days, we would call a white woman and I'm a red-blooded brown man. But we did away with racial classifications which only served to disunite us. We realised that individual histories and identities were dangerous. So we began the process of erasing past lives; tore up the flags, burnt the history books, deleted the archived memory projects and eradicated every shred of nationalist pride instilled in the dark heart of man. In a clean strike we eradicated the collective and the individual. We were triumphant.

Jenny wakes up and, in her hurry to get out of bed, straddles her legs wide enough for me to catch a glimpse of her underwear. It is white and damp and it curves perfectly over her mound, which rises and falls gently as if it was alive and breathing all on its own. It is not quite the expected V-shape but more like a capital U with its bottom flattened out. From either side emerge stray pubic hairs and two long caramel coloured legs which she now dangles effortlessly off the bed. Above the underwear, her frail torso sprouts like a young tree of bony branches, and large-sized cushiony pink buds with hook-like nipples, carelessly falling out of her terrycloth bathrobe.

I stare out the window trying to ignore the stiffening between my legs. Such sensory processing is unlawful. If the authorities get wind of it, that I, a former Lieutenant in the war, was experiencing such things there would be repercussion; long counselling sessions, in solitary confinement, where a white-coat would try to cure me.

The smell of the disinfectant in the room is overwhelming and Martha is already shuffling about the dormitory changing the bed-linen. Martha occasionally remembers the time before the war but she was a young girl then, and is happy to live in the new age. 'I couldn't live like that,' she tells me, 'with everyone doing exactly as they pleased. It was chaos.'

Ginger, our communal cat comes by my bed. Overfed and fat, she has two tails. This is not how things used to be. Cats had one tail back then, which they would wiggle delightfully if you placed them on your lap, and purr contentedly. But then came the campaigns by animal rights activists. Culling and euthanasia were strictly forbidden and punishable by law. Owners were mandated to clone those that eventually died, and that's when their DNA started mutating until the domesticated tabby became a caterwauling predator lacerating their unsuspecting owners to death.

I can see Jenny. I'm one of the lucky ones; my peripheral vision still works. Most people lost that ability in the years of rapid mutations. She is sitting with her legs tucked under her. She is so young; born after the apocalyptic wars. She doesn't know any world except the one she was born into. Has she taken lovers? Has a man ever pulled down her pants and penetrated her? It can't be, of course.

The lack of interest in sexual activity began first somewhere in the east and then spread. Children were the first casualty. People simply chose not to have children. Then they chose not to fall in love, or cohabitate. For a long time, and I remember this well because my generation called it, *d'une sorte de morte*, we simply had recreational sex. We mastered the techniques and prolonged the orgasm, but eventually, it felt too great an effort and we preferred to pleasure ourselves with stimulation devices and holographic aids. That, in the end, saved us. The laboratories took over the production of human beings based on a demand and supply statistical model. That's when the relentless race for resources came to a halt.

I try to concentrate on the rain coming down. I begin to count the drops; making mental notes of the times they hit the aluminium gutter before running its length and cascading downwards.

I try to pray. I can't remember any of the prayers I'd been taught as a child. That was something else we fought hard to eradicate; the myth of the divine protector. The tyrannical dictator residing in the popular imagination as God had to be ruthlessly destroyed; sometimes with bombs, sometimes with cold reasoning. I am proud of the part I played. I was head of the anti-religious squad and oversaw the imprisonment of countless clerics and the mass burnings of religious books. Yet, as I stand here, I feel that old familiar lump at the back of my throat and I recognise it as that most despairing of human prayers – hope.

The rain has stopped. I wrap an oversized coat around me and go for a walk. The air feels fresh and clean. I cross the field of red poppies. The bees have made a comeback. The field is fenced in by barbed wire, beyond which are the grey slums of derelict malls and museums, without sewage or water or electricity; home to the forgotten. We couldn't save everyone; just a few. And millions live in the squalor of post-war poverty.

I turn back and find Jenny walking in the field. She bends to pick up a poppy. She is wearing black tights which reveal the gentle swell of her young buttocks; the twin orbs separated by a deep cleft.

I turn and walk away.

'Wait up,' she shouts, motioning to me to slow down.

She catches up and begins walking apace.

'I want to ask you something,' she says, her breathing hard and unconstrained. It feels odd for anything, even breathing, to be unconstrained.

'What?'

'Some of us girls were talking and we thought maybe, since you're one of the older ones in the commune, you would know.'

'What do you need to know?'

'I want to know what sex is.'

I feel like the wide-eyed eleven year old I was when I asked my mother the same question. She had looked away in embarrassment but the next day an anatomically correct and instructive book had appeared on my writing desk. It told me nothing about the anatomy of desire. That I learnt the following year at the encouragement of my mother's friend.

'Why now?'

'The girls – those of us, I mean, who were asked to keep going with the empathy simulation games – are beginning to feel things now, that we don't understand.'

This was dangerous territory.

'Talk to your Advisor?'

'He wasn't very helpful.'

'I don't see how I can help.'

'I want to know if sex is the same as feeling empathy?'

Yes. And other verbs too.

Loving, lusting, wanting, desiring, bonding, breeding, withdrawing, feeling pain, inflicting pain, depression, a living death.

How could she know sex when she hadn't experienced any of that?

'I'm sorry, I can't help you.'

'You must or...'

'Or what?' There was nothing left in our world that a young girl could use against an old horny man.

'I watch you every morning. I know what you're looking at. That's why I wake up with my legs wide open.'

I walk away. Ahead of me the bees are learning anew to pollinate. I feel myself slipping into a blurry unconsciousness and I imagine that's what death feels like.

Pillar of Salt

Alison McBain

Some people are fascinated by the past. They can trace their family history all the way back to the Science Wars – if you can believe them, of course. If everyone who claimed to be descended from 'Mad' Mike Sheffield were true survivors, half the world would be linked to the hero of the 23rd century.

Not me. I never looked back.

Then again, I knew I wasn't descended from those elite few, from the scientists who ended the war and pulled us back from the brink of apocalypse. My family was halfway around the world two hundred years ago, deep in the heart of agricultural China. Farmers, in other words, real 'salt of the earth' folk. My parents were the first to emigrate to a city, and I'm the first engineer in our family, so history isn't my strong suit.

But I'm not alone in that. As soon as Zimmerman took that fateful trip in his prototype time machine and came back to tell us our future, we were all focused on one thing. And it wasn't the past.

Annihilation. The Earth, a burnt black cinder.

Zimmerman died a couple days after his first trip. We had some miracle medicines, but his cells simply broke down after exposure to such intense radiation.

We had some guesses as to what happened in the future. But we had no *proof*, no idea of how to prevent it. Or even if we could.

The consensus was that the cataclysm occurred a hundred years from now. Perhaps a little sooner or later – it was hard to tell for sure. But all the theorists agreed that everyone in the future was dead. Gone, kaput, finis.

What we didn't know was why.

'Approximate location, 36.972° N, 122.0263° W. Five samples, half-mile radius. Results: Sample A at 36.971° N, 122.0263° W contains cesium-137 at 3.975 GBq/kg...'

A familiar voice behind me interrupted, 'Look alive. HQ here in fifteen. Conference room, now.'

'Pause,' I said to the recorder. I looked up from the grubby sheets brought back from the latest trip. Because we had limited tech on the other side, we couldn't scan the same way as if we were at home. The radiation quickly broke down the machines' finer capabilities, and samples couldn't be brought back with any reliability. On-site testing made for a lot of data entry and analysis down the road. That was my job.

I started to ask something of my boss, but he was already zooming to the next work station. Damn.

I got up and headed to the conference room. We were government funded, but that meant we had to justify our costs on several levels. They were still duking it out at the capital about if what we were doing even mattered. Those who were against it argued that we didn't know for sure what we had found. Or that it was a hoax.

As for the cost of our research, it was pretty easy for detractors to claim that it was a drain on the country's resources. All our expensive equipment was one-time use only, since the radiation on the other end fried it. The trip wasn't a walk in the park, either. Ground teams could only go through the process a few times before bad things started to happen to them. The first teams were still in the hospital, as far as I knew, if they weren't dead already.

I was one of the first people in the conference room. I nodded to Bob, who already sat at the far end of the table. Must be bad, if he wanted to hide in a corner. I walked around the table to join him.

He had his coffee mug in front of him and was stirring its contents obsessively with a spork. Aside from the first glance at the door when I first opened it, he hadn't raised his eyes from his cup.

'What's shaking?' I asked, trying to act casual.

'Nothing. The usual. I mean, everything's fine.'

Ri-ight.

I wondered if someone else had discovered the same discrepancy I had – if we were about to be prepped on what to say to the press. Since I'd found out, I'd had no idea what to do, or how to act, or who to tell.

Maybe now I wouldn't have to say anything.

The pressure that had been bearing down on me since I'd discovered the truth seemed to lighten at that thought, just a little.

I sat down next to Bob and he scooted his chair as far as he could away from me. This was not the good kind of strange behavior, and he was a bit of a nutter to begin with. A tip? Never ask him about his collections.

There was a sudden rush at the door and the rest of the floor trooped in. Sandra handled the ops end of things with her team, and Phil's guys the rest. My boss and the rest of my co-workers, the data-crunchers, were last into the room. They arranged themselves around the table, huddling together with their own groups. There wasn't competition, per se, but a general lack of camaraderie between sections. Ours was the smallest group; data analysis.

A section of seats near the door remained empty. People chatted and shuffled, but quietly, like at a funeral. Ten minutes later, the suits from HQ banged open the door and sat down at the front of the room.

We cowered before their shiny teeth and slicked-back hair. I might have a boss, but these were the numbers men. What they said, we did. They were the bosses' bosses.

'Okay, I'll jump right in.' Abhay Singh, Mr. Singh to most of us, had not taken a seat. Instead, he stood at the front of the room, vibrating with energy. 'No need to mince words. The House finally swung the vote. Unless we can produce something concrete, they're pulling the plug.'

Shock. Outrage. Gasps.

'How can they do that?'

'Why?' 'Shortsighted, egotistical…'

I said nothing. Neither did Bob. I guessed he'd probably heard ahead of time. He was pretty much a nonentity, very good at lurking and picking up information from eavesdropping. The type of guy who nobody noticed. Also, the type of guy with several restraining orders against him, but that's another story.

Mr. Singh held up his hands. 'Please, please. Right now, this just means a restructuring. We're being dropped by one backer. But there are others out there.'

That brought immediate silence. My stomach sank. This didn't seem to be leading where I had hoped it would lead.

'We're in talks right now about private purchase. Our lawyers are working out the details, but it's getting the green light from the top. It would recoup some of the taxpayers' losses, and an election's coming up.'

The silence continued. Mr. Singh frowned, as if he had expected a different reaction. 'That's good news, people! We get to keep our jobs. Well, most of us.'

Bob trembled next to me, and I suddenly knew I hadn't made the cut. Probably he had. Of course, he didn't know what I knew. No one did at this point, since I hadn't told anyone.

I realized I had raised my hand only when Mr. Singh looked at me and gestured impatiently for me to speak.

'What is the private enterprise?' I asked. 'Why would anyone want our research? Are they planning on picking up where we left off?'

A pause. The pause said *confidentiality clause* more loudly than a room full of lawyers. 'No, Ms. Lee. They have a new direction for this project.' His attention turned back to the room in general, and I think he expected his tone of voice was quelling enough to stop me.

I remained un-quelled. 'But what direction? We're trying to save the future of the human race,' I lied. 'What's more important than that?'

Singh gritted his teeth in a smile or a grimace – I couldn't tell which. 'Details to discuss later, Ms. Lee. Right now, we're looking at the big picture.'

'Our mission *is* the big picture,' I argued.

'But not commercially viable. And rather than let this company die, we're saving jobs, okay? So let's focus on that.'

I wasn't the only one bothered by this. I glanced around and noticed even the bosses seemed uneasy. They weren't in on this little secret, either. This was the first they were hearing about the change. And they didn't like it.

'We have new contracts for each of you to sign once the deal goes through. In the meantime, carry on. We should have more news in about a week. Thank you.' And the money men swept out as abruptly as they had arrived.

That opened the floodgates. I sat back in my padded chair and let the words of the others wash over me as I thought about what had happened.

Mr. Singh might be the big boss, but he wasn't the one who mattered. And my boss was just a cog, as helpless as I was. Who could I tell about what I had discovered? Who could make a difference?

Although what was the point, anyway? This changeover would get me fired but, more importantly, the new direction would have to be something that involved making money. No corporation threw funds away on dead-end research.

Ha! Dead end. An end where we were dead. There was that. That was exactly what we were studying.

'Ms. Lee, Ms. Graham and Mr. Yurkov. If I may see you in my office, please?'

Here it came. I followed my two co-workers to the boss's office, just a tiny shut-up box against the wall with one small window at eye level. I wondered if he ever sat in his chair and stared out the window aimlessly. He seemed to do a lot of aimless wandering around the floor.

Once he was seated behind his desk and we were in the three hard-ass chairs in front of it, he furrowed his brow with what he probably thought was a sympathetic expression. But he went right for the gut.

'I'm sorry, but I've been informed that the changeover requires some reorganization of staff. You three have worked tirelessly to promote our project, but I'm afraid we're going to have to let you go.'

Mr. Yurkov got teary and Ms. Graham shouted. I sat and stared out that little nubbin of a window, thinking through my options, and came back into the conversation as things were winding up.

'–and I don't need to remind you about the confidentiality of this project. We've put together a generous severance package and will be sending you the details.'

'I'd like a meeting.'

I was as shocked as everyone else as I realized – yep, that voice was mine.

'What did you say, Ms. Lee?'

'A meeting. With the head – the CEO.' I waved my hand nonchalantly. It would have made more of an impact if I knew a bit about corporate culture, but I was, and had always been, just a data rat. 'It's important. It's about the project.'

He raised a disdainful eyebrow and spoke with his insincere, big-man-boss voice. 'I'll be happy to pass on any information. What is it about the project that you would like to share?'

I studied his little pig eyes and knew there was no way he would say anything to anyone, no matter what came out of my mouth. It just wasn't worth his effort.

'Nope, sorry,' shaking my head. There really was nothing left to lose. I had worried before they might think I was as crazy as Bob and sack me. *What if I was wrong?* But it didn't matter anymore, did it? They were firing me anyway.

'I'll only tell the CEO. Get me a meeting or I'm going to the press.'

I heard a few irate sentences involving the words 'lawyer' and 'jail time.' I shrugged it off.

'I'll do the time, pay the fines. But you won't get your information back, and the whole world will know the details. What do you think that'll do to the sale of the company? What will happen to the project if all the buyers jump ship?'

He glared at me. Finally, he said, 'I'll see what I can do.' I stood up without another word and walked back to my desk. I tried to log into the system, but my passcode was already blocked. Cindy – Ms. Graham – stopped by my desk on her way out.

'That was the most awesome thing I've ever seen,' she said in her slightly breathy voice. I'd heard her normal, commanding voice come through when we got fired and she had shouted, so the reversion to her soft-sounding voice seemed strange to me. The face we showed to the public was not always the real deal.

'Thanks.' I smiled at her. She pressed my shoulder with one hand and was gone.

'Come with me,' my boss growled an hour later from behind me. I had been leaning back in my chair with my hands behind my head, day-dreaming, and hadn't heard him come up. His voice made me jump, and I laughed in embarrassment. Needless to say, he didn't laugh with me.

'Okay.' I followed him to the lift, and he pressed the top button.

'You know you'll be unemployable after this,' he said as the doors closed. 'No one will touch you with a ten-foot pole.'

'Doesn't matter. We're all going to die in a fiery apocalypse soon, aren't we?' At my jovial tone, he looked like he wanted to say something, but the words seemed to get strangled in his throat. We reached the top in silence.

This floor was more spacious. Instead of rows of desks all crammed together to fit as many bodies as possible, this one had an open-air feel. Plants graced the ski slopes of virginal white desks bent in odd, artistic contortions. People walked at a slow pace, not the frenetic one below. If there was any emergency activity here, it was well hidden.

The secretary seated at the front desk smiled at us, stood up and escorted us to a set of double doors made out of real wood. She opened them and waved us inside.

A woman sat behind a desk. Her hair was three different shades of blond, indicating a professional and very expensive dye job. I didn't recognize her, but I'm not really up to date with most high-up corporate things. She smiled with her teeth, not a wrinkle marring her artificially smooth forehead, and offered us a seat.

'I'd like to talk to you alone, Ms.– ' I scanned her nameplate, '–Morris. This won't take long.'

'As you wish.' She nodded at my boss, who looked like he would protest, but left without saying a word. He closed the doors behind him. 'Now, what would you like to say? I must warn you that this meeting is being recorded, so perhaps keep any threats at a minimum.' Her smile never faltered as she said it.

'No threats, Ms. Morris.' I sat on a white leather chair and stretched out my legs. 'But if you are planning on selling this project and all that goes with it, you might want to know that it's flawed.'

'Yes?'

'The data. It isn't adding up, not even accounting for the variations of surveyor and faulty instruments. There's something wrong about the time lapse.'

'So you don't think that this event we're studying will take place so soon?'

Ah, the word *event*. What a sanitizing way of saying the end of the human race.

'No, ma'am. I'm saying that it has already happened.'

She laughed. I didn't, but her eyes now had a new label aimed at me. *Crazy*. Perhaps I had put it too baldly.

'If it's already happened, then how are we here? I don't feel dead – at least, not today.'

I studied her face. How much would she make with this deal? 'I'm just curious. What does the company want the prototype for?'

'I'm sorry, but I don't know what you're talking about.'

'The potential is amazing. But it's like trying to hit a bulls-eye in the dark on the other side of the world with a slingshot. It can't be done for political gain, not with any accuracy. Even though Zimmerman went back in time, like he was supposed to, it didn't make a difference. It would have been a miracle if he got to the time period he wanted. As it was, he didn't hit the right mark, and so here we are.'

'*Back* in time? What do you mean?'

She'd picked out the relevant words I'd wanted her to. Good puppy.

'We assumed forward, because that's what he told his team before he died. And it would be pretty hard to miss an apocalypse, right? But, no, he went back. He found out it had already happened and he went back to prevent it. He didn't create "The Event"', I did air quotes in the most exaggerated way I could, 'but his trip created the time loop in which we find ourselves.'

'Can you prove this?'

'Yes.'

'How?'

I sighed and crossed my hands over my stomach. 'Do you ever look up?'

'Up?' She glanced at the ceiling. 'Why?'

I laughed, but it wasn't intended to be mean. 'No, no. When you're outside.'

She laughed too. More to play along, than because what I said was funny. 'Of course.'

'Stars, Ms. Morris. They move at a measurable rate. We've been so focused on finding out what will happen and trying to prevent it that we put two and two together and got five. I asked a team visiting the site last week to do some measurements off the record. And I got back star data from two hundred years ago.' In case she didn't understand, I emphasized, 'Stars don't lie.'

She sat back in her chair and crossed her arms. I saw something in her eyes as she studied me, the first sliver of fear.

'And you can prove this,' she finally said.

'Yes.'

'So what does this mean? How can we exist in the future after an apocalypse in the past?'

'We can't,' I said. 'The only thing holding us here is the time lapse and displacement. My best calculations? It can go any day now. Zimmerman's trip was the focus and the catalyst, like a rubber band stretched back in time. Once it's broken, once the time lapse plays out in reality, then the apocalypse will have happened and none of us will have existed. If you're looking for measurable profit--you won't find it, at least not with the prototype.'

I saw she believed me. At last. She leaned over her desk and whispered, 'What do you think happened? What went wrong?'

'The Science Wars,' I said. 'I dated the radioactive decay and did the math. It matches up. Mike Sheffield never saved the day.' Her expression was stark, and I saw that she guessed what I was going to say. I paused before stating the obvious, but I said it anyway into the face of her understanding, said it to another person to share the burden, to make it real. I couldn't help it – I didn't want to be Atlas. I couldn't bear the weight.

'The prototype failed. Zimmerman didn't make it far enough back on that first trip, and it was a one-shot deal. He set the fixed pattern with the machine, so there's no way to save us unless we build a brand new one from scratch. The majority of the plans were in his head, and they died with him. If we take apart the prototype we have, there's no guarantee we can build another one at all, and we sure as hell can't build one in time.

'So,' I told her. 'Barring a miracle, we're already dead.'

We sat and stared at each other for several heartbeats, and then she leaned back in her chair, fingers steepled. After a few moments, she swiveled around so she was in profile to me and looking out the window.

Past her, I saw the colorful spires and boxlike towers of the city I had grown up in, the city in which I had lived for my entire life. All of those millions of people, unaware.

'How can we solve this?' she asked quietly, almost under her breath.

'Weren't you *listening* to me?'

My harsh tone brought her head around. I got the strangest sensation she had temporarily forgotten me. Or, if not forgotten, had deemed me unimportant to the new situation.

'Ms. Lee,' she said briskly. 'I am not in the habit of giving up. I will need to verify what you've told me before I can believe it, but if what you're saying is true, it only means one thing to me.'

The pause was expectant, so I filled it with the obligatory, 'What?'

'It means it hasn't happened yet.' She raised her head slightly and said in a louder tone of voice, 'Call a meeting with the directors.'

It took a second for me to realize she wasn't talking to me. She hadn't been bluffing when she said we were being recorded. A second later, the door opened and the pleasant-faced secretary walked in, trailed by two security guards.

'We are reinstating Ms. Lee in her old job on a temporary basis,' Ms. Morris said, her eyes flicking past me. 'She will inform the ground team of what data we need to look for. As soon as the team returns, I want the results brought to me immediately.'

Hours later, after the team was gone and back, and the data had been presented to the directors, I was called back to Ms. Morris's office. Everyone else on my floor had gone home, and the lights had turned off one by one as the automatic sensors deemed the place empty. I waited for the summons without knowing when it would come, adrift in a small and singular pool of light. I felt like the last person on Earth.

I watched the overheads flicker on near the elevator, and stood up from my desk in anticipation. She had sent two security personnel, different men than from this afternoon, and they were friendly and chatty as they escorted me up to Ms. Morris's office. But it was hard for me to concentrate on them saying casually, 'What a late night,' and telling me they hoped I got overtime pay.

'Yes, yes,' I said, not realizing how rude I sounded. They fell silent the last bit of the trip, depositing me into Ms. Morris's office and shutting the doors behind them as they left.

'Okay, Ms. Lee,' Ms. Morris said grimly when I took a seat across from her in the same chair as before. She didn't bother with the usual niceties of offering me a drink, even though I could certainly have used something – I was having trouble keeping my eyes open from the late hour. Come to think of it, she hadn't offered me a drink when I was in her office earlier.

I felt a little spurt of irritation at the lack of this polite convention, and I had to stifle a laugh at the absurdity. Our world was ending – but where's my damn coffee?

She didn't seem to notice my distraction. 'Now is when the real work begins. I know there doesn't seem to be much of a point in offering you more money and bonuses – you can't spend it when we're all dead.' I realized she'd made a joke, but couldn't do much more than give her a wan grin. 'But you were the only one to notice this and bring it to my attention, so I can guarantee you a spot with us in finding a solution.'

I felt dull inside. Perhaps it was the late hour, perhaps it was the fact I was no longer alone. I had played out the scenario so many times in my head since I had discovered the discrepancy, but had never been able to get this far in my thoughts.

It seemed too improbable. I was *believed*.

'Thank you, Ms. Morris.'

She smiled, and this time, her smile didn't have the insincerity of before. This smile was a little tired, a little worn around the edges. A glimpse at the face of a real woman.

'Let's get started as soon as possible. Let's fix this,' she said with a trace of her former brusque energy.

And for the first time since I had taken up the burden of knowledge, I felt an answering spark rise up inside me to meet her challenge. I didn't have to look behind me anymore at that giant looming behind all of us in the past – maybe, for once, I could look ahead.

I felt something new then. Perhaps it might have been hope.

Four Horsemen

Chris Iovenko

Sirs, I'm telling you again, all of you, you can't ride your horses here. All four of you need to move it along. There's a riding path in Central Park, quite pretty this time of year, that I'd suggest. Nice shaded areas and it won't be crowded, not during lunch hour on a Tuesday. So get your show on the road. I repeat; you cannot ride your horses here down the middle of Wall Street. You're blocking traffic and frankly you're spooking people a bit.

And you, what is that thing you're waving around? It's a scythe? What the hell is that, a rake of some sort?

Hi Sergeant; didn't believe me and had to see it for yourself, huh? Look at these four. Just parading around in the street. Yes, I've told them to go to Central Park. Identification? They're tourists. They say they're the four horsemen from the Acropolis. I don't know where that is. Greece? Maybe. Sounds familiar. That would explain the weird clothing. Yes, it's strange and yes, I noticed it. But what am I supposed to do? There's no law on the books about having to have your horse's hooves touch the ground. The law of gravity? Very funny.

How long? Ten minutes I guess. Yeah, I know the crowd is grow-ing. But these fellas aren't doing anything. They're looking weird – and this is New York. Looking weird ain't a felony and what do we even do with those horses? Stick them in your squad car? Disturbing the peace? Yeah, that would be it. You go arrest them and I'll stand over here and back you up.

What – they need you back at the precinct? So you're leaving me here to deal with it? I am shocked. Just shocked. No, I don't need backup or SWAT or anybody else. This is my beat and I can handle four kooks on ponies.

Guys, I'm giving you one minute to clear the area. Otherwise, you and your horses are going to jail. You will be arrested, detained and charged with a crime. I've been very patient with you because I know you're not from our country. But here in America we don't ride our horses through the center of the city, especially not the financial district. Thank you for your understanding. Yes, I'm sure the end is nigh. Whatever that means. Have a nice day and be sure to visit the Big Apple again soon.

Thank You

Thank you for taking the time to read our book.

We are interested in how *Apocalypse Chronicles* worked for you, and hope that you won't hesitate to write to us with any thoughts or reactions you may have. Please consider leaving a review on one of our sales platforms to keep potential readers informed and to support the community.

Also from Almond Press

If you enjoyed this volume, it might be worth checking out *Broken Worlds: Dystopian Stories, After the Fall: Tales of the Apocalypse* and *The Russian Sleep Experiment*.

Broken Worlds: Dystopian Stories

In a future of bleakness and roboticism, a totalitarian government enforces upon the people a lifestyle that lulls them into a state of obedience. Your career and social status are predestined and you cannot alter it – this is a reality that walks a fine line between evoking sensations of fear and inducing a sense of futility.

A dystopian reality can sometimes turn out to be as powerful and strong as it can be fragile, collapsing in on itself from one second to the next. As a race, we are fascinated with what comes next, what's over the hill and, inevitably, what happens if we're left all alone. How can things go on? What lessons can we learn?

Broken Worlds takes a peep into an all too possible future. Narration and style change from story to story, but the core of this volume is human emotion. Coloured by their cultures and backgrounds, the storytellers featured in this volume take the idea of a society at extremes and weave a variety of outcomes.

After the Fall: Tales of the Apocalypse

A desolate landscape, wracked with upheaval, the uncanny nature of a place once so familiar. A revelation of what was formerly undisclosed, the harbingers of apocalypse are edging ever closer...

The wasteland of abandoned memories, the end of the world or a chance for a new beginning. Be it a personal apocalypse, or one of great cataclysm, the stories that arise from the rubble are tales of aftermath and tales of survival. Bridging the gap between Science Fiction and Horror, the gothic overtones of the apocalyptic imagination are explored to their full extent in these short stories.

After the Fall is a collection of twenty short stories, all apocalyptic or dystopian in nature. Some bringing laughter and others bringing tears, but each unique in its interpretation of the theme.

The Russian Sleep Experiment Horror Novella

If you are promised freedom, how long would you endure a nightmare?

Siberia: the height of Stalinist terror. Four political prisoners from all corners of the Soviet Union, exiled to the frozen wastes, and sentences to ten years hard labour, are promised their freedom if they endure 30 days without sleep, fuelled by gas 76-IA.

Soviet researchers look on, neutral, and take careful notes on this new wonder drug as insomnia causes words and pleasantries to break down. Only Luka, a junior researcher, believes the experiment needs to be stopped. A lone voice of reason, he is shot down. However, when this experiment ends, one thing is clear: the nightmare has only just begun.

Printed in Great Britain
by Amazon